D1826472

ONE TO SAVE

By Tia Louise

This book is a work of fiction. Names, characters, places, and incidents are products of the author's imagination or are used fictitiously. Any resemblance to actual events or locales or persons, living or dead, is entirely coincidental.

One to Save
Copyright © Tia Louise, 2015
www.AuthorTiaLouise.com
Printed in the United States of America.

Cover design by Steven Novak, Novak Illustration
Photography by Perrywinkle Photography

All rights reserved. No part of this publication can be reproduced, stored in a retrieval system, or transmitted in any form or by any means — electronic, photocopying, mechanical, or otherwise — without prior permission of the publisher and author.

For Mr. TL, always.

And for Derek & Melissa fans everywhere:
another sexy, exciting adventure for you to enjoy.

CONTENTS

CHAPTER 1: GAMES

Melissa

In the cool darkness of the semi-crowded bar, I study the glass in front of me and consider my journey, how many steps I've taken in the last two years, how far I've come. Memories of my old life fade like smoke in a glass. The shame that held me so tightly now dances at the edges of my mind like the whisper of a bad dream, a flicker of shadows that no longer make sense in my world.

Young women in shiny slip dresses twist and laugh on the dance floor, but instead of resentment, my lips curl into a smile. My old self—cynical, bitter, defeated—is a memory I have to work hard to recall. These days I could dance all night with them, but I'd rather spend my energy on other things.

The slim glass holds a pale amber liquid, and I can't resist taking a sip. An involuntary wince pinches my eyes as I put it down. Seven and seven. Refreshing citrus dragged down by the heavy undertone of whiskey. *So gross.*

Sliding my palms over my thighs, I realize my outfit isn't much different from the girls' on the dance floor. The deep red silk is fitted at my waist, and drapes loosely over my torso. My long, dark hair is swept over one shoulder revealing a thin spaghetti strap. I lightly touch the delicate gold chain around my neck leading to the floating heart pendant that sits between my collarbones, and light glances off the thick gold cuff on my wrist.

Unlike that night almost two years ago, I'm alone. My best friend Elaine is miles away with her new husband, most likely indulging in that blissful honeymoon period of early marriage. Make that, most *certainly* indulging. I know those two well.

No, I came by myself to this bar in Princeton after finishing my business with a client in town. My infant son is in Wilmington, spending the weekend with his grandmother. Studying my hands, I admire the deep blue sapphire ring on my finger, but I have no wedding band.

At thirty-two, I'm an unmarried mother of a beautiful little boy, and I wouldn't change a thing... Yet. The tiny silver scar at my hairline reminds me of what a bad marriage looks like, and with my successful marketing business and the gorgeous cottage at the beach I own, I'm satisfied with my life. Calm, not desperate. I'll take my next steps deliberately, with certainty.

All these thoughts preoccupy my mind when I blink up and catch him watching me from across the square-shaped bar. Blue eyes, strikingly blue because of the way they stand out beneath his dark brow, coupled with collar-length thick dark hair.

He's massive, at least six-two, and elegantly dressed with a thick stainless watch on his wrist. I can spot his type a mile away—rich, powerful, accustomed to getting what he wants. I can't deny the hum his gaze sets off under my skin. *I know what he wants.*

Catching my lip in my teeth to stop my grin, I know what I want, too, and it's no coincidence I happened to look up at that exact moment to meet his stare. Still, I'll make him work for it.

He starts to move, his eyes never leaving mine. I don't look away either. Thick cords of muscle ripple beneath the thin black sweater he wears as he glides past the oblivious patrons talking and laughing. Some are more animated than others, waving their arms and putting their drinks in peril.

Yellow lights hidden in the recesses above the bar illuminate rows of liquor bottles in all colors and shapes. Glasses hanging upside down above also catch the flickering light. It's a raucous atmosphere, but this man and I are in our own secret place of longing and desire.

As he rounds the final corner, and I see him in full, my breath quickens. My eyes drift from his broad shoulders to his narrow waist, grey slacks and black shoes, then back up just as he reaches me. A close beard shadows his face, and the muscles low in my pelvis tighten at the thought of how it feels brushing the soft skin of my inner thighs.

"Can I buy you a drink?" The low vibration of his voice touches every part of me, and the intoxicating hint of his cologne surrounds me.

Casually, I motion to the glass. "I have this." My voice is softer and higher compared to his.

"You don't like it." A tease twinkles in his eyes, and I almost forget my line.

"How can you tell?"

He leans in close, "You make a face every time you sip it. I've been watching you."

Soft lips graze my skin, and I catch his forearm to steady myself. "Why?"

The tables have turned, it seems, and now I have to work to stay focused. My body is like a spoiled child accustomed to instant gratification, and my insides are clenching, demanding him.

He straightens and clears his throat. "Maybe I should introduce myself. Derek Alexander."

I slide my noticeably smaller hand across his large palm. "Melissa Jones."

"A last name, Miss Jones?" A sexy grin curls his small nose, and a million pornographic memories flood my mind of that nose nudging into my dark spaces, those lips plundering areas of my body he knows will drive me wild as I moan and twist in white sheets, my fingers threading in his dark hair.

Clearing the thickness in my throat, I say under my breath, "I messed up."

His fingers close over mine. "Sweet Melissa, that's impossible."

At once I remember, and I take back my hand. "I'm not so sweet."

"Let's skip the cava." His eyes are dark, but I'm back to coy.

"Aren't we celebrating?"

"We can celebrate after I show you the stars."

"Where exactly are you planning to do this star gazing?"

"I have the key to a condo just across the street. It has a private balcony."

For a moment, I consider how intimidating this mountain of sex standing in front of me is. At the same time, I've never felt afraid. Thrilling anticipation, yes, but never fear. "Why do you have a key?"

"Because I used to live there."

"That sounds dangerous." My elbow is in his firm grip, and I allow him to help me off my barstool. Even in my tall stiletto heels, my head only reaches the top of his shoulder.

"I'll keep you safe."

"You're not safe." My voice is a low purr.

Straight white teeth are revealed with his smile. "And you're not sweet."

* * *

Derek's condo hasn't changed—spare, little to no accessories on the very masculine furnishings, which are dark with stainless accents. It's all hardwood and straight lines. A massive flat-screen television hangs on the wall above the gas fireplace. Only a few low lights are on. The air surrounding us on the balcony is slightly chilled, but it can't compete with the blazing heat flooding my thighs as he holds me against the secluded outside wall.

He lifts me as if I were a doll, and our mouths open and move together, tongues touching, breaths mingling. With every kiss our panting grows faster. As many times as we've been here, the tension could be visible it's still so hot.

"You wore red," he groans moving to my jaw, tightening my stomach muscles. "You're beautiful in red."

The hem of my dress is pushed all the way to my waist, and his large hands grip my bare ass. My fingers slide into the sides of his hair, and I pull his face back to mine, consuming his mouth. His teeth pull my bottom lip before he moves to my temple, inhaling deeply the side of my hair.

"I don't do this," I gasp, still playing the game. "One night stands are incredibly risky and dangerous."

My legs are around him, and he jerks my thong aside. "I won't tell anyone."

A moan scrapes my throat as he invades my core, testing my wetness with two large fingers as his thumb circles my clit.

"Oh, god..." He knows just how to touch me, and the metallic *Clink!* of his belt meets my ears.

Anticipation tightens my stomach, and opening my hazy eyes, I catch his reflection in the large mirror facing us from the guest bedroom. His slacks drop around his thighs, and the dim light highlights the planes of his ass.

"Mmm..." I slide my hand from his shoulder down, leaning into him so I can clutch that perfect muscle.

Just then he thrusts into me. We both moan loudly. He's so big, it's always a surprise. Flexing my thighs, I push myself higher, catching his shoulders so I can ride him. The movement slams my clit directly against his pelvis, driving him deeper into me.

"Shit, Melissa," he gasps.

He's always the lead, the aggressor, but tonight, I feel powerful. Our little pretense helped me remember how far I've come since the days when I was the victim. That time is over. I survived, and now I am strong.

He clutches my hips, jerking me forcefully against him. "Fucking amazing." It's the same movement only now he's in charge, and he's right. It is amazing.

"Oh, don't stop!" I cry. He's driving deeper, hitting me harder, and we truly let go, riding the waves, oblivious to our shouts and moans of pleasure. It's a privilege that's become less frequent now that our little son is old enough to be disturbed by us.

My back is pressed against the rough fabric of the patio drapes, and I look again at his body in the mirror. His ass flexes as he drives into me, over and over. It's erotic, and the sight combined with the friction of our touch, the force of his movements, has me dancing on the edge. One last thing—I reach around to unfasten my bra and arch up. His lips clamp firmly on my beaded nipple, and with a tender bite, I fly over the edge.

"Oh, god!" My orgasm shatters my core. He doesn't stop, and in three more hard thrusts, my entire lower body is shuddering. I'm coming again, and the intensity of the pleasure radiates under my scalp. "Oh, god, Derek."

He's keeps going. His forehead is at my brow, and I notice the faint sheen of sweat touching his lip. Pulling forward, I run my tongue over it, pulling it between my teeth as he sinks deeper.

With a flick of his chin, he consumes my mouth, and the moan of his orgasm fills me. His body tenses as he takes one last, slow thrust.

Salt is on my tongue as I hold him. His arms surround me, and his kisses move to my neck. We're locked in an embrace, our bodies touching everywhere, as we melt together. It's the most intense satisfaction combined with such familiar comfort.

"I love you so much," I whisper.

Slowly he kisses me again. "I love you more." A gentle suck, a light nibble at my jaw. His lips sweep my cheek before our eyes meet. "Happy anniversary."

Smiling, I trace my fingers along his beard. "Our anniversary is in the fall."

"It's our mid-year anniversary."

"It's spring. That time when men's thoughts lightly turn to—"

His sexy grin is irresistible. "What I've been thinking about all winter."

We both laugh, and he slips out of me. My lips poke in a pretend sad face, but I lower my legs to stand in front of him. "I'll freshen up. You owe me a cava."

As I step through the balcony door, he playfully lands a *Slap!* on my bare backside. "Don't be long. I'm not finished with you Miss Jones."

Shaking my head, I make my way through the large master suite. It's practically empty since Derek's been with me full-time in Wilmington almost a year. Stuart Knight, his original business partner and Patrick's older brother, briefly lived here before getting his own place—the identical condo across the hall. The only personal items left are a photo of us together on the beach and a new one of me holding Dex.

Stopping, I lift the small frame. Derek took it of us, and my love for him glows on my face. I'm looking up at the camera, and our son is holding my shoulders. His big blue eyes, more the color of mine than his daddy's, gaze out at the ocean.

Warmth stirs behind me, and two strong arms wrap around my waist. "Miss him?" Derek's voice is at my ear. His chin rests on my shoulder.

Turning my head, I kiss his cheek. "I do, but I'm glad we have this weekend."

"Me too." He kisses the top of my shoulder before releasing me. "Meet me in the kitchen?"

"Be right there." Setting the frame down, I step into the bathroom to quickly clean up. My thong is ruined. "I should buy these in bulk," I mutter under my breath.

Returning to the bedroom, I pull open the top drawer that was designated as mine when we lived apart. A few outfits and luckily, panties are still here. I'm refreshed and joining him seconds later.

"Do you think we should still keep this place? It feels like bad luck."

He's just finished pouring two slim flutes of cava. His lined torso is on full display, and the recessed light under the bar casts shadows, making the cut of his muscles appear even deeper. *Sigh.*

"It's good that I have somewhere to crash when I'm in town. If I need to check in at the office."

I take the glass he hands me and sip the crisp, sparkling wine. "I'm sure Stuart wouldn't mind if you stayed in his guest room the few times you come here."

His dark brow creases. "With Mariska sleeping over? That's not very considerate."

"Hmm." My thoughts travel to the beautiful girl who only recently captured his stubborn partner's heart. "I guess you have a point."

"Besides, I like my place. Walter takes care of things, and if we need a quick getaway, we don't have to deal with hotels and luggage…"

"Yes, I'd miss Walter." The friendly doorman-slash-butler is like a doting grandfather to all of us. "I'm convinced. For now."

With a grin he kisses my forehead. "How was Aunt Bea?"

"Lovely as always. She's sending you a box of her recommendations for your groom's cake." He smiles, but as he turns, I see that shadow in his eyes again. Lately I've been seeing it more and more.

"Is that a problem?" I nudge.

He's back with me in a blink, shadow gone. "The only problem will be trying to pick one."

It's not a satisfactory answer, and I take another slow sip as I watch him thumbing through takeout menus. "Hungry?"

He nods, still flipping. "Nothing here looks good."

"Walter could order something. I'm sure he knows what you like."

Steel blue eyes flicker to mine, and he's hesitating, holding something back. It's confusing after the way we just made love. Everything about the way he's been acting these last weeks has been confusing. One moment he's with me, the next he's distracted, and it always happens when I start talking wedding plans. Derek has never been mercurial, and I'm trying not to let it spook me.

My visceral reaction is to remember how quickly Sloan went from doting fiancé to cheating and later, abusive husband. But Derek's not Sloan, my heart argues. I know he's not, yet I shudder remembering how Derek has kept secrets from me before. How we originally met because Sloan had hired him to track me—a fact I never knew until I found the emails on my ex-husband's laptop.

"I think I'll take the car and see what I can find," he says. Scooping his black sweater off the couch, he leans forward to kiss my mouth briefly. "Sure you don't want anything?"

I watch as he straightens and pulls the thin material down his bare chest. He's still wearing his black loafers. "I ate so much cake this afternoon with Bea, I might burst if I eat another thing."

With a wink, he's headed to the door. "When I get back, we'll see about working off those extra calories."

Despite the tension, I can't help smiling at his suggestion. "If I'm still awake."

"I seem to recall you like the way I wake you."

He's out the door before I can make another quip. It's probably for the best. He's right, after all. I do love the way he wakes me, especially when he starts with slow, lingering kisses below my waist.

Warmth curls my toes and I sigh. "Oh, Derek. What are you hiding now?"

CHAPTER 2: THREATS

Derek

I'm not hungry. Maneuvering my black Audi through the empty streets of Princeton, I pass under traffic lights blinking yellow, block after block, taking me further away from what I have to do. I've never run from a problem, but the reasons driving me on are inescapable.

They're a woman who smells like roses mixed with the ocean, who fulfills me in a way nothing else does, and a little boy with round, sapphire eyes just like hers. My fiancée. My son. The second-chance I thought I'd never have that dropped in my lap one week in the desert. The future I could lose just as fast.

Gripping the steering wheel, images trickle from the corners of my brain—a dark conference room, Patrick and me cramped in the adjacent tech booth, fighting with all my strength. On the other side of the glass is our target. He's holding a woman—our bait—by the throat, strangling the life out of her while he hisses his poison in her face.

Star's cheeks go from red to purple as he grips her, and the sound of her sniffs, her nose running as her life is twisted from her body, is a noise that still ignites an explosion of rage in my chest. *He touched Melissa that way...*

The necklace was the final nail in his coffin. When that fucker pulled it out, holding it for all of us to see, I knew I didn't have a choice. He'd been in her cottage and taken it from her somehow. She didn't even know he'd done it.

I'm at the Alexander-Knight building. I don't remember driving here, but I park the car near the front entrance and kill the engine. That night is like a dream. With one word, *Sangria*, Patrick released me. The shock and recognition barely registered on Sloan's sick face before I had him in my hands.

Closing my eyes, I can still feel his wretched skull against my palms. No hesitation. Immediate action. The satisfying *Crack!* of his fucking neck as I twisted it echoes in my brain. In one motion, I ended his threat to my family forever, then I stood over his dead body and smiled, the warmth of satisfaction flooding my veins like hot liquid.

I have to tell her. I have to do it before the wedding. It's not like she loved the guy. It's not like she probably didn't wish him dead. It's not like he didn't beat her, leave her with that scar at her hairline... My jaw clenches so hard at the memory of the photograph she showed me. Her beautiful blue eyes rimmed in ugly purple bruises, the jagged cut extending into her scalp, gaping open like a blood-red mouth. A tiny silver line is all that's left to remind us what he did to her, yet the memory of him hurting her that way... I've never felt such consuming wrath.

I'm breathing too fast. I need to get out and think. I need to calm down and clear my head. I walk under the security lamps to the obelisk fountain in the center of our courtyard. It's cool out, but not frigid. Spring is breaking all over, and the fresh scent of new growth fills the air.

Dropping onto a nearby bench, I lean forward and jam my hands in the sides of my hair. I know why this is so hard. Lowering them, I study my palms. With malice aforethought, I placed my palms on the sides of Sloan Reynolds's head and murdered him. It wasn't wartime. He wasn't an enemy combatant. He wasn't even coming at me with a weapon.

I charged out of that tech booth with one thing on my mind, and I walked straight up to him and snapped his neck like a twig. Then I stood over him and allowed the sick satisfaction of what I'd done to wash over me like some fucking psychopath. I reveled in that revenge. I drank it in like the finest Scotch.

How can I tell her that? It's a side of me Melissa has never seen. It's a dark and brutal part I'm not sure she could love. It's useful in combat, but it doesn't make me proud. Clearly, I can't even control it.

Patrick, Toni… or Star, and I have never talked about it directly. None of us has ever named what I did. We only reference it sideways. It's our secret. The variable we didn't plan for. The thing we're all so ready to sweep under the rug and forget.

Patrick's position is to walk away. He and Star both say it was justice, and telling Melissa will only make her blame herself. For a little while it worked. I'd believed my only reason for keeping it from her was to protect her from somehow adopting the blame for my actions.

Time has pulled the curtain back on that half-truth. Protecting Melissa is only part of why I can't tell her. The other part is much more basic, more black and white. In one moment of authoritarian rage, I turned my back on everything I believed, everything I dedicated my life to defend. I sank all the way to his level that night. I became the monster I killed.

With a growl, I clench my fists, and I know with painful certainty Melissa won't understand. How could she? Over and over she begged me to put it behind us. She wanted to move on and be stronger than her past, and now I've chained us to it forever.

No statute of limitations applies to what I've done. I didn't simply take the law into my own hands, I put our family in jeopardy. I'm a felon, a murderer. No matter how many years go by, how far we get from that night, how old we are or how much she might need me, if I'm ever discovered, I'll go to prison. Depending on the circumstances, I could get the death penalty.

"Fuck." Pushing against my thighs, I stand, staring out across the courtyard. "He deserved it," I try, but the words ring hollow.

Who the fuck am I to decide what anyone deserves? When did I buy into vigilante justice? I'm a Marine. I took an oath. I trained as a cop. Everything I've ever done has been to uphold the laws of this country. I put my life on the line over and over to defend our way of life, yet in one moment, I turned my back on all of it.

I'm no anarchist. I'm an American hero. At least, I was.

"Melissa… Melissa." Closing my eyes, I say her name like a prayer for forgiveness. Will she forgive me? Will she understand?

I killed a man in cold blood with the very hands I use to touch her… with the same hands I use to hold our son.

"God dammit!" My shout echoes off the concrete walls, and I know what has to happen. I have to look what I've done in the face. She has to know the truth and decide if she's willing to live this life with me. If she can marry me knowing what's hanging over our heads.

If she wants me to turn myself in, I will. If she can't love me anymore… *Shit.* I can't even think that.

Either way, I have to say it out loud to the one person who makes everything real, and I have to do it soon.

* * *

When I return to the condo, I've mentally prepared myself to say it, and she's in my bed asleep. Lying on her side, curled in her familiar sleeping position, I can't bring myself to wake her. It would ruin her night, and a few more hours won't make a difference.

Climbing in beside her, I pull her into my arms. As always, she melts into me as if she belongs there.

She always belongs there.

Since that first night in Scottsdale, I've known she belongs to me. Yet… that night I'd been hired by her husband to watch her. Is it possible the wheels I set in motion, taking her instead of doing my job, doomed us from the start?

Pressing my face into her hair I inhale deeply, allowing her scent to relax my mind. These thoughts will drive me crazy if I let them. Sloan tricked me as much as everyone else, and my role in this has always been to save her from him.

Still, my mind can't let it go. How will our beginning appear to a jury? I can only imagine how a prosecutor will take our situation and run with it. I've worked on prosecution teams. Shit, I'd been the key witness in the case against Slayde Bennett. They'll crucify me.

I followed her to Scottsdale, seduced her, then killed her ex-husband. It would drag all of Melissa's past out of the closet and expose it to intense media scrutiny. She once called Sloan her humiliating truth, and now thanks to me, it could all be put on display for the world to see. The beatings, the prostitutes... adultery, murder. It's a sensational, juicy story. The press would eat it up.

Tightening my hold on her, I hug her to me as my chest collapses. The weight of the position I've placed her in destroys me.

When morning finally rolls around, I'm exhausted from wrestling with my thoughts all night. Melissa's still asleep, so I slip out of bed and go to the kitchen for coffee. Just as I've sat down, my phone buzzes. Stuart.

"What's got you out of bed so early," I ask.

His voice sounds surprised. "I was planning to leave a message."

"Now you don't have to. What's going on?"

He clears his throat, and it sounds as if he's been wrestling with his thoughts all night as well. "Nikki gave her notice on Friday."

My brow rises. Not what I expected. "Didn't you just get back to the office?"

"Yeah. She said she only stayed to keep things running until I came back."

She could've told me, I think but don't say. "What's her reason?"

A soft voice sounds in the background on his end, and I hear a brush over the phone as he answers what I assume is Mariska. A few moments pass before he returns to the line.

"Hey, I can't really talk about this now. I'd rather discuss it Monday. Suffice to say, it's because of something I did."

Shit. Nikki has never been one of my favorite employees, and I'm ready to let her go without a fight until he says those words.

"You've been in Saudi three years. You were in the office in Princeton a week. Now you're with Mariska. What the hell could you have done?"

"When I get to the office Monday, I'll call and explain." His tone has an urgency that makes me relent.

"Fine. Monday. Enjoy your weekend."

We end the call, and I sit back to think as I sip my coffee. I can only find one reason why Stuart would call me early on a Sunday morning to discuss Nikki resigning, and that reason is Mariska. He doesn't want her to know. She should've been asleep, which leads me to believe it has something to do with sex.

I can't believe it. Stuart is as committed to professionalism and following a code of conduct at work as I am. At the same time, when he came back from Saudi, he was addicted to narcotic painkillers and basically hitting rock bottom. Patrick and I feared he might take his life.

As much as I can't imagine Stuart crossing a line, I can't imagine Nikki suing us. The lion's share of her duties has been working with me, and I've always treated her with respect. She and Melissa are close... Still, I know she carried a torch for my partner for years, and when he got back, well, he didn't go to her. Mariska had been the woman to heal him.

Finishing my coffee, I stand and walk to the sink. I'll figure out this problem, solve it, and return to handling my shit. I'm just passing the table when my phone buzzes again. Patrick. *Isn't anybody sleeping this morning?*

"Why the hell aren't you in bed with your wife? You're supposed to be in your fucking honeymoon period."

"We've got a situation." My younger partner's usual cocky greeting is absent, his tone tense. "Will you be back tonight?"

"We'll probably leave in about an hour. Melissa needs to pick up Dex at her mother's—"

"Toni called. She's in trouble." My chest tightens at his words. This fucking snowball just keeps getting bigger. "It's better if we discuss it in private, but it can't wait."

"I'll drop Melissa off and head over as soon as we get in."

"Meet me at the satellite office in town."

Disconnecting, I notice Melissa has joined me. She's standing at the large windows gazing out over downtown. Based on her expression, I know she's curious about my early calls. Melissa is one of the smartest people I know, and the fact I've been able to keep my shit from her so long blows my mind.

"Everything okay?" She gives me a little smile, and dammit, she's so beautiful. Her dark waves ripple over her shoulders, and she's wearing a satin pajama top that displays her long, smooth legs.

I can't tell her what Patrick said, so I say what I can. "Stuart called. Nikki gave her notice Friday."

Her mouth drops open. "Nikki loves working for you guys! What happened?"

"I'm not sure. Stuart's only been in Princeton a week, but apparently there's a story."

Crossing her arms, I can see her brain working behind those beautiful blue eyes. "It doesn't make any sense. Nikki was excited he was coming back. She managed to work it into nearly every text or email she sent me leading up to his arrival." Quiet settles over us, her eyes slowly move to mine. Despite all my conflict, warmth spreads across my chest. Stepping closer, I slide my hands over her hips, around her waist.

"Are you going to let her go?" she asks softly.

"Stuart will have to make that decision." Pulling her closer, I drop my chin and take a deep inhale at the top of her head. Ocean roses. "I know you like her, but trust me. Nikki can be a challenge as a secretary."

Her arms are still crossed, and I can tell by her tone, she's not buying it. "That explains why Stuart might fire her. Why would *she* quit?"

"I'll know tomorrow."

"So you're going to talk to her about it?" Arms uncrossed, she returns my embrace at last. I love holding her this way. I love her holding onto me.

"I'll talk to Stuart first. He couldn't discuss it in front of Mariska."

Again she's quiet, thinking. "You think this has something to do with Mariska?"

I exhale and kiss her head. "If it were Patrick, I'd say yes without hesitation, but Stuart's different. He keeps it in his pants."

Pulling back, she barely hides her surprise. "You think he slept with Nikki?"

"I'm not jumping to any conclusions. The reason Stuart and I agreed to start this firm is because of how alike we are. If something happened, my guess is it was before he left the last time."

"He wasn't planning to come back."

I nod, remembering the night he left. He was pretty jazzed about going overseas. I left him and Nikki alone together at the bar. "Three years is a long time to keep a secret," I say, thinking out loud.

Her eyes narrow, and I realize I've given her an opening. "Even three months is a long time."

One problem at a time. I turn my gaze out the window and watch the bright green trees swaying in the early spring breeze. "Sometimes people have reasons for keeping quiet."

CHAPTER 3: SECRETS

Melissa

Loud, impatient squeals echo from Dex's room down the hall, forcing my eyes open. Looking around our bedroom, I see no signs of his father. He'd been late again last night after meeting with Patrick, and I wouldn't have known he was back if he hadn't pulled me into his arms in the darkness.

Our son is only playfully complaining, so I take a moment to reflect on last night. It's the second time in a row I've gone to bed alone. Combined with Derek's increasing withdrawal, it's getting to be more than I can take.

Last night, when his strong arms circled my waist, pulling my back against his chest, it wasn't like his usual embrace. His face moved into my hair, against my neck. "Melissa..." His voice cracked in a low whisper against my skin.

He hadn't been trying to wake me, yet the sound of that break tightened my throat. Anxiety moved across my chest, and I slid my palms down his forearms to entwine our fingers.

Sensitivity to my environment is a skill I learned the hard way during my final months in Sloan's mansion. I'd slept with a can of pepper spray clutched beneath my pillow, all my senses on alert against any changes as I slept.

Only one thing has ever scared Derek, according to him, and that "thing," that threat—my ex-husband—has been dealt with. How exactly, I still don't know, but I believe Derek's words. So if Sloan is no longer a threat, what's tormenting my love?

I whispered his name in the darkness. Clutching our hands, he wrapped them around my waist as his mouth moved to the top of my shoulder. My head dropped back against him, and we held each other several long, quiet moments, our hearts beating together, our bodies touching head to toe. We were home, our son was in his bed asleep, we were together. What could be wrong?

Releasing one of his hands, I reached up to thread my fingers into the side of his thick hair. I knew how to ease his tension. I wanted to ease his tension.

The climate in Wilmington is warmer than Princeton, so I only sleep in a thin cami and panties. His large hands spanned my bare stomach, tightening my muscles. Derek's touch is a delicious mixture of gentle and rough. Soft lips, scruff of beard; smoothing hands, firm grip. From the first night we were together, his touch has always made me hotter, wetter than I've ever been with anyone.

Shrugging off my lace underwear, my eyes don't open as he parts my thighs. His thick erection sinks deep into me, stretching me. "Oh, god," I gasp. It's so good.

Arching my back to allow him further access, another soft moan scrapes from my throat as his expert fingers find my clit.

Quiet words of desire, love, and appreciation rumble across my skin, and my mouth opens to release another little cry as I buck against him. Pleasure snakes up my thighs. He goes deeper, his length massaging my tightening insides.

I want it harder, and I tell him so. He's quick to comply. Large hands grip my breasts, and we're working together, meeting each other thrust for thrust. Moving

faster, gasping and grinding, our bodies tense as we reach the crest of orgasm.

"Come, Melissa." It's a low order I don't need.

I'm riding him as the pleasure lifts me out of myself. A quivering little wail comes from me as he clutches my thighs so hard, I'm sure he'll leave a mark. We ride our orgasm to the end, moaning and trembling, then holding each other, breathing hard.

"I love you so much," he exhales against my skin, yet even in the sparkling afterglow, that tone is still in his voice.

My chest clenches. I don't understand. "I love you more," I whisper back, stealing his usual line as I tighten my grip on him.

He doesn't speak. His arms never loosen their hold. His lips touch the back of my neck, followed by the scratch of his beard. Derek's arms are always a safe place for me—they have been since our first night in the desert. He's sexy, wildly passionate, and deeply safe, the most erotic combination my guarded heart could desire. Whatever's bothering him, I know we can fix it. Our love hasn't changed. The thought comforts me as I drift to sleep again.

Sometime before dawn, my eyes open and he's still holding me. My back is against his chest, and I'm tight in the confines of his strong arms as if I might slip away while he sleeps. I've become so used to it, I practically have to relearn how to sleep alone when he travels, which is rare nowadays.

A more insistent squeal from Dex brings me back to the present. It's time to start the day.

Dragging myself out of bed and staggering down the hall, I catch a glimpse of my fiancé in the kitchen already dressed and talking on his cell. His brow is lined, and I can tell we're back to where we left off. With a sigh, I enter our son's room.

He's standing in his crib, holding the side. When he sees me, his blue eyes sparkle and he starts to jump. My worries about his daddy fly away, and I can't help laughing.

"Good morning, pumpkin," I coo, lifting him over the rail. His legs pump against my waist as he struggles to get down, out of my arms. "You want to walk, big boy?"

A week short of his first birthday, and he's already tearing through the house. We've had to move all small items to the top shelves in every room as his favorite thing is pulling whatever he can reach down on his head.

"I can drive to Raleigh if I need to." Derek's voice is low as he speaks into his cell. That makes my brow crease. Raleigh hasn't come up in more than a year.

When he sees me, he smiles, but it's not his usual flood of appreciation at my presence. It's that tight smile, the one accompanying his subtle mood-swings. He gets an impatient smile from me in response.

"We can talk more at the office. I'll be there in ten minutes." He disconnects and walks over to pull me into a hug. "Sorry I was late last night. I hope I made it up to you."

I press my nose against his chest and inhale the warm, slightly woodsy scent I've come to associate with the greatest love of my life. I feel him kiss the top of my head. "Still working on the Nikki situation?" I ask.

Releasing me, he picks up a leather portfolio and grabs his keys. "I'm heading to the office to meet Patrick and talk to Stuart. Are you working today?"

"Later," I say, walking to the coffee maker. I drop in a small, plastic pod, slide my mug in place, and hit the button. "Elaine and I are taking the boys to do their fittings this morning."

His expression is confused, and I'm ready to have it out with him. I knew he hadn't been listening to me on our drive home yesterday. "Their tuxes? For our wedding?"

"Oh, right." He steps back to me and kisses my forehead before heading to the door. "Don't let Dex knock over the mannequins."

I give him a little growl, but his comment still makes me smile. Our toddler is a menace to anything in his grabbing space. Derek's gone, so I grab a baby breakfast bar and a sippy cup of milk. Dex is in front of the flat-screen television attempting to turn it on when I return to the living room.

"Come on, little man, I'll put on your show." Scooping him up, I deposit him in the pack and play in my bedroom, pulling up his show on the Internet television. "Be sweet while Mommy showers!"

My shower is fast, and I listen for any changes in the bedroom as I step into jeans and pull on a loose, charcoal tee. I tie my hair in a low, side ponytail, and drop a few necklaces over my head as I step into black ankle boots.

Running down the hall, I stop at Dex's room and grab his little jeans, long-sleeved polo, and an extra diaper. He can still wear the cowboy boots we bought him for Elaine's Christmas wedding in

Montana. He wasn't walking yet, and we intentionally bought them a few sizes too big. He's adorable in them.

When I return to the room, he's engrossed in his favorite train show, and just like a little man, he doesn't even look at me when I enter. "Okay, mister. Time to get dressed."

"May, tank," he says, twisting and pointing over my shoulder as I scoop him up and carry him to the living room.

"Yes!" I nod. "A blue tank."

Flipping on the flat screen, I'm about to sit when I hear banging on my back door.

"Guess who it is, Dexy? It's Aunt Elaine and Laney!"

That sends him wiggling again, and I let him down, following him to where they're smiling and waving at the back glass. Shouts and squeals fill the kitchen as the boys greet each other and my best friend and I hug.

"I tell you," Elaine says, stripping off her coat and dropping it on the back of a kitchen chair, "After how cute they were in my wedding, I can't even imagine how they'll look surrounded by the guys in their dress whites."

"Blues," I correct. "Derek told me in spring it's blues."

"Are you sure about that?" Elaine has a sour straw hanging out of her mouth. "I think you have it backwards."

"Hell, you're probably right. I'll have to double-check. Properly addressing the invitations was enough to drive me crazy."

She follows me into the living room where Lane is sitting in front of the television making engine noises as he moves his ever-present truck back and forth across the rug.

Dex is parked in his tiny leather armchair with matching ottoman—identical to his daddy's right behind it. Love spills through my veins as I pause to study his baby profile. He looks so much like Derek.

"So? How was the weekend getaway?" Elaine drops onto the couch.

"It started out amazing, but then…" I'm trying to figure out how to end that sentence when she cuts in.

"Stop! Don't say you had a fight. I'll lose all my faith in happily ever after!"

"You're so freaking dramatic." I flop on the couch beside her. "Give me a sour straw."

"Am I the worst mother or what?" She digs in her purse and pulls out two—one for me, and another for her. "Lane loves these things, and I'm completely addicted."

That makes me laugh. "I'm sure you only give him one a day."

"It's true! But only because I've eaten all the rest!" She falls back on the couch, a fresh straw hanging from the side of her mouth. "I'm going to get a cavity, I can feel it."

"What does Kenny think?" Lane's birth mother, a young artist Patrick was involved with briefly before he met Elaine, keeps their two-year old one weekend a month.

After a rocky beginning, she and my bestie bonded last fall over a situation involving Kenny's boyfriend Slayde. Kenny is also how Stuart met Mariska—in a crazy twist of love and fate.

"She's the one who started it! He came back from Bayville demanding sour straws and Coke floats."

"Oh, wow. Coke floats." I try to remember the last time I had that creamy, bubbly deliciousness. "So old-school, and so good."

A sharp kick to my thigh makes me yelp. "I'm trying not to gain a hundred pounds! I'm convinced Kenny has a worm. It's impossible she can stay that skinny with all the crap she eats."

"She's a fitness instructor," I snort laughing. "A worm. You sound like my grandma!"

"I'm not lying. She eats the worst shit!"

Lane's towhead pops up at once. "Mommy, bad word!"

"Good grief." My friend flops back against the couch. "Don't tell daddy."

Lane goes back to engine noises, and I chew on my sour straw. "I thought Kenny was lactose intolerant."

"Goat's milk doesn't bother her. It's been life changing, apparently. She eats goat ice cream and chévre nonstop now." I exhale a little laugh, and Lainey's green eyes blink to me. "So what the heck could've spoiled your romantic getaway?"

Leaning beside her on the sofa, I straighten my legs and rest my heels on the coffee table next to hers. "I'm probably overreacting."

She kicks my leg again. "Spill!"

"Ow!" I cry. "You're so violent."

"Mel."

With a loud groan, I just say it. "He's keeping something from me again, and it's kind of making me crazy."

"Oh, shit." Elaine's eyes narrow.

Lane's little head pops up again. "Mommy, bad word!"

"Mommy said *spit*," my best friend casually corrects him.

I can't help noting the obvious. "Lane's pretty good at spotting the swear words all of a sudden."

"It's Patrick!" she shrieks, slapping her leg. "I said he swore too much, and now all he does is point out when I drop a bomb. I'm ready to kill him!"

That makes me grin. "I love him."

Her bottom lip goes under her front teeth, and she wriggles out an arm to squeeze me. "I know. Now finish telling me what happened."

With a sigh, I lean back. "Derek is wonderful and attentive and sexy... and I can't take how he hides things. It's like this invisible shield or something, and it's too... It reminds me too much of living with Sloan. I lived so long in his house of secrets and lies. I just... I can't do it again, Lainey."

We're both quiet, and in my peripheral vision, I see her chewing a sour straw as she thinks. "I get that," she says quietly. A few more moments pass and she adds, "but you know, the grass isn't really greener. Now that we're married, Patrick wants to tell me all this sh-spit he's working on. You know, because wives can't testify against their husbands?"

"Yeah?" I can't hide the eagerness burning in my chest that she might know something.

"I don't. Want. To know!" She waves her hands over her head. "I'm married to the master of pushing the limits. He's driving me crazy with worry!"

That gives me pause. I sit back and think a moment. I remember my request from Patrick—the promise I'd asked him to make to keep Derek from doing anything "hazardous or potentially life threatening" as Patrick put it.

"I guess that makes sense," I say quietly.

"We both love Patrick, but oh my god. He takes too many chances."

Shaking my head, I catch her hand. "It's not like that. Derek and Patrick are different people, they have different styles." Searching for the right words, I just say what's eating up my thoughts. "Derek's hidden stuff from me before, and it hurt when I found out. It hurt badly."

My friend's eyes are round as she turns to me, all teasing gone. "Derek loves you, Melissa."

"I know that. I know." Pushing up I go and pull Dex out of his baby chair, ignoring his complaints as I strip off his pajamas. "I'm not a little girl, Elaine. I don't want a daddy. I want a partner. I want someone who views me as an equal, not someone who keeps things from me—even if he does believe it's for my own good."

The best part about having the same best friend since childhood is sharing a deep understanding of each other. Her expression is serious as she watches me. "Have you told him that?"

"No," I confess, standing my son in front of me and pulling his jeans over the puff of his new diaper. He's content to let me change him so long as he can see his trains. "He should know how I feel by now. We've already been through this."

"Wait." My best friend holds her hands up. "Are you saying a *male* should *know* how you feel? Is that what I'm hearing you say?"

"Lainey." I can't suppress my irritation. "This is Derek."

She shakes her head, her light blonde hair spilling over her shoulders. "Who happens to be the most manly male we know? Except for maybe Stuart?"

"Patrick's pretty manly. And stop defending him!" Dex is dressed, and I grab the remote. "We've got to go."

Once the TV is off, both boys get restless, and I can't help wondering about that Y chromosome. We scoop them up, grab our bags and head out the door. They're secure in their car seats, and we're heading to town when Elaine grabs my forearm.

"Stop at the office for a sec."

My eyes narrow at her. "We don't have time for a quickie."

"Just... it's not that." She grins, and I can't help it. I have to know.

"What is it, then?"

"Mel."

"Lainey."

She lets out an exasperated breath. "I visited Patrick at the office Friday, and... well... you know, and I forgot a *personal item*."

"Do you have a checklist? Shit! Where have you not done it?"

Lane pipes up from the back seat. "Aunt Mel, bad word."

"Lane!" I cry, defensive. "I said *spit*!" Narrowing my eyes at my bestie, I grumble. "You've got me lying to babies now."

"I blame Patrick."

We both snort as we laugh. "Oh my god." I shake my head, turning into the parking lot of the long, one-story building where Alexander-Knight's satellite office is located.

"Besides, we're newlyweds! It's our honeymoon period!" She climbs out of her side, and I call after her.

"That excuse might've worked if I hadn't known you before the wedding."

"Grab the boys. The guys will want to see them."

I lean into the backseat unbuckling them before we all follow her into the rented space, but it's empty. "We must've missed them," I call as she heads to the back office.

I stand in the reception area while our little boys resume their usual positions—Lane is on his knees making engine noises as his favorite truck runs over the tracks on the rug, Dex is beside him watching. It's hard to know how long that will last before my little wrecking ball is up and exploring.

"Hurry up," I call to her as I pick up an issue of *People* magazine. "I can't believe they subscribe to these. Who reads them?"

I flip through the magazine as Dex toddles to where I hear Elaine searching.

"Heads up!" I call. "Here comes my little wrecker."

"I can't find it!" My friend's voice is a muffled reply.

Lane is content being the soundtrack for his truck as it follows the lines on the carpet. I'm scanning a movie review, when the monotony is broken by a *CRASH!* a shriek from my friend, and the slow siren-whine from my son.

"Dex!" I rush to the back.

My little boy's heartbroken cries grow louder, and I drop to the floor beside Elaine who's trying to comfort him. He's rubbing his eyes, and I look around at the scattered photo prints and a large paperweight he knocked off the desk. I'll have to clean this up.

"It's okay, baby," I whisper, shushing him as he pulls my shoulders and buries his face against my chest. "He's only scared, not hurt." I glance up at Elaine. "Did you find what you were looking for?"

"No," she says, but her voice trails off. She's on her knees collecting the photos and looking at them, eyes wide.

"What is it?" I reach out and take one of the prints from her. Turning it over, I have to blink twice to understand what I'm seeing. She hands me another, and my heart starts beating faster. My breath comes in pants as the images click together. I realize what I'm seeing, or rather *who* I'm seeing.

"Oh my god," I whisper as my hands tremble. My stomach turns like I might vomit.

Dex is still clutching my arms, and I hold my lips, taking a slow breath and trying to calm down. *Breathe, Melissa, breathe...* Leaning forward, I pick up another photo and notice my hand is trembling.

The images are horrible—a dead man, his face a sick grey color and his neck bent in an unnatural angle, clearly broken. He's lying on the floor in what appears to be a dark, hotel conference room.

"It's..." But everything tilts. The room seems to move out, away from me, and I'm afraid I might faint.

I can't finish my sentence. It doesn't matter because my friend whispers it for me. "It's Sloan."

Lane makes a loud engine noise from the front, and Dex releases me, running to see what his friend is doing. I can't move. I can barely breathe. I'm paralyzed and numb—and confused. I don't understand why I'm reacting this way, why I'm so terrified.

My voice shakes like my hands. "Why do they have these?"

Clearly, he was murdered in some gruesome manner. *No.* I stop myself. I'm jumping to conclusions. Maybe he had an accident. *Could he have fallen? But from where? And how?*

This is why Derek has been so preoccupied. Rising to stand, my light-headedness almost makes me fall. Dropping all but one print, I catch the side of the desk.

"Melissa?" Elaine jumps up and holds my arm. "Are you okay?"

"I have to talk to Derek."

"Of course." Her face is lined, and she holds my arm as we head back out to the front. "Come on boys. Lane, get your truck. Dex, hold my hand."

It feels like a thick fog is wrapping around me, clouding my vision. Derek doesn't want me to know about this... But why? I'm afraid I know the answer without needing to ask.

We're in Elaine's car heading back to the beach, and I barely register her telling me she'll keep Dex for the afternoon. When she stops at my cottage, I see his black Audi sitting in the driveway.

"Call me when you're ready for me to bring him home," she says.

Nodding, I glance back to check on my little son before I go. He's happily chattering baby-gibberish at Lane, unaffected by the sudden change in my mood.

"Thanks," I say softly and start toward the door.

Pausing, my eyes close, and I listen to the soft whisper of the waves in the distance trying to find calm. I know I have to talk to him, but I'm so afraid of this conversation. My emotions are all over the place. Sloan was an abusive, sick, evil man, who hurt me and kept me living in fear for more than a year. I should not feel emotional at discovering he's dead. I shouldn't be shocked or disturbed… I shouldn't… care. Why do I care?

Opening the door, when I see Derek sitting at the table, I know why I'm so torn up and twisted. I care because I know why my abusive ex is dead. I don't have to ask who did it. I know who did it.

That leaves one question: What now?

* * *

Derek

I'd been late getting back to the beach cottage last night, and Melissa was already asleep for the second time in a row. I know she's growing increasingly annoyed with my evasions, and she has no idea how her talk of our wedding plans and Dex's first birthday party are killing me. The drive back from Princeton had been difficult, but leaving her as soon as we'd arrived home was worse.

"You have to meet Patrick *now*?" Her hands are on her hips as she follows me to the door.

"He found out about the Nikki situation. He needs to go over a few cases." Lying to her burns in my chest, but it's the last time I'll do it.

"What about Dex? He hasn't seen you in two days!"

"Patrick and Nikki are close." I pull my keys from my pocket. "She's heavily involved in several of his cases. Her leaving probably impacts him the most."

"Then let him convince her to stay." She catches my sleeve in her hand. "I can't believe this can't wait until tomorrow."

Covering her small hand with mine, I look into her eyes. "I won't be long."

I'm going to make this right, I vow as I walk to my car. *I'll make all of this up to her, and we'll never be in this situation again.*

Patrick is waiting when I arrive at our satellite office in Wilmington. Dressed in his usual faded jeans and a maroon, short-sleeved tee, his light-brown hair is a messy bedhead, and if he didn't have his son Lane at the house, I'd guess he came straight to meet me from sleeping with Elaine.

Hell, he probably did that anyway. Those two have been known to leave a house full of dinner guests for a quickie in the bathroom.

Standing in our small office space, I hold the fax and read the typed letter. It's on nondescript, white paper in a basic, serif font. Nothing distinguishes it. Nothing gives us a clue as to who might have sent it.

The message is short and clear:

Ms. Durango:

I know about your involvement in the death of Sloan Reynolds. An item belonging to you, containing your DNA, is in my possession along with digital files of the enclosed photographs.

Lowering the sheet, I glance up at my partner. "Photographs?"

He hands over cheap prints showing Sloan's corpse from a distance, lying on his back, his head cocked at a sick angle. The images gradually move in closer, frame by frame, until the focus is on a black lace thong in his pocket.

My jaw clenches. "Her fucking underwear."

Patrick's bicep flexes as he bends his elbow, pulling a fist to his chest. "We forgot he had it."

I also know about your record and the child in Myrtle Beach. If you want her to remain safe, you'll do as I say.

My next letter will contain instructions. Tell anyone, and you can kiss your baby goodbye.

Signed,
A Friend.

"A *friend*? Is that a fucking joke?" I'm ready to slam my fist through the wall. "What the fuck do they want?"

"Letter number two hasn't arrived yet. Toni called me as soon as she read this. She's pretty spooked, which you know takes a lot." He walks around the only desk in our two-room satellite office. He and I both do the majority of our work on the road or from home, so this space is for the rare occasion we have to meet with a client in person.

Sitting in the chair, his hazel eyes laser into mine. "You get what this means, right? This asshole was there. He or she saw what we did and is looking to exploit it."

"But why go after her?" My voice is flat. "Why not come straight to me?"

"That's the part neither of us can figure." He leans forward, elbows on the desk. "You clearly have more money if it's blackmail. Maybe whoever it is sees her as the weak link in our chain."

Growling, I try to think. "What's this about a kid?"

"A little girl, Camille. She had her about a year ago, but the baby lives with her sister."

Confused, I look up at him. "Could it be the father?"

"My first question." He stands and walks around the desk again. "She says no. He still lives in Raleigh. They're friends, just not together."

Scrolling through my thoughts, I try to remember the last time we'd heard from Toni... or "Star," depending on whether she's running a con. She'd enrolled in community college and was working toward a degree in criminal justice. I'd offered to help her find a legitimate job when she finished.

"She's sure he's not after the baby?"

"From what I understand, Cammie lives with her sister because of Toni's... work history."

"She expected something like this to happen?"

"I don't think she expected Sloan Reynolds to come back from the dead, but apparently she's been involved in some pretty high-risk jobs. She didn't want to elaborate. I think she was afraid I might arrest her."

"So that's it. Whoever is sending this is trying to drag up her past for some reason."

"Maybe." He leans against the desk and crosses his arms. "Only she can't figure out why. As we've both already noted, she's not rich."

"What do you want me to do?"

"The fact this person addressed her as Durango and not Brandon, her stage name, has her scared. It means he or she knows the real Toni." He slips the letter back in his pocket and grabs a manila envelope. I watch as he drops the photographs in it and places it under a paperweight on the desk. "She's afraid for her little girl."

"How old is the child?"

"Almost a year."

Same age as Dex. "I guess I understand how she feels."

Patrick nods. "She's tough, but you know how it is. Hit somebody where they live, and you can pretty much get whatever you want."

Inhaling deeply, I nod and start for the door. "Speaking of, I need to get home. Let me know as soon as you hear from her. Tell her not to be afraid. We'll take care of this."

CHAPTER 4: THE LAST STRAW

Melissa

Derek is at the kitchen table when I open the door to my beach cottage. The images of Sloan's gruesome, broken neck churn my stomach. I'm still holding one of the prints.

"Melissa?" He crosses the room as I step inside. "Are you sick? What's wrong?"

I lift the photograph, holding it so he can see what I know. "Dex knocked this off your desk."

His jaw clenches, but he doesn't speak. I don't need him to. I remember the night he'd told me he could kill a man with his bare hands. We'd been discussing "special skills." He'd said he wasn't proud of that one.

"You did this." My voice is so quiet, yet it feels like the loudest thing in the room.

His eyes close, and for the second time, my head grows suddenly light. Only this time, the whiteness overpowers me. I'm going down, until I'm scooped up in his strong arms at once.

"Hang on," he soothes, carrying me to the sofa and gently helping me sit. "Stay here. I'll get you something to drink."

"No!" I catch his arm and hold him. "I need you to tell me if it's true."

With a deep sigh, he lowers himself beside me. My head hurts. Pressure is behind my eyes, and my limbs are weak.

His voice is quiet, resigned when he answers me. "It's true."

"Oh, god, Derek!" Tears flood my eyes, and my whole body is trembling now. "Oh, god!"

The tears spill down my cheeks, and he gathers me to his chest. I can only clutch his shoulders. Breathing is hard. Thinking is hard—past the one thought of *What now?* Repeating over and over in my brain. My worst nightmare is coming true.

"I'm sorry." His voice remains quiet, and he continues holding me, softly running his hand up and down my back.

"When were you going to tell me?" My whisper is accusatory. I'm angry, but more than anything, I'm terrified of losing him.

I feel him take a deep breath, his hold on me loosens as his arms lower. "In the beginning? Never."

Pushing back, I catch his eyes. "You were never going to tell me you killed a man?"

"I didn't want you burdened with that knowledge." His tone is closed, but his steel blue eyes tell me he's not saying everything.

All the shock and fear that had just been swirling through me binds together in a fist of anger in my chest. I push to my feet, adrenaline driving me now. "You didn't want me to be burdened with the knowledge that you've committed a crime? That my ex-husband is dead at your hands?"

I'm pacing the living room, but he's not moving. His eyes follow me.

Finally, I stop and shout at him. "How could you keep this from me?"

He looks up at me, and his expression is so pained, my chest clenches again. As angry as I am, I still love him so much. His suffering tears me apart.

"Melissa," he breathes my name in a way that nearly melts me. "I've wrestled with this decision so long—"

"Because you know it's the wrong one."

"Because I love you." He stands and steps toward me. His massive size makes me feel very small. "I couldn't risk you assuming any of the blame for what I did. This crime is solely on me. I wouldn't let him hurt you again."

With that one statement, understanding washes through me. "He threatened me?"

Derek's chin drops, and I reach up to cup his cheek, sliding my palm over his close, dark beard. Our eyes meet then, and his are filled with so much regret. "Yes," is all he says.

Reaching for him, I surrender to his embrace, and for a few moments, we simply hold each other. Our breathing swirls together, and images fill my mind of how something like that would affect this man who spent the first part of his career as a commanding officer, leading men like Stuart on combat missions. It would be like tweaking the nose of a lion.

My cheek is against his chest as I consider it. "How did he do it? How did he make that threat?"

Silence settles over the room, and I lift my head to look at him. He smooths my hair back from my face, his lips tightening as he views the tiny scar at my scalp. "He had your necklace."

"What?" The icy fear is back.

"We were watching him, and he had it. He pulled it out and showed it almost as if he were taunting me..." Derek's voice trails off, but I can see the anger darkening his blue eyes. "The idea that he had been here, in this house, close enough to take something so precious to you without our knowing…"

Memories of the dream I'd had that day so long ago trickle into my thoughts. I remember the squeak of his shoes, the spicy scent of his cologne burning my nose, the sound of scissors. Shivering, I step forward again to hide in the shelter of Derek's arms.

He only holds me, breathing in the top of my hair. My eyes close as guilt rolls over me like a flood. I'm to blame for this. If I hadn't been such a stupid fool to marry Sloan Reynolds, none of this would be happening. Derek Alexander, one of the most honorable men I've ever known, a hero, wouldn't have ruined his reputation and possibly his life for me. He'd be free from guilt, he'd be away from this nightmare. It's the horrible truth, my humiliating truth, that started this chain of events.

"It's my fault." My voice is so low, I'm sure Derek can't hear me, but I'm wrong.

He catches my upper arms and holds me in front of him as anger fills his eyes. His dark brow lowers, the muscle in his jaw moving as his teeth clench. In this state I imagine he's intimidating to others, but I feel no fear. He'd never hurt me.

"That is exactly why I didn't tell you," he growls. My eyes start to close, but he gives me a gentle shake. "Look at me, Melissa." I obey and meet his steely gaze. "You are not to blame for this. Sloan Reynolds was a master manipulator. He fooled everyone, including me, and the last thing I'll let you do is blame yourself."

"If I hadn't married him—"

"Stop." Another gentle shake, and I'm back against his chest, surrounded by his arms. "You had no idea what he was hiding. No one did. We've talked about this."

I want to argue, but he won't let me.

"I should have had more control," he continues. "I'm trained to be in control at all times. What happened is entirely my fault."

I don't agree with him. I know him too well, but that means, I also know he's convinced himself of the truth of his words. Only one person is as stubborn as he is, and she's locked in his arms right now. Struggling to get free, I look up at his face again, so strong, so handsome, so intense in his commitment to keeping his family safe.

"We're not going to agree on this." A few beats of silence pass, and for the first time in so long, he smiles. It's small, but it's better than the dark veil that's been clouding his eyes.

"If anything ever happened to you… " His voice is soft, and he cups my cheeks. "I can't live without you, Miss Jones."

My anger dissipates as his lips lightly cover mine, but I pull back. One enormous part of this is still unresolved.

"You can't hide these things from me." My voice is low, and I'm deadly serious. "Something this big… you have to include me in this, in your life."

"I know." He blinks down. "I told Patrick—"

"Patrick is in a shit load of trouble with me, too! He specifically promised to keep you out of trouble."

"He's already predicted your response." That little smile is back, and he glances at me. For a moment, I forget I'm mad as his sexy gaze holds mine. "What's all this making deals with Patrick behind my back anyway?"

"He promised he wouldn't let you do anything dangerous or... potentially life-threating. Nothing that could take you from me forever."

My final sentence is the big question hanging over us now. Our blue eyes meet, and I know the fear twisting my insides is plain on my face. He sits on the sofa and pulls my body to him. I'm standing in front of him, my hands resting on his broad shoulders.

"Nothing can take me from you," he says, placing his cheek against my torso.

We hold each other a moment, before he slides my tee up so he can kiss my skin. The touch of his lips on my stomach, the scratch of his beard pulses need in my lower body, and I lean down to kiss his head, curling my fingers in the sides of his thick, dark hair. He pulls back to unbutton my jeans, sliding them over my hips along with my panties as I step out of my boots.

A deep inhale and he speaks against the crease of my thigh. "You smell so good." His kisses move closer to the center, and my knees grow weak.

"Derek," I sigh. With one slow circle of his tongue over my clit, I rise on my tiptoes, crying out as electricity snakes up my legs.

"Oh, god!" I'm gasping and clutching his hair as he sucks and pulls at me until my thighs begin to tremble. All at once, I'm off my feet. I clutch his cheeks and cover his mouth with mine. The adrenaline, the anger, the fear, the frustration, all of it is burned away as he carries me to our bedroom.

* * *

Derek

Melissa is so beautiful coming apart in my arms. I have her in our bed, thighs parted, and I slide my tongue over her clit then down, tasting her deeply. I don't want her angry. I don't want her blaming herself. I want her to understand nothing in this world is ever allowed to threaten her in my presence. I'll take any chance, any risk to keep her safe.

"Oh, god, Derek!" Her soft moans are shocks of pleasure straight to my cock, which is aching to be inside her. "I'm almost there," she gasps, and I give her another firm suck, resulting in a high-pitched cry.

Her body is soft and wet, like honey on my tongue, and as her legs start to convulse, I rise up to kiss her belly before sinking deep into her. It's the most incredible feeling, her clenching and holding me, hot and wet.

She's in my arms, my weight supported on my elbows. Every thrust piques the pressure growing in me, and I can't stop a groan. I kiss then bite the soft skin of her shoulder. She moans, and all I can do is hold her as the most intense sensation of relief explodes through my body. My orgasm shakes me like blinding light.

"Melissa." Her name is a prayer on my lips.

Two more hard thrusts, she's so tight and willing. Rolling onto my side, I have her in my arms as we slowly come down together. Our breath mingles, our bodies melt. It's beautiful and perfect... until she twists away. I release her, and she rises up on an elbow. A dark lock of her hair falls over her ivory shoulder.

Reaching out, I touch her lightly. "God, you're so beautiful."

"That wasn't exactly fair, you know." Her blue eyes sparkle with her tease, and I do a quick internal evaluation of how long it might be before I can take her again.

"What wasn't fair?"

"I'm mad at you, you distract me with mind-blowing sex —"

"Did I blow your mind?" We're both smiling now.

"You must've. I don't feel angry at all."

Pushing myself up to sitting, I gather her in my arms. Her cheek rests against my skin, and I thread my fingers through her soft, gorgeous waves. "You're not angry."

I feel her brows move against my skin. "Oh, I'm not?"

"No. You understand why I did it, why I couldn't tell you, although I'm glad you know."

"Derek," she exhales, frustration in her tone. "You have to include me in things like this. You can't keep them from me." Lifting her head, our eyes meet, concern filling hers. "I'm your wife. Your partner."

"I can't wait to make that official."

Her expression is still agitated. "So what happens now?"

"Nothing."

She pushes all the way to sitting, the sheet clutched under her arms. "You think you can get away with it?"

"Sloan was in the wrong place committing a criminal act. Patrick's theory is his handlers will sweep it under the rug, protect the shareholders and the Reynolds name from what was clearly happening when he was killed."

"What was clearly happening?" Her voice is so quiet, just above a whisper.

"He was engaging in criminal activities with a prostitute."

Her eyes slide closed. "Star." It's not a question, and she doesn't give me time to speak before continuing. "And you killed him."

We're quiet a moment, and I can see her internal struggle. "What are you thinking?"

She shakes her head slowly. "I never understood… I guess now I never will."

Catching her chin, I make her look at me. "Understand what?"

"How he could be so duplicitous. Smooth. Seductive even. When we were engaged, he was completely different." Her eyes shine with forming tears, and my stomach tightens. "For the longest time I stopped trusting myself, my ability to judge people."

I reach for her, smoothing her hair away from her beautiful cheek. A tear falls, and I touch it with my thumb. "You lived through hell."

She sniffs and wipes her cheeks roughly. "It was all a lie. He lied to me every day." Taking my hand, she threads our fingers. Her strength shines in her eyes. "You helped me learn to trust myself again. I'm so lucky to have you."

"I'm pretty sure I'm the lucky one in this scenario." She lifts her chin and smiles, and I kiss her hand. "I wanted to kill him for hurting you."

"Shh!" Pulling it away, she lightly touches my lips. "I'm always safe with you."

I'm ready to show her how much more than safe she is, how loved and appreciated she is as well, when her phone rings from the kitchen.

"That's Elaine with Dex." She's up and heading for it before I can do anything more.

Sitting alone in our bed, my eyes drift past the light-olive colored walls, out the window and over the miles, over time, to that night. I can still hear the sounds of Star's life being choked from her body, still feel the rage at the overwhelming knowledge that he'd touched Melissa that way. My jaw tightens, and I know I'd do it again. I'd kill him every time. Control be damned.

Patrick's right. We have to ride this out, track down whoever's blackmailing Star, handle that asshole, and then put this case to rest.

Melissa's back. Her shirt's over her head, and she goes to the dresser to pull out a fresh pair of panties. Red lace. I smile, thinking it's only a few more hours until we're back in bed together.

"Elaine's bringing Dex home, so you'd better get dressed."

Throwing back the covers, I stand and catch her by the hips, running my fingers under the elastic of her underwear. "I like where your head's at with these."

She gives me a little grin and a quick peck on the lips. "Later, soldier. For now we have to get dressed."

I smile at her using Stuart's and my favorite "diminutive." It started when we'd first joined the Corps, and a civilian kept calling us *soldier*.

My pants and boxer briefs are where I quickly discarded them earlier. "It's not like Patrick and

Elaine ever worry about being discreet," I say, stepping into them.

"Listen." She stops in front of me, and I stand, pulling up my jeans. "I'm serious about what I said earlier. No more secrets."

Her blue eyes are so round and beautiful. I grab her by the waist, pulling her into a hug. Her hands rest on my bare chest. "No more secrets," I repeat.

"Promise me?"

A slow kiss, a little nip on her bottom lip, and I meet her gaze. "I promise."

* * *

The next day, Patrick and I are in my car speeding to Raleigh. He explains the latest in our evolving case as I weave us through the morning-commuter traffic.

"Toni's getting panicky. She wants us to find a safe place for Camille."

My teeth clench, tightening my lips as I think. "Did you explain to her that's not something we're prepared to do?"

"Whoever this is knows exactly where the little girl goes to daycare, her schedule, everything."

"And we still don't know what this fucking '*friend*' wants?"

"Toni seems to think he's after you."

Silence fills the car. My eyes flick to my partner's. "What the hell?"

His face is dead serious. "Her last letter referenced 'the big guy.' Her idea is you're the biggest guy connected to the case in every way — physically, financially, professionally…"

"Then fucking come get me," I growl. "Why go through her?"

"Safety. Insurance." Patrick releases a long exhale. "Our man's smart, which is not good. Going directly to you will only get him killed."

"Damn straight it will." Tightening my grip on the steering wheel, my thoughts go immediately to the ones I've left behind. "You should've told me this before we left today. Melissa and Dex are home, unprotected—"

"I think they're okay for now. I told Elaine to be aware of their surroundings, take precautions if she notices anything suspicious."

"You told Elaine?"

"Of course." His hazel eyes narrow at me. "You need to tell Melissa more than you do. She's a tough chick."

"She's a beautiful, smart woman."

"But you didn't tell her about Toni."

"I'll tell her when we have answers. I'd rather tell her our solution than our problem." My promise to her yesterday lurks in the corner of my mind. "What makes you think they're not in danger?"

"Toni said the letter is very specific. She was too afraid to fax it. Doesn't want it out of her possession in case he goes after Cammie."

"That's not going to happen. This asshole's not going after anyone."

Soon we're pulling into the parking lot of the Skinniflute, the biker bar where Star works and where we've met on several occasions in the past.

"I can't believe she's still at this dump," I grumble as I lock my car.

"Working her way through college." Patrick's dressed in his usual Skinniflute attire—faded blue jeans, a black tee, and combat boots. I'm in slacks and a thin navy sweater. I'm no fucking biker, and I don't have to dress like one.

"She could get a job in an office. Be a secretary or something respectable for a change."

He heads inside the all-wood establishment with neon beer ads shining in the windows, but I take a moment to text Mel.

You okay?

It only takes a moment for her to respond. *The boys are hilarious. Just like little men. Wish you could see them.*

Me, too.

Everything okay?

I pause a moment, considering. *So far nothing new.*

Working on the Nikki problem?

Shit. I made this trip without telling her. *And other things.*

Tell Patrick to call her. She loves him.

I will.

Check this out. A picture of Mel kneeling beside my little boy in a tiny tux appears on my phone, and my chest warms.

I love you both.

We love you more. Want us to stop by the office?

No. We'll talk tonight. Be safe, okay?

This is Wilmington, babe. We're good.

I exhale deeply. I can't believe some new asshole is threatening my family. He'd better be ready for the hell he's inviting.

It takes a moment for my eyes to adjust to the dim interior of the establishment. A few pool tables are situated in the back corner, and the usual cast of regulars in their faded jeans, leather vests, and bandanas are stationed around the center bar.

Lylah, the other Amy-Winehouse-looking waitress, is hanging on the polished wood separating them laughing and talking trash. It's just after noon on a Tuesday.

We slide into a wooden booth and she calls back over her shoulder. "Toni! Got a couple of regulars in your section."

Toni, a.k.a., "Star," walks out, and I'm surprised to see she hasn't changed her look since the last time we saw her. Instead of the blood-red lipstick, jet-black hair, and white tank showing off her matching sleeve tattoos, she's wearing a navy shirt-dress and leopard print cardigan. Her hair is smooth and hanging down her back in chestnut waves, and while she still has the cat-eye makeup, her lips are a pale shade of glossy pink. She's a ringer for Melissa. It's the look we used to trap Sloan. The only thing missing is my fiancée's sapphire-blue eyes.

"Thanks for driving up," she says in her low smoker's voice. "I know it's a haul, but I didn't know what else to do."

"No worries, girl," Patrick steps forward and kisses her cheek. "You look great. How's school treating you?"

She slips in across from us and picks up a cardboard coaster. Lylah appears smacking gum and looking every bit the biker chick with her side ponytail, short shorts and tight tank. She's still sporting the look—Priscilla Presley hair and red-velvet lips.

"What can I get you fellas today? The usual?"

"You bet." Patrick drops a twenty on her tray. "And a little privacy."

Lylah's eyebrows rise. "When have I ever been a concern?"

Star cuts in. "Just get us the drinks, Lyle."

Her friend spins around and swings her hips back to the center of the room. I turn my attention to the woman in front of us. "Show us what you've got."

Her dark-brown eyes flicker slowly over mine, and her face flushes. I don't know what that's about, but she reaches into her sweater pocket. The letter is folded into a small square, and we watch as she spreads it open on the table then hands it to me.

Ms. Durango,

If you follow my instructions, your daughter will be safe, and you can return to your normal life. If you involve the authorities in any way, be sure my offer is null and void. I will make good on my threats.

You have one task: Let the big guy know I'm coming for him. Let him know if he tries to run or retaliate in any way, you and your daughter will suffer for his crimes.

It's time to pay up, and revenge is a dish best served cold.

Signed,
A Friend

Anger fires in my chest at the nerve of this fucker. "This is about money."

Star's voice is soft. "It says revenge. And crimes."

She's looking pointedly at me like all that bullshit means anything. I'm ready to punch whoever this is in the face for harassing a mother and her child.

"It doesn't make any damn sense," Patrick interrupts. "I thought Sloan didn't have any family left."

"His parents died years ago," I say. "Melissa was his only wife as far as I know, and they never had children."

Leaning back in the seat, I try to think. "My job is putting criminals behind bars or turning bad guys over to the cops. It could be anybody."

Star's doe eyes are round with worry. "What do we do?" She blinks and a tear falls. "I can't have this asshole threating Cammie. She's too little. She wouldn't understand. She'd be so scared..."

Her voice goes high, and I reach across the table to grasp her hand. "Look at me." When I've got her attention, I put as much meaning behind my words as possible. "I won't let anything happen to you or your daughter. I promise."

She blinks a few times, eyes glistening with unshed tears, but I can see her body start to relax. "I believe you. I do. I just wish..."

Her voice trails off, and Patrick jumps in. "Has your daughter ever lived with you or has she always been with your sister?"

"She's always been with my sister." Star's voice drops a few decibels. "I'm no kind of mother for a little girl."

He sits back with a deep exhale. "Well, that fucks my plan."

"What are you thinking?" Patrick might color outside the lines, but he's smart. He's good at our job, and I've learned to trust him.

"Your condo's sitting empty in Princeton, right?" I nod, and he continues. "I was going to say Toni and Cammie can hide out there until we solve this. Stuart's across the hall, and Walt won't let anybody suspicious past him. The parking garage is secured... Unless it's too stressful for the baby."

"It's a good thing you're so fucking smart, partner. Otherwise your screw-ups might be more noticeable."

Star looks from Patrick to me. "I don't understand."

Patrick leans forward and smiles that ridiculous smile of his that makes women act like idiots. "How would you like to live like a queen with your little girl completely safe while we figure this shit out?"

Her brow lines, and I almost laugh. She's unaffected by his charm — probably because she's already been there. "Can you be a little more specific?"

He gestures to me. "This guy has a huge, two-bedroom penthouse condo in Princeton with a doorman, secure parking, and my Marine older brother right across the hall. I think you and Cammie should stay there until we've nailed this fucker. He'll never know where you are, and if by some chance he figures it out, he'll have three layers of security to get through."

Star's eyes flicker to me again, and a note of relief is in her voice. "You'd let me stay at your place?"

"Of course. I don't know why I didn't think of it myself. You're in this situation because of me.

This idiot wants me. It only makes sense."

"Okay, then!" She actually smiles, and relief shines in her eyes. "I'll call Nan and see if I can get the baby tomorrow...? Is that too soon?"

"Not at all." I give her a reassuring smile. "Go home and pack. I'm sure you're worried about your daughter."

Her eyes flood again, and she jumps out of her seat, rounding the table and giving me a tight, unexpected hug. I lightly touch her waist as the scent of honeysuckle drifts around us.

"Thank you so much." Her voice cracks.

Star might be a tough girl, but her Achilles is Cammie. Having Dex has shown me the power of children. They can bring even the hardest characters to their knees.

"I gave you my word. I'm going to fix this."

* * *

On the drive back to Wilmington, my thoughts are preoccupied with what this asshole wants from me, and how I can find him so I can rip his dick off and shove it up his ass. Patrick's preoccupied with his smartphone, and it reminds me of my text chat with Melissa.

"That was a smart move with Star," I say, catching his attention. "I'm glad you thought of it."

"It just came to me as we were sitting there." He exhales a laugh. "I'm glad you're not pissed I volunteered your place without asking."

"Nah, it was good." Pausing a beat, I continue to our "other business." "You had a chance to talk to Nikki?"

He nods, looking back at his phone. "Seems Captain Asshat is also Captain Hypocrite. He fucked her."

That makes me wince. "Shit. When?"

"The night before he pulled out last time."

Fuck. My grip tightens on the steering wheel. "I can't believe he'd screw up like that."

"Ah, give him a break." My younger partner stretches in his seat. "He never planned to come back from Saudi." We're quiet a moment, and my thoughts go to how messed up Stuart was when he did come back.

Patrick breaks the moment with a laugh. "So I'm officially off the hook. At least my office fuck-up was also a set-up."

"I'm glad you're both on a leash now. Makes my job easier."

"I am a happily married man. That is the truth."

"As if we don't have enough shit going on." I grumble. "Is she going to sue us?"

"No fucking way. It was consensual— apparently very consensual. It's why I never made any progress with her. She was hoping to get back in his pants when he came home. Ahhnd now she can't work with him."

"So she's pissed about Mariska?" Jealousy is a fucking nightmare to deal with. I rub my brow, trying to think. "I don't have time to train somebody new."

"I thought you hated Nikki." His laugh irritates me.

"She's a terrible secretary, but at least we know her weaknesses." Filtering through my options, I land on one. "Maybe if I talked to her…"

"Won't work. This is more than simple jealousy. She pulled some stunt in Montana, got Stuart all riled up, ran Mariska off. She said she's too humiliated to stay."

"What kind of teenage drama is this?"

"Don't yell at me. I tried to keep her out of their way."

Frustration twists in my chest. I've got a fucking psycho threatening Star and now the Princeton office is a circus. "I'll talk to Stuart and see what he thinks."

"It's possible if I asked her to stay, told her we need her, the office can't run without her —"

"Just hold off on that. I don't want to make any false claims."

He chuckles as we're pulling into the parking lot of his and Elaine's condo. "I'll run more background checks on Sloan tonight. See if he has any nutjob relatives we overlooked."

"Thanks. I'll see if I can come up with anything."

"You might try talking to Melissa about it. She was married to the guy."

That reminder burns my chest. "Yeah, we'll see."

My eyes flicker over Patrick's shoulder as I pull out, and I catch Elaine standing in the doorway. She's watching me with a worried expression that bothers me, and I drive a little faster than legal to get home. Patrick should have told me this case had gotten so specific. I never would have left Wilmington today if I'd known.

Quickly killing the car in our driveway, I hustle up to the door when I see something that slows my pace. Three large black suitcases and my duffel bag

68

are stacked on the porch. My eyes travel over the house, and I can see the flicker of the television through the sheer blinds in the kitchen. Melissa and Dex are here, but clearly something's wrong.

My chest tightens as I walk toward the entrance. Lifting one of the bags, I notice it's heavy. I pull the zipper down, and inside are my clothes. *What the fuck?* Standing, I push my key in the lock and try to open the door, but it stops short. The metal chain prevents it from opening. I can only see a few inches into the kitchen.

"Melissa?" I shout through the crack. "What's going on? Let me in."

Footsteps thud on the other side, and all at once the door is shoved closed, pushing me back. The sound of the deadbolt locking follows next.

"Melissa?" I shout, banging on the door, but she doesn't answer. I'm simultaneously pissed and confused. All my shit's out here... *Is she throwing me out?*

My key is back in the lock, and I open the door again, but again it's stopped by the chain. "Melissa, unfasten the chain."

"No." Her voice is just on the other side of the door.

I can't see her, but I can hear the anger in her tone. Dex's train show sounds in the background, and I don't want to argue in front of him.

Taking a deep breath, I stay calm. "Please open the door and talk to me."

"Oh, *now* you want to talk?" Her voice goes high. "I'm sorry. You're a day late and a promise short."

The muscle in my jaw clenches hard, but my voice stays calm.

69

"Open the goddamn door, Melissa."

"No."

I step back ready to snap that chain with a swift kick, when she pushes it closed and the noise of that fucking deadbolt sounds again.

"God dammit!" I shout as I shove my key back into the lock. I'm turning it open when I hear scraping noises on the other side. This time when I push against the wood, it doesn't move at all.

Resting my forehead against the door, I take another deep breath, fighting for control. "Please let me in."

"You promised!" She yells from the other side. "You looked in my eyes and *promised*."

"Baby, I didn't know how serious this was."

"I won't hear any more lies from you. Take your shit and leave. It's over."

She's crying now, and all semblance of control I had is gone. This is not happening. Stepping back, I hit the door with my shoulder as hard as I can. A low growl escapes my throat on impact. The door doesn't budge.

"Open the door," I repeat.

Again, she shouts. "No."

Stepping back, I kick it with the sole of my foot. The doorjamb shudders, but it doesn't give.

"Don't make me call the police," she shouts from the other side.

That nearly sends me into a rage. My shoulders are rapidly rising and falling as I step back and survey this situation. The woman I love has thrown me out and is now threatening the cops on me. *Am I having some kind of fucking bad dream?*

The only possible way I might get in the house comes to mind. "I want to see Dex."

She's angry, yes, but if we can look at each other, talk it out... Maybe she needs to yell at me. I can listen, hear what she needs to say, and everything can go back to normal.

"I'll talk to my mom. We'll work out a schedule for you to visit him."

My fist is pounding on the wood before I even realize what I'm doing. This is fucking idiotic, and I need to get on the other side of this fucking door and hold Melissa in my arms.

"Stop it!" I can hear the break in her voice, and it rips me apart. "You're scaring Dex."

Breathing hard, I rest my head against the wood again. Looking to the side, I can see the cracks that have formed around the doorjamb from my attempts to break it down. Sound filters through the spaces easily. The noise of my Melissa crying is just on the other side. I can't take this.

"Melissa." This time I'm pleading with her. "Please open the door."

"No." She says softly, between sniffles.

My heart is twisting in my chest. "What do you want me to do, baby? Just tell me what to do."

"I want you to go away." Her voice shakes as she says the words.

"I can't do that." I'm breathing hard now. "I love you."

"Not enough to keep your promise."

"I love you more than enough." Gripping the wooden frame, I fight my emotions. "Let me in."

"I'm done talking. Take your bags and go."

Noises on the other side sound like Dex whining. I hear her go to him and attempt to soothe him. Stepping back, I look at the windows and consider breaking one of them. For several long seconds, I visualize myself doing it. I look around the perimeter and see every place I can force my way inside, go in there and gather her in my arms, make her stop saying these things.

But I don't. It would scare Dex, it would anger Mel… It would only make things harder for me.

Instead I do what she asks. Ice is in the pit of my stomach as I pick up my duffel and the largest suitcase and carry them to my car. Popping the trunk, I put them inside and go back for the remaining two.

Once everything's loaded, I turn the car back toward Wilmington, stopping briefly at a liquor store for a fifth of Dewar's. It doesn't take long before I'm in a hotel room trying to figure out my next steps. One thing is certain, no matter what she says, this is *not* over.

CHAPTER 5: HEARTBREAK

Melissa

Tears coat my cheeks as I rock my whimpering little boy back and forth on my lap. My entire body is shaking, but I'm struggling for control. I have to keep it together for Dex. He's only a baby. He's too small to understand why Mommy can't stop crying, why Daddy has to go away.

Rocking him in my arms, his little cheek is against my chest, and he's sucking on his finger. His little fist grips my sleeve tightly. I shush him and kiss his soft dark hair, rubbing his back until he slowly calms down from the explosion of his father trying to break down the door. Derek's anger is terrifying and his determination formidable. Only one thing is just as strong—my refusal to make the same mistake twice.

The memory cramps my stomach and fills my eyes with fresh tears. A hiccupped breath jerks my throat, and I'm on the verge of sobbing again. Packing Derek's bags had been the hardest thing I'd ever done in my life, but I will not live in another house of lies and deceptions. At least this time I've found out before it was too late.

Elaine and I had spent the day taking the boys for their fittings. Derek had even texted me to check on us. He'd texted me from Raleigh and never said a word about being out of town or what he was doing. He'd pretended he was dealing with Nikki! I can't believe the extent of his deception, and after just promising me...

The never-ending train show makes a cheerful whistle, and Dex wiggles to get free of my arms. At least he's young enough that what just happened is quickly

forgotten. Mommy's here, he's safe in my arms, back to the trains.

Standing on shaky legs, I take his little hand and a train and slowly lead him to my bedroom. Upon entering, it appears the same as it did when Derek was here, but if I open the closet, I'll see the gaping hole where his suits used to hang. If I open his drawers, I'll find them empty where his jeans and tees once were. His exercise clothes are gone, his socks. In the bathroom, his toothbrush, razor, shampoo, shave cream... All gone.

The pack and play stands waiting as I gently lower my little boy into it before pulling up his never-ending show on the television. He's contented as I crawl onto the bed, silently weeping as devastation tries to pull me under.

My phone rings. It's Elaine's tone, but I'm too weak to pull it out of my sweater pocket. I know what she wants. After the fitting today, we took the boys for ice cream. Lane wanted a Coke float, but Dex only had half his dip cone before hopping down and running to the indoor playground.

"Derek said not to, but we should drop by the office since we're in town." I watched our little boys play. Dex stormed across the top level with such determination, so much like his father, I couldn't help but laugh.

"Did you forget something?" Elaine winks at me, but I shake my head.

"I just wanted to stop in and say hey."

"Wait, what? Stop in and…" Her voice trails off, causing me to turn and catch her confused expression just before she tries to hide it.

"What's going on?"

She looks at her lap, and I can tell she's trying to think of an excuse. I'm not having it. "Lainey. What are you not telling me?"

"It's not me not telling you." Her voice is soft, and she won't meet my eyes.

"Then tell me what I don't know."

"The guys drove to Raleigh today."

She doesn't have to elaborate. I remember all too well what's in Raleigh. "Has something happened to Star?"

"She's been getting threatening messages. It's where the photographs came from." Shaking her head, she looks away from me, over her shoulder to where Lane has joined Dex on the playground. "After the last one, she wanted to meet in person. She's scared. Somebody's been blackmailing her about the crime. Using her to get to Derek."

With every word, my throat goes tighter and tighter, and I'm sure I'll start screaming. I've never been this angry… *ever!* We made love yesterday—sexy, passionate love—and I forgave him for keeping secrets, for not telling me he'd murdered my ex-husband… *Murdered*. My. Ex-husband.

He kept a secret from me so big it could change all our lives. Police could break through our door at any moment as long as we live and take him away, and I would be clueless.

No more secrets. I can still see his steel-blue eyes fixed on mine as he said the words. *I promise.* He looked me in the eye and gave me his word. Yet here

I sit hearing he's doing it again. We spent the rest of the day together, we slept together last night, had coffee this morning, and he never mentioned it. Never told me what he was doing today. Didn't say anything in his text. My head feels so hot, I wonder if my face is red.

"I have to go." Standing, I collect my bag, Dex's train.

Elaine is on her feet just as fast. "What are you going to do?"

"More like what am I not going to do." My breath is coming so fast, but at this point it's only anger. I'm unable to be still. I have to move. The tears come later, bathing his clothes in salt water as I shove them into his suitcases. Crying and cursing, unable to believe he would put me in this position.

I never dreamed I'd feel this way towards Derek. At the same time, dancing at the edges of my memory is the day I discovered his email to Sloan. That day long ago in that horrible mansion when I thought I'd lost my last shred of hope.

"Tell me what you're going to do," my friend repeats as we catch the boys and carry them to the car. Both struggle and complain, but I'm too distracted to worry about Dex wanting to stay.

Buckling him in his car seat, I say one word. "Pack."

Now, a half-day and a nightmare later, my phone is ringing again, and I know Elaine won't stop until I answer. Forcing my arm to move, I reach into my pocket and pull out the device. Sliding my finger across the face, I hold it to my ear.

"I'm here, Lainey."

"Melissa?" Her voice is tentative and high. "Are you okay?"

"I'm okay."

"Patrick talked to Derek." She pauses, and my eyes close. Pain twists in my stomach, and I know I'll start crying again if I have to talk about it. As if knowing this, my best friend doesn't make me. "I can come over if you need me. Help with Dex?"

"It's okay. We'll be okay."

"Call me if you need me." She hesitates then continues. "You don't even have to call. Just send me a text—911."

"Thanks. I will."

We disconnect, and I push myself off the bed. I have to make Dex's supper, bathe him, get him ready for bed. He can sleep with me tonight.

* * *

Mom's in the kitchen when I open my eyes the next morning. I vaguely recall her coming over last night, having to shove the heavy table I'd moved in front of the door back to its place and unfastening the chain. She'd wanted to talk, but I couldn't do it. I'd been crying off and on all evening, and I'd only just managed to fall asleep with Dex in my arms. Being outside the tight grip of his daddy's embrace would take getting used to, but I'd get there. I had to be strong.

Now I hear her talking to our little boy, and I stretch out my hand to Derek's empty side of the bed. Pain twists in my stomach, and I push my face against the pillow to muffle my cry. It hurts so bad. On my nightstand is the photograph of Derek and me sitting on the beach. His arms are around me, and it's a painful reminder of what a beautiful liar he is.

Oh, god! I jump from the bed and run to the toilet. I barely make it before I lose what little contents are in my stomach. I collapse on the cool tile floor and weep, holding onto the handle. I don't know if I can pick up the pieces this time. I've been through this with him before, forcing myself to get over him, but that was in the beginning. I'd only had a week. Now it's worlds different. So much of his life is woven into mine.

Five minutes pass, and I force myself to get up. Scooping handfuls of water into my mouth, I look in the mirror. My eyes are puffy from crying, and I lean forward to hold a cool rag on them. After a few moments, I straighten, pat myself dry, and take my robe off the hook. I can do this. I *have* to do this.

"I made eggs," Mom says quietly as I enter the room. Dex is already down and in the living room running his trains all over the lines of the rug.

"Thanks, Mom." My voice is thick with unshed tears. "I'm sorry about last night. I just... couldn't."

"Derek called me. He's worried... He sounded a little desperate."

I can't answer that. I don't even want to hear that. My insides clench, and I'm fighting the crippling sobs as I go to the coffee machine and drop in a plastic pod. Waiting as my mug fills, I know she's watching me for some sign. Anything.

"He said you kicked him out?" she nudges.

Taking my coffee to the bar, I don't look at her as I pour in a dash of creamer. My jaw tenses. *Be strong, Melissa.*

"Was it another woman?" Her voice strains.

I glance up at her worried face and shake my head. I can't tell her about Sloan's murder—I don't know what I can tell her that won't get Derek in trouble with the law. So I stick to the facts.

"He lied to me," I say. "He kept secrets from me and then lied about it."

Her face scrunches as she tries to understand. "Can you give me an example?"

"I don't think so. It involves his work."

Mom exhales and drops into a chair. "Sweetie, I have to say, it must be something incredibly major. I've never seen any man love someone as much as Derek loves you. Your father — "

"Mom." My voice is sharp, and I hope she can tell how serious I am. "You have to trust me this time. Just like you had to trust me with Sloan."

She looks down at the table. I take the chair across from her and hold my mug in both hands. The warmth of it soothes me, even if I don't feel like drinking it. I don't trust my stomach yet.

When she speaks again, her voice is quiet. "I've also never seen you so in love with a man." Her eyes are full of concern even as her words gut me. "Maybe give it time. I'm here to help you any way I can — with Dex, with the cottage. Do you need to stay with me a few days?"

My first instinct is to say no, until I consider the week ahead. One important milestone is coming, and I'm not sure I can get through it alone. "If you can help me with Dex's birthday. I want him to have a happy first birthday."

"Of course!" she answers quickly.

My insides clench at what I have to say next. I feel my stomach again on the verge of losing its contents, which at this point is nothing.

"After that..." I pause to steady my breathing. "If you can help me cancel the wedding plans." She makes a little noise of shock, and my grip tightens on my mug. "If it's too much, I can ask Elaine — "

"No! I just... What if we just say the plans are on hold?" The flicker of hope in her voice spears the pain in my heart. I want to crawl into a dark place and never come out. I want to turn back time and never have met Derek Alexander. I want to scream and throw things, and...

I hear Dex in the other room. Only, I'd never give up my little boy. If all of this means I have him, it's worth it.

Steadying myself, I shake my head. "The wedding is off. I can't marry him."

"Darling, I'm afraid you're being too hasty. You've been hurt — badly, I can see that. At the same time, you and Derek have something so special — "

I can't listen to any more of this. She's killing me little by little and she doesn't even know how or why. I can't tell her the extent of his deception or how deep it goes without risking police involvement.

Holding out my hand, I grasp hers. "Let's focus on Dex right now. Help me get through his birthday. We can deal with the rest after."

She's satisfied, and I'm exhausted. I leave my full mug on the table and head back to my bedroom. I only barely hear her say she'll take Dex for the day before I push through the blankets. I curl into a ball surrounded by the scent of warmth and woods that used to soothe me. The scent of a man I trusted with everything, and who couldn't trust me with anything. It's a scent I used to crave when we were apart. Now it only breaks my heart.

CHAPTER 6: SAFE HOUSE

Derek

Pacing the small hotel room, I pour two fingers of scotch in a glass and call Patrick. I should be at the cottage. I should be sitting in my chair with Dex in front of me playing with his damn trains. Melissa should be sitting beside me with her laptop or ordering takeout. I should be with my family, dammit.

Melissa and I have been a foregone conclusion so long, I can't get my mind around what's happening. It's almost comical to think of me being trapped out of our house with her on the other side of the door telling me to go away. I'd laugh if I weren't so fucking ready to kill somebody.

My phone buzzes, and I snatch it up without even looking.

"Hey, man. I just heard." Patrick's voice is a mixture of concern and his usual swagger. "What can I do?"

"You've fucking done enough," I growl before taking a long drink of scotch.

"What the fuck does that mean?"

My eyes squint and I shake my head. "Nothing. It doesn't mean anything. I'm just… I'm fucking pissed as hell. I don't know why Melissa's doing this."

"It's what I told you before. Women don't like being left out of the loop."

I'm ready to strangle him, considering the whole *Don't tell her* approach was his fucking idea. "This is way past a simple tantrum, Patrick. Melissa doesn't make dramatic gestures. This is serious."

He's quiet a moment, thinking. "What are you saying? You think she means it?"

"Fuck yeah, she means it." My fists clench, and I have to count to ten before I slam the tumbler against the wall. Trashing my hotel room won't help me. "What I don't know is if she'll forgive me this time."

"Melissa loves you. That is a fact."

"Sloan hurt her too badly. I fucked up when I didn't tell her about Star. I wanted to have more information before giving her the whole story, but she won't listen to that now."

"Give her some time. She'll come around. You have Dex, after all."

Setting the tumbler down, I pour two more fingers into it. "His birthday is this week."

A hiss of air fills my ear. "Shitty timing."

We're both quiet a few minutes while I think of my little boy, my beautiful bride. Patrick's back in problem-solver mode.

"Or it could be really good timing," he says. "It'll give her a few days to cool off before you see her again. Then you can try talking to her."

"I want to talk to her now." The scotch has my insides warm. My anger is soothed, and I want to hold her, kiss her, love her until she forgives me.

"You need to give her space."

"That's going to be impossible." Being in this shitty hotel room is already impossible.

"I know what you can do." His voice brightens. "Help Toni and Cammie with Princeton. Meet up with them, spend the night, and when you get back, go to Dex's birthday party."

I think about what he's suggesting. At least it will fill these hours. "It's not a bad idea," I agree.

"You can get Toni set up in your condo, make sure she knows her way around, introduce her to Stuart and Walt…"

"Us traveling together might attract attention. Reveal her hideout."

"All the better." Patrick has an edge in his voice now. "I'd love that fucker to make a move in Princeton. Get Stuart involved, and you won't have to kill him. Asshat'll dismember him."

"Stuart's pretty ruthless in a fight." I finish my scotch and look out the window toward the beach. My chest is heavy. I want to be home. Still, I know my partner's right. "I'll do it."

"I'll message Toni and tell her you'll meet her in Princeton. She's spending tonight with her sister Nancy and Cammie. She hopes it'll ease the transition."

"Great. I'll get on the road first thing. And Patrick?" He makes a noise in my ear. "Keep your eye on Melissa for me."

"Just like always. I'm the Guard. I got her covered."

* * *

The first thing I notice when I enter the condo building in Princeton is Cammie. She's a tiny little thing, wearing a purple dress with a big white flower pattern on it. Her dark hair is brushed up into a purple bow the size of her head, and she's holding a saggy pink bunny over one arm.

She seems calm, which is in direct contrast to her mother. Star's hands flutter over her daughter's hair every few seconds. She shifts the little girl from one hip to the other, then she digs in her bag and pulls out what looks like a small packet of jellybeans. Just before she hands them to Cammie, however, she pulls them back fast. I enter the double doors and greet Walt, whose eyes are twinkling at this new development, and Star hustles over to me.

"Are jelly beans a choking hazard?" she whispers, blinking huge brown eyes up at me.

"Maybe," I answer in what I hope is a calming voice. She's clearly nervous as hell around her child.

"Right." She nods fast and shoves the plastic package back in her bag. "What the hell was I thinking?" Then she gasps. "Shit!" She gasps again, and grips her mouth with her fingers.

I can't help it. My insides are shredded, my head hurts from drinking myself to sleep last night, but despite it all, this makes me laugh. She's a complete screw up as a mom, and she can't even stop swearing.

Catching her arm, I give it a squeeze. "Relax. She seems okay for now. Cammie's what? A year old?"

"Ten months."

"She won't remember any of this. All she knows is how you feel, so be cool. Let her know you love her."

She's blinking fast, and I'm afraid she might cry. Unsure how my own battered insides will respond to that, I catch Walt's attention.

"Mr. Alexander?" He steps over, ready to serve.

"Walt, this is..." I hesitate, unsure which name we're using on the record.

"Star," she says quickly.

"Star Brandon and her daughter Camille." Walt gives her a friendly nod, and as if by magic, pulls a sucker out of his pocket. The little girl takes it and smiles. Her brown eyes are bright, and a little dimple is in her cheek.

"She's a cutie," Walt says, giving her arm a light tap.

Touching his shoulder, I pull him aside and lower my voice. "Star is one of our clients. She's gotten some threats. No one is to come near these two."

He's immediately serious. "I'll alert the other doormen. We'll be on the lookout against any new delivery guys, postmen…"

I give his shoulder a squeeze, and the level of appreciation I feel for him at this moment is indescribable. "You're a good man, Walt. I confess, I miss you."

"Ahh, you traded up, Mr. A." He laughs in his warm, scratchy voice. "How's Miss Jones and your little look-alike?"

I can't help the wince of pain at his question, and he seems to notice. "I'm sorry, sir. I hope everything's okay."

Patting his shoulder I nod and swallow back the thickness in my throat. "Everything will be fine, Walt." It *will* be fine.

* * *

Mariska is at Stuart's place, and the minute she hears us arrive, she's at my door. As usual, she's wearing some filmy, red handkerchief-print dress, but she's pulled an oversized, drab-grey fisherman's sweater on top of it. It falls off one shoulder, and with her loose, brown waves pulled in a high ponytail, I don't know how she does it. She actually makes her bag-lady outfit look sexy. Stuart's fucking happier than I've seen him in my life.

"Drop off your stuff and come across the hall!" Mariska says, giving Star a huge hug.

"Okay!" Star's tension seems to melt slightly.

"Do you think Cammie will come with me?" Mariska holds out her hands to the little girl, who's sucking a pacifier now and still clutching her limp bunny.

Star and her daughter share those huge doe-eyes. "I don't know." Her mother's voice is hesitant as she studies the little girl on her hip.

"Let's see." Mariska holds out her hands with cheerful confidence. "Cammie! Come here, baby! Come with Aunt Mare Mare!"

Mariska's slim hands are covered in rings of all shapes and colors. The little girl looks up at her smiling face and instantly smiles back, leaning forward. Mariska gives her a twirl, and the baby laughs, losing the pacifier Star had shoved in her mouth on our way up even though she wasn't even crying.

"Oh!" Star jumps forward and grabs it. Mariska doesn't pause. The two of them are out the door and headed to Stuart's place before we even have a chance to respond. All we hear are Mariska's sing-songy coos trailing behind them.

Star looks at me in wonder. "She's really good with kids."

"Kids, animals... stubborn jackasses," I say under my breath, heading to my room. "Make yourself at home. After tonight, you can have the master bedroom if you want it."

I stop just inside my old room and drop my duffel on the floor. The photo of Melissa and Dex at the beach is on my dresser, and it hits me like a sucker-punch to the gut. Leaning heavily on my hand, I pick up the mahogany frame and look at my beautiful family as several painful moments pass.

"Melissa," I whisper, touching her face. "What are you thinking?"

"Hey, you okay?"

Straightening, I put the frame back on the dresser. "Yeah. You need something?"

Star's eyes narrow and flicker from mine to the frame and back. "I wasn't expecting you to meet me here. I wanted to say thanks."

"No worries. Patrick suggested I drive up. It made sense."

"Shouldn't you be with your family?" She's watching me, and I remember what I observed the last time we worked with this girl. She's smart. She should be so much more than a fucking part-time hooker. She should be in college, which is what she was doing until some asshole thought he'd start blackmailing her.

"I'm not going to let an opportunistic thug steal your future. Especially not to get to me. They understand."

Her voice softens. "I don't know if I'd understand. If I was your family, I mean."

Not going there. "You'd better get across the hall. Mariska is pretty persistent from what I understand."

She nods and takes off. Finally, I'm alone.

Holding my phone, I stare at Melissa's face on my screen. She's so beautiful, sitting on the beach, the wind wrapping one of her perfect waves around her neck. My body physically aches for her. I need to bury my face in her ocean-roses scent and tell her I love her.

Patrick said not to call. He said he has his eye on her, give her space, give her time. None of that matters. I have to hear her voice. Touching the number, I wait as it rings in my ear.

It rings and rings. I've almost given up when the call connects.

"Hello?" her voice is so soft. I can tell she's been crying, and it rips through my chest. I want to hold her.

"Melissa." I exhale her name. "Baby, please talk to me."

Silence first, a few moments where I only hear her shaky breathing, then she clears her throat. I know her so well. She's building that wall against me. I can't let her do it.

"What do you need?"

"I need you."

Silence again. The sound of brushing covers her phone, and I wonder if she covered it with her hand. When she comes back, the slightest tremor is in her voice.

"If you need something, please tell me. Otherwise, I'll have to block your calls."

"Don't do that. Just hang on." I think fast, hoping to derail that notion. "I need to know about Dex's party. What time and where."

Another deep breath in my ear. It tightens the knot in my chest. She's so close but still so far. What will it take to get her to listen to me again?

"I didn't realize you were coming."

"Melissa." My voice is low. "It's his first birthday."

"I thought you'd see him another time. Later in the day, I mean. At Mom's."

I'm not invited to his party? This is fucking getting worse and worse. And it hurts like hell. "I'd like to be there. If that's okay?"

She's quiet again. We were just in bed together less than two days ago. I know this is killing her, too. She can't turn on me that fast.

"I'll talk to Mom." Her voice is quiet. "We can have the party at her house."

"Okay." I'm keeping my tone gentle, like I'm approaching a wounded animal. "Do you know what time?"

"Dex naps at three…" her voice breaks off, and I can hear her losing the battle against her tears. I'm on the verge of losing my battle with all of this. A sharp breath, and she's back in control. "I'll text you after I've talked to Mom. I need to go now."

Not so fast. "If you can, give me some lead-time. I drove Star to Princeton so she can stay here. Hide out until we know who's blackmailing her. It was Patrick's idea, but it's a good one. Stuart can watch over her, and Walt guards the door. You know the setup."

She makes a noise, and I go for it.

"I'm telling you everything, Mel. Full disclosure. Whatever you want to know." I wait, but I only hear the soft sound of her breath. She's got to be thinking the same thing as me: *This is so wrong.* "I love you, baby. I miss you so much."

I've gone too far. A whispered, "I'll text you," and the line disconnects.

Setting my phone on my dresser, I clutch my forehead. I've trained for torture, prolonged periods without sleep, food, or drink. I've gone days staring at the desert sand until I thought I'd go blind. I've been in combat, injured... Nothing compares to this.

Turning, I go to the kitchen and reach over the stove. My supply of alcohol is relatively untouched. Melissa prefers wine, and nobody's been here for months. I pull down the Johnnie Walker and a tall glass. My front door opens just as I've taken the first sip, and I hear Stuart's voice.

"Hey, man. Looks like Mariska's found a new friend." He rounds the corner, and stops in his tracks when he sees me. "What happened?"

Taking another long drink, I stare at the amber liquid and just say it. "Melissa kicked me out."

"What the hell?" He takes a step forward and stops. "What did you do?"

It's funny because I've known Stuart so long. I can remember a time when his response would've been *Fuck her. There's plenty of fish in the sea. I'll get the boat.* Apparently Mariska's changed everything.

I lean back against the cabinets and take another drink. "She found out about Sloan. Then she found out about Star."

My friend's brow lines, and I know he isn't following me. I'm not making sense. Saying it out loud makes it all sound so stupid to me.

I clear my throat and start over. "She was mad I didn't tell her about Sloan."

"You didn't tell anybody about Sloan. You didn't even tell me."

"The fewer people who know about a problem, the better the chance it *won't* get discovered."

"It's Security 101," he agrees.

Shaking my head, I wonder why women aren't as reasonable as men. "Well, my fiancée isn't in the security business, and she didn't like that answer." Taking another sip, I confess. "In fairness, I understand her being mad about it. I should've told her. My role in what happened to Sloan impacts her and Dex…"

Stuart doesn't speak. I can tell he's waiting for the other shoe to drop.

"I promised not to keep her in the dark on these things anymore."

He nods, and I see the pieces click together for him. "And then she found out about Star."

"And then I found all my luggage on her front porch."

"Shit." Stuart leans against the opposite cabinets, crossing his muscled arms. On his face is stunned empathy. "You must be going crazy."

A female voice interrupts us. "What's up with you guys?" Mariska is standing in the doorway watching, and I don't care anymore.

"Melissa and I are… taking a break."

"Oh my god!" Mariska swirls to me in an instant, touching my arm. "Is there anything I can do?"

Stuart leans forward and catches her around the waist, gently pulling her back against his chest. "You could order up some food?" His voice is tender, and he leans down to kiss her ear. I turn away from the sight of her touching his cheek and take another long drink of scotch.

"I've done something even better!" She's smiling when I look up. "I made a big pot of sarmale this afternoon. It's the ultimate comfort food."

"Is that the tomato-cabbage..." Stuart's still holding her against him.

"Cabbage leaves stuffed with tomatoes and rice and pork... It'll warm you to your toes."

"I'm not cold," I say under my breath.

"It's delicious," Stuart says over to me. "Can't have my CO getting his dinner from a bottle."

Mariska kisses his mouth briefly before going to the door. She pauses before leaving and looks back. "Derek?" I glance up at her. "It's going to work out, okay?"

My brows rise briefly. "Thanks."

She's gone, but Stuart's still watching the place where she stood. I'm glad I'm not staying because being around these two still so fresh in love would push me over the fucking edge.

"Take your time," he says before following the trail she left. "Come over when you're ready."

"Thanks," I nod.

"If you don't come over, I'll send a plate with Star and Camille."

"I like that even better."

He nods. "Brothers. Always there for each other."

* * *

I'm sitting on my leather couch staring at the black screen of my enormous television when Star and Cammie bump through the front door.

She doesn't speak, so I look up to see the little girl is fast asleep on her mother's shoulder. I put my empty glass on the coffee table. I've only gone through half a bottle tonight. I'm trying to pace myself knowing I'll see Melissa and Dex tomorrow. I want my head to be clear.

Star motions to the guest room, but I don't respond. I'm tired and numb, and my insides are shredded. I just want to go to bed.

It doesn't seem like enough time has passed before she's with me again in the living room, plate in hand.

"Mariska made this. It might be the best thing I've ever eaten." She's beside me on the couch, but my mind is miles away with Melissa. What is she doing right now? Can she sleep without me? I can't sleep without her.

"Take a bite." Blinking up, I realize Star's been talking, and she's now holding a fork with a square of cabbage roll on it.

Clearing my throat I straighten up on the couch, taking the fork and plate from her hands. "Thanks," I say.

She relents and sits back on the couch. The spicy tomato dish tastes like dishwater. I'm in no mood to eat. If I'm honest, I want to go to my room and finish off that fifth until this fucking pain is gone. The only thing stronger than that urge is me not wanting to look like shit tomorrow.

"I hope Cammie sleeps tonight." I glance up and Star's chewing her lip. "If she asks for Nan, I don't know what I'll do."

"You're doing okay with her."

"You think so?" Worried eyes meet mine.

"Yeah. You're not born knowing these things. I've learned a lot being around Dex, watching him." I mechanically cut another piece of cabbage, put it in my mouth.

Star exhales, shaking her head. "That's the problem. I've never even babysat. I don't know what the hell I'm doing."

I don't want to say it shows. I'm trying to be encouraging. "You love her. That's what's important. Try to be calm and smile more. Use that voice like Mariska does."

She nods, blinking fast. "I'm afraid I'm going to break her."

"Kids are pretty sturdy."

We're quiet again, and Star watches as I force myself to take another bite. "It's good, yeah?"

"I don't know."

She laughs then. "You've taken four bites. Either you like it or you don't."

Leaning forward, I set the plate on the coffee table. "I'm not really hungry."

We're quiet again, and I'm about to excuse myself when she speaks. "I wanted to thank you for something else."

Sitting back on the couch, I look at her, blinking those brown eyes at me. I'm trying to figure out when she got so vulnerable. "Okay?"

Reaching out, she takes my hand and holds it in both of hers. I start to pull away, but somehow that feels mean. "This is going to sound pathetic."

She does a little laugh, and I confess I'm curious. "Shoot."

"Nobody has ever believed in me like you did." Her eyes move from our hands to my face. "Or do?"

Shifting my position to face her, I take my hand back. "You're a smart girl. I believe you can do better than your past."

"Right," she nods, looking down again. Now her hands are clasped in her lap. "You're the reason I applied to college. I wanted to see if you were right. At the same time, I was scared. You didn't know me or anything."

I'm sorry her life has been such a shit hole. "It's my job to read people. We spent a week together, and I saw your potential. I'm glad if I helped you see it, too."

She smiles, and for the first time I concede she's a pretty girl. Without all the makeup, her features are delicate, and even if her eyes aren't stunning blue, they're lively and full of emotion.

"So I owe you more than I can repay. First with the believing in me," she exhales a laugh again. "That sounds so dumb, I know. Now you let me stay here with Cammie…"

"It's the right thing to do. Only an asshole threatens a helpless mother and child."

"I'm not so helpless." She cuts me a look from under her lashes, but I let it pass.

Anger burns in my chest. Star's blackmailer has pulled her out of college, dislocated her and her daughter, wrecked my home.

"You're not as strong as I am," I growl. "I'm ready to kick this fucker's ass. You have no idea."

Her lips press together and she nods. "Either way, you're really special to me."

With that, it's time to say goodnight. I stand and pat her shoulder. "There's more good people in the world than bad. Keep doing the right thing, and you'll meet them."

She touches the top of my hand on her shoulder, but I pull away heading to my room. I don't expect to get any sleep, but I'm hitting the road early. My chest aches at the thought Melissa might not text me, but just as I'm plugging in my phone it lights up.

Mom said we can have the party at one. If that gives you enough time.

Pain mixes with relief at her words. *I'll be there. Thank you.*

She doesn't respond, but I'm still encouraged. I still have a chance of getting back inside that wall, and when I do, I won't fuck it up again.

CHAPTER 7: BIRTHDAY BREAK

Melissa

Mom is in the living room with Dex, and I can hear her playfully chatting with him while he lines his trains up on her coffee table.

"Is this the station?" she asks in a high-pitched tone. "Are the trains wishing Dex a happy birthday?"

His little voice answers a loud *Yes!* And they continue chattering.

My hands tremble as I stand in the kitchen dropping slinkies, tiny containers of bubbles, and toy trains in decorated plastic bags. I'm doing my best to stay calm, breathe through my growing anxiety as I finish the party favors for his few little birthday guests.

They'll all be here in less than ten minutes. Lane is invited, of course, and two little boys from Dex's Mom's Day Out class. They'll only stay for an hour, then I'll be alone with his daddy. Another tremor moves through my stomach at the thought.

I'm not strong enough for this yet. Mom's being very supportive, although she repeatedly slips up and makes some comment about how she can't believe this is happening. She blames herself, saying if she hadn't gotten sick last fall we wouldn't have postponed our ceremony, and we'd already be married. I counter saying yes, and again I'd be stuck in a marriage built on secrets and lies. Elaine also blames herself, which is ridiculous. She didn't force

Derek to break his word. I haven't even spoken to Patrick.

A quick glance around the kitchen, and the blue and red train decorations are all in place or draped over the table. His cake is an elaborate blue tank engine with red and yellow piping and a bright yellow 1 on the side. It's a special delivery from my favorite client and baker "Aunt Bea," and a bright red candle is waiting to go on top. It's so cheery, Dex will love it. I can hardly look at it.

I'm not sure how much longer I can take the building tension waiting for his guests to arrive. Silently, I pray Derek won't be the first one here. Then I silently add another prayer that I won't cry during my son's first birthday party. I've been crying every other time of day. My determination is to make it one hour without tears.

The doorbell rings and I jump. Stepping to the passage between the kitchen and the living area, I watch my mom catch Dex's little hand and help him toddle to the door.

"Let's see who it is, Dexy!"

My eyes close as I hold my breath, releasing it in a rush when I recognize the squeals of children and realize it's Hannah and Evan from Mom's Day out. Right behind them are Cheryl and Tatum.

"Hi, guys!" I manage to say, surprised at my ability to act so calm.

I *will* be calm. Dex *will* to have a happy first birthday party. Hugs are exchanged, and I take the gifts into the kitchen. The little boys go immediately to Dex's train station setup on Mom's coffee table and start picking their engines.

"Such a lovely apartment," Hannah says, giving Mom a hug. "It's so nice of you to play hostess!"

"I thought it would be easier for everyone if we had the party in town," I lie. The truth is I can't have Derek back in the cottage. I'm afraid he won't leave, and I won't have the strength to force him.

"It is closer to everyone," Mom agrees, supporting my fictitious excuse.

"I suppose it's easier for Derek to pop over from the office, too," Cheryl says.

My breath stutters, and thankfully Elaine and Lane are coming through the door at that exact moment.

"We made it!" she calls cheerfully, and Lane makes a beeline to the little boys. "Where's my mimosa?"

"Good idea," I say, heading for the kitchen.

My hands shake violently as I reach for the cava. It's only a matter of moments before he'll walk through the door, and I'll have to face him. What the hell made me think I could do this? I should've insisted he wait to visit Dex at a later time when I could be elsewhere. Several deep breaths, I have to compose myself. It might have made things easier for me, but I couldn't ban him from the party. It would be too cruel, and Dex would want his daddy.

Tears threaten in my eyes, and I quickly pop the cork. Elaine walks up behind me. "How's it going?" Her voice is low, concerned.

"Okay," I nod as I pour an inch of cava into her glass of orange juice. I take my wine straight, sipping it fast. "If I can make it through this party."

A low voice from the living room interrupts my sentence. My heart stops then restarts beating painfully fast. In a gulp, I finish the rest of my wine and quickly pour another glass.

Elaine's green eyes are fixed, and she holds my forearm. "Ready?"

Taking another sip, I see my hand tremble too much, and I set the flute on the counter. "I don't have a choice."

Holding hands, we start back for the living room. Rounding the corner, my entire body flushes with heat when I see him. He's wearing dark jeans and a long-sleeved chambray button-down shirt under a brown tweed blazer. The shirt makes his eyes glow and the blazer accents the natural highlights in his dark hair. It's ridiculous that he looks even more handsome than when I saw him two days ago. He's carrying a soft brown teddy bear with a huge blue bow and a bouquet of red and white roses. I have to look away quickly before I lose the tiny bit of control I'm desperately clinging to.

"Oh, Derek, they're beautiful." Mom takes the flowers, holding his arm as if it's a lifeline. "Did you drive straight in?"

"Yes," his low voice cuts through me, and I can feel his gaze on my skin. "Had to get an early start, but I wouldn't miss Dex's party."

"Were you out of town?" Hannah's sitting on the floor near the boys.

"I had some business to take care of in Princeton," he answers, and his long explanation last night on the phone of exactly what he was doing filters through my mind.

It's too late, I stubbornly argue. Am I going to set the precedent that every time I need him to take me seriously, I have to throw him out of the house? My thoughts swirl with frustration and anger, and I realize Mom is asking me something.

"I'm sorry?" I say, blinking up to her.

"I said would you get Derek a drink?" My eyes land on his and lightning flashes to my toes.

"I-I…" I'm trying to recover when Elaine jumps in and rescues me.

"I'll take care of it. Mimosa, Derek?"

"Just a soft drink will be fine."

"Anybody else?" My best friend makes her way through the room, and I glance over at the clock. Fifty more minutes.

"We can head into the kitchen for cake if everybody's ready," I say, wishing my voice didn't sound so fragile.

"You ready for cake, Dex?" Derek squats down beside our son, who suddenly recognizes his presence.

"Day!" Dex squeals and holds Derek's shoulders, trying to climb him. Derek laughs, and my stomach cramps. I turn and head to the kitchen to light the candles.

An hour has never gone by so quickly. The little boys are full of cake and ice cream, goodie bags are passed out, and they're chasing each other around the coffee table as Hannah and Cheryl say goodbye and snag their little guys. Mom sees them to the door, and I busy myself cleaning up.

Elaine has done her best to run interference between Derek and me the entire party, trapping him in the living room with discussions of all things Patrick, Stuart, little boys, buying a condo versus buying a house, car buying versus car leasing, basketball or football, fly fishing… I swear to god, if she feels responsible for our present situation, she's redeemed herself a thousand-fold today.

Lane's whining is the only thing able to pull her from between my ex-fiancé and me. "I guess I'd better get him home," she says, and I can hear the worry in her voice. "Do you want to come with me, Derek? I'm sure Patrick wants to see you."

Nice try, I can't help thinking as Derek declines her offer. He's here to see his son, but I know who else he's here to see. Picking up my flute, I take a last gulp of cava. Elaine and I essentially split the bottle.

"I'll walk you out," Mom says. *Traitor.*

Dex is back to playing on the rug, but I can tell from the energy behind his train noises, he'll be crashing soon. I'm standing in the kitchen clutching the counter when I hear him enter.

"It was a great party." His voice is soft, and my insides twist painfully.

"Thank you," I manage in a voice far calmer than I feel.

"Dex seems really excited about his new toys."

"He really likes the stuffed bear you got him." I'm still facing the counter, afraid to turn around.

"Yeah," I hear a smile in his voice. "I know he's a train guy, but sometimes it's good to try new things."

His casual tone makes me glance up at him. It's a huge mistake, because the pain I'm feeling is reflected in his blue eyes. My heart clenches hard, and I have to look away again. He saw my response, however, and he's at my side.

"Mom sure is taking a long time with Elaine," I say around my rapid breath.

"Melissa." The torture of our separation is bound up in one word. I can barely stand it.

"I think I'd better go for a walk or something." I try to pass when he catches me by the arms.

"Wait." His voice breaks on the words, and my eyes flood. "Won't you talk to me just a moment?"

"It's too late for talking."

"It's not too late if you still believe in us."

Cutting my eyes up at him, I let out all the anger I'm feeling. "I *always* believed in us. You were the one who held me apart."

"You know it wasn't like that." His low voice is urgent. "I wanted to protect you."

"That excuse is only good once, not after you promised me—"

"Dammit, Melissa! I wasn't trying to break my promise."

"Still, you lied—"

"No. Lying implies deception. I never tried to deceive you."

"You conveniently omitted the part where you drove to Raleigh because Star was being blackmailed!"

"I didn't want you to feel responsible."

"Responsible? How could I feel responsible? You never let me in!"

"May, tank?" Our voices have grown too loud and Dex toddles in the room. He's holding his toy in one hand and his new bear in the other. I bend down to pick him up, but I have to look away from the break in Derek's eyes.

"I need you to give me your key." My voice is quiet, and I feel my body trembling as I say the words.

Derek steps toward us, but I turn my back.

"Stop this," he pleads. "Why are you doing this?"

"I've lived that life. I've been with someone who acted one way before we were married, and once we said *I do*, everything changed."

"I'm not like that." It's a low growl.

"Neither was he."

"Goddammit! I am *NOT* Sloan Reynolds!"

Dex starts to cry, and I clutch him closer to me. "I need you to give me your key and go."

I'm doing my best not to back down from what I have to do, doing my best to hold myself together. Doing my best not to dissolve into the fountain of tears I feel welling up in my chest. Shifting Dex on my hip, I again try to step past Derek, but again he stops me. "I won't let you do this to us."

"NO!" Now my voice is raised. "You're not putting this on me. You did this to us when you lied to me. When you swore you would be honest with me and the very next day you broke your word."

He's holding my arm too tightly, and I'm about to give in to my tears. "Let me go, Derek."

"I can never let you go."

My voice trembles. "Let me put Dex down for his nap."

His grip relaxes, but he doesn't move. "I'm not finished talking to you."

I push past him speaking softly to my little boy, who's sucking his finger. Once we're in his room at Mom's, I lay him in the crib and pull his favorite blanket beside him. He clutches the bear close and turns his head away, ready to sleep.

For a few moments, I stand beside his crib and rub his back, blinking as the first tears drop onto my cheeks. I have to stay strong. I have to make it through this. I have to believe I'm right.

A few more moments pass. Finally, I feel like I can go back to the living room. Dex is slowly drifting to sleep as I step out and close the door. A mirror hangs in the hallway behind me, and my eyes land on the gold chain around my neck. My breath hitches, my stomach cramps, and new tears flood my eyes. Reaching around my neck, I can barely unfasten it for my trembling fingers.

Holding the necklace in my hand I walk into the living room. "I should give this back."

"You will not." His face looks as if I've slapped him. "My heart is yours. Nothing has changed. You still love me."

More tears flood my eyes until they can't be contained. Drops fall on my cheeks, and I have to turn away. "I do. I love you more than I've ever loved any man."

"Okay, then." He's behind me, holding my shoulders. "I'm moving home."

"No, you're not." I step forward, out of his grasp. "I'll deal with my broken heart the way you'll deal with yours."

"Dammit, Melissa." His words are sharp even if his voice is low, and I appreciate him not wanting to upset Dex any more. "How can you say that?"

"I made a vow when I left Sloan's mansion that I'd never live that way again."

"If you compare me to that bastard again—"

Looking back over my shoulder, I meet his eyes now. "You're not an abusive asshole who frequents prostitutes, that's correct. Otherwise, you treat me the same as he did."

His jaw moves as anger flashes in his eyes. "Nowhere in the fucking universe is that true, and you know it."

"I'm not your equal. You hold me apart from your life—"

"You're so far in my life, I don't know where you begin and where I end. It's why we can't be separated."

105

From somewhere deep in my heart comes a question I'm not sure I want to ask. Yet out it spills. "Did you keep secrets from Allison?"

"Of course not, but—" His answer is so fast, so automatic, it crushes me.

"I need you to give me my key and go."

His fists clench, and for a moment, I'm afraid he might grab me. His voice grows louder as he speaks. "Stop this goddamn stubbornness, Melissa. I hear you now. I understand what you need, and I'm ready to give it to you."

Dex's whimpering from his room matches the quaking of my own insides. My head is light as I back away. I can't argue with him anymore. I don't have the strength. Putting my necklace on the end table, I clutch it for a moment, saying my final words.

"I can't do this anymore." Holding the walls I make my way to Dex's room.

At this point, I'm feeling so broken down, I don't know if I'll make it through this. If I won this battle he wins the war. When I'd said I still loved him, I'd spoken from the depths of my soul. My heart is battered, broken, and torn, and all I want is to crawl into his arms and let him hold me. Take this pain away and come home.

Only how can I say that? He doesn't treat me like he should. He flat out admitted he never hid things from her... He knows this isn't the way we should live, and I have to mean more to him than that.

Dex is standing in his crib, blue eyes round, a tear hangs on his little dark lashes. I lift him into my arms and walk to the glider in the corner. He snuggles into me, and the closeness of him, his baby scent eases the bleeding hole in my chest.

It would be so easy to give in, to say it doesn't matter and take him back. At the same time, everything inside me revolts at the prospect of going back to a life of half-truths and double-lives. Even if I know Derek isn't Sloan, I can't shake the ghosts of how my life used to be. The faintest hint of it sends ice water running through my veins.

If I willingly go back and nothing changes, I can only blame myself for making the same mistake twice, and this time, I can't blame it on ignorance. This time I'd be making the decision with my eyes wide open.

Dex scrubs his little head against my shoulder, and I hug him closer. As much as it hurts being away from Derek, I also have to consider our little boy. A baby is something I never had with Sloan, thank goodness.

His little fist grips my sleeve, and I kiss his dark hair. His little humming noises as he soothes himself actually soothe me.

Derek would never hurt me the way Sloan did. His lies are different from Sloan's in that while my ex-husband cheated on me and humiliated me at every turn, Derek has only risked everything to protect me—and then kept it a secret.

My survival instinct says to protect myself from even the hint of how my life used to be. What if my survival instinct and the man I love are on the same team, fighting the same battle? Derek says he'll change, and maybe he will. But if he doesn't, can I overlook this side of his personality?

"I'm going to figure this out, baby," I whisper, kissing Dex's ear. "I'm going to make the right decision for us. I promise." I just need more time.

CHAPTER 8: HARD LINES

Derek

Leaving her is the hardest thing I've ever done, but I'll be damned if I give that fucking key back. I'll be damned if I give any of it back. Melissa is mine. She and Dex belong with me. I won't back down from that.

Listening to her say those words was like being gutted with a dull knife. She fucking compared me to Sloan. God dammit. The mere suggestion rains acid all over my shredded insides. I would never treat her like that bastard. I killed that fucker because of what he did to her, what he wanted to do to her.

Anger pushes me too hard. I'm at a hundred on I-95, and I don't even see the cars as they pass. I have to drive back to Princeton tonight. I don't know what I'll do if I stay in Wilmington, but I know it won't help my case any.

Melissa is my heart and my soul and my life and my love, and every word she said made me want to grab her and shake her until... No. I'd never do that. I've just never been in that position where every word out of her mouth was so impossibly insane. My skull feels like it's coming apart from the pressure in my head.

I've suffered through someone I loved slipping away from me. When Allison had cancer, and all I could do was watch her die, I never thought I'd survive it. Yet, Melissa stands there with our little boy in her arms talking to me like nothing we've done even matters.

"Fucking bullshit!" I shout inside the car, slamming my fist against the steering wheel.

Yeah, getting out of Wilmington is the right call. Staying wouldn't lead anywhere productive. I'll step back, decompress, do some work, and see if I can figure out a better solution than tearing her door down with my bare hands.

The eight-hour drive is done, and I'm parking in my usual spot, heading into the building by eleven.

"Welcome home, sir," Jason, Walt's regular backup greets me.

"Hey, Jase." I pause inside the doors. "Did Walt mention my guests to you?"

"Yes, sir." Jason's overgrown eyebrows pull together like two black caterpillars. "We've alerted the other staff to be cautious of new runners and such. We won't let you down, sir."

Clasping his shoulder, I nod. "I appreciate it. The mother's okay, but her baby—"

"She's a cute little girl." Jason's oval face splits with a smile. "Dark hair and eyes. A real show stopper."

"Thanks." Nodding, I head to the elevator, wondering what Star was doing with Cammie in the lobby. I'll have to talk to her about being more discreet.

My condo is empty when I enter, which surprises me. I can only assume they're across the hall with Stuart and Mariska. It's late, but the little girl could easily sleep on a palette or a bed, and honestly, I appreciate the time alone. I need to recover from Melissa's blistering words.

Opening the cabinet, my scotch is gone. A bottle of Belvedere sits in the background, and I pull it down. Amber last night, clear tonight. My insides are loose and shaken. I haven't felt this helpless in years.

Walking to the couch, tumbler of ice in one hand, bottle in the other, I kick off my shoes and collapse into soft black leather. My phone is in my pocket, and I pull it out. Holding it in my hand, I stare at her beautiful face smiling, blue eyes glowing.

I want to call her. I want to shake her. I want to pull her to me and hold her until these fears in her melt away. Sloan put them there, and now from beyond the grave, his ghost still threatens us. I can barely take the thought, and I pull the cork out with my teeth. God, what am I? A fucking pirate?

Setting the phone on the end table, I pour until the tumbler is full. Fuck control. Fuck sensibility. I'm killing the pain tonight.

Leaning back on the sofa, my head drops back against the leather. I haven't checked in with anybody. I haven't answered the calls from Patrick. I'm sure Elaine told him I was there, but fuck if I feel like discussing it.

Another long pull, and the tumbler is half empty. Behind me, I hear the noise of my front door open. I expect it to be Star bringing Cammie back for the night, but the voice is my partner's.

"Patrick suspected you drove back." Stuart walks into the living room and takes the bergere facing me. "How long you been in?"

Lifting the tumbler, I finish my drink. "Five, ten minutes."

His eyes move from my hand holding the glass to my face. "That bad?"

"Shittier than bad." Leaning forward, I take the vodka and start pouring again.

"Give me some of that." He leans forward and catches the bottle before I've topped off my cup. Walking past he goes to the kitchen, and I drink while he fishes out another glass. "Did you talk to her?"

"She compared me to her fucking ex."

"The abuser?" Stuart's back, taking the seat across from me, keeping the bottle closer to him on the coffee table.

"One and the same."

"She knows better than that."

We're both quiet. He's nursing his drink, but I lean back and polish mine off then reach across for more. Before I grab it, he's picked the bottle up and is pouring more for himself. My brows lower as I watch. *If he's trying to piss me off...*

"Why don't you come into the office tomorrow," he says. "It'll take your mind off things."

"Why don't you fucking back off."

He actually has the nerve to chuckle.

"Don't fuck with me, Stuart. I'm in no mood."

"You don't have to tell me," he leans back, holding his glass. "It's been a long time since I've seen you this way."

"Buckle up. It's about to get worse."

"Strike that." He's in my way again, holding the bottle so I can't refill my glass. "I've never seen you this way."

"Fill it up," I growl, slamming down my tumbler.

He opens the bottle, but he only pours a shot. "This isn't going to change anything. It's only going to make you feel like shit."

"I already feel like shit. This is going to keep me from trashing this condo."

He stands and goes to the kitchen. "What about Cammie and Star?"

I'm leaning forward now, shoving my hands into the front of my hair, gripping the sides of my skull. "She asked for the key. She tried to give back her necklace. I'm surprised she didn't think of her engagement ring."

"Give her time. She'll think of it."

"Who's fucking side are you on?"

He walks back and leans against the wall of windows facing me. "I've only been around Melissa a few times, but I can tell she loves you. You crossed a line."

"She keeps saying it's over." Dropping my hands, I stare at my fists. "If she says that one more time."

"Grab the reins, and give her space. At least this time, she's still here. You still have a chance."

My fists open, and I reach for my glass. Only one sip is left, but I've made it through the scorching burn of rage. Now my pain is dulled from the vodka, and all I'm left with is the helplessness.

"Losing Allison is nothing like losing Mel. It was out of my hands. I couldn't do anything to stop it."

"The situations might be more similar than you think."

Glancing up, I study his face. "How so?"

"You can't do anything now. You're going to have to let her come around in her own time."

"I don't know if I can wait that long."

We're interrupted by the sound of the door opening again. Looking back, I see Star enter with her daughter asleep on her shoulder. She does a little wave, and I stand.

"I'm sorry. I needed to come back," I say softly.

"Were you…"

She shakes her head and points to the guest room. "I'm sleeping with Cammie."

Stuart pats my shoulder and heads for the door, leaving his full glass of vodka by the sink. "I'll pick you up in the morning. Get some sleep."

The two doors close simultaneously, and I pick up my phone. She doesn't want to hear from me, but I'm sticking to my policy of full disclosure.

I drove back to Princeton tonight. I'm going to go in and talk to Nikki, see if Patrick's found any leads on Star's situation, see if I can find anything. I'll be home this weekend. I'll be thinking of you every minute until then.

I hit *Send* and wait. Seconds tick past, and there's no answer. A minute, and I let it go. Stuart's right. It's tearing me apart, but I have to let her take the lead.

* * *

Nikki doesn't even look up from her desk when we enter the glass doors of the Princeton office. It's not until I speak that her white-blonde head snaps to attention.

"What's this I hear about you quitting?" My tone is mock disapproval, and her blue eyes go wide.

"Derek!" Her pinup mouth drops open, and I can't help shaking my head. Of all the secretaries I expected to stick around, it wasn't this airhead blonde.

"Can I see you in my office?"

She hops up and follows me in the same too-tight dresses she's worn since Day one. We step inside the office, and I push the door closed.

"What's going on?" I go around and sit behind the desk, and she takes the chair in front of me, not meeting my eyes.

"I got a better offer at another firm. A law firm."

"You don't know anything about being a legal secretary." She's bluffing, and I know it. "Try again."

Clearing her throat, she shifts in her seat, pulling on the hem of her skirt. "Okay, well, I just thought I'd take a break. Maybe go back to school…"

"Remember when it was just the two of us in this office?" She nods, and I continue. "I got pretty good at knowing when you weren't being completely honest with me."

"I can't work here with him anymore." She says it so fast, I lean back in my chair. I hadn't expected her to cave in the first round of questioning. "I did everything right. I waited. I… I…"

Her eyes well up, and she drops her chin, pressing her fingertips to her forehead. "I wasted three years, and now I'm too old to meet anybody." Her shoulders shudder as she cries, and I'm at a loss.

Scanning my former office, I spot a tissue cube in the back corner. Going to fetch it, I cross back and hold it out to her.

"First, you're young and fit. I'm sure plenty of guys would want to ask you out." Not me necessarily, but I prefer brunettes. I prefer Melissa. "Second, I don't think he was expecting you to wait." It's a shitty thing to say, but somebody has to tell her the truth.

"I know!" She wails, breaking down even more. She's full-on sobbing now, pressing a handful of tissues against her nose, her glittered fingernails catching the light. "I'm the loser here. I'm the one who gambled and lost."

She cries harder, and I flip through my papers trying to think of an excuse to send her home. "Tell you what. Why don't you take the day, and maybe you'll feel better tomorrow."

"No!" She wails shaking her head. Mascara is smeared on her cheeks, and she's starting to look pretty bad. "It's so much worse than that. I have to resign."

"Settle down, now." Walking around the desk, I put my hand on her shoulder. "If you have to resign, I won't stop you. At least stay and train your replacement."

All the bone-headed mistakes I've put up with from her, she can do that much.

"I don't know," she sniffs. "As long as I don't have to see... them."

Considering this, I figure we can make it work. "Stuart will be in the office, but if we can get a replacement this week, it shouldn't be a problem. Will that work?"

She nods still looking down, still wobbly from crying. "I'm going to miss you guys. I really liked working here."

Patrick's lines drift through my head, but I don't have it in me to lie to her. "You've been here a while... we'll miss you, too."

It's not a lie. Patrick will miss her, and I know Melissa was her friend, whether that still counts, I'm not sure. Nikki's reaction to my words comes out of the blue.

"Oh!" She jumps out of her chair, catching me around the neck. "I always knew we were friends, even if you are a hard ass at the office."

"Take the morning off if you need it," I say, patting her arm then pulling it off my neck.

"It's okay," she sniffs, straightening up and wiping her eyes. "Let me know if you need anything." She's at my office door when she stops and looks back. "How's Melissa and Dex?"

Doing my best not to wince, I open my MacBook. "Good. Thanks for asking."

She pauses for a moment, and I can see curiosity stirring in her eyes.

"Thanks, Nikki." I pull open files and try to appear busy. She shakes her head and leaves.

The rest of the day, I comb through every file I have on Sloan Reynolds. After Melissa showed up in my office that day in November, I became mildly obsessed with nailing him. I tracked down every dirty deal, every misstep, every possible way I could expose him. Going through all of those files, looking for anything I might have thought insignificant, I'm struck again by how well he'd been able to cover his tracks.

"Fucker," I mutter under my breath. "You will not win. I didn't let you win then, and I sure as hell won't let you win now."

"That's the spirit." Glancing up, I see Stuart standing in my doorway. "It's after six. Let's call it a day."

Leaning back in my chair, I realize I worked through lunch. Brown accordion files surround me on the desk and the floor. "I collected a lot of shit here." My eyes travel over the mess.

"This is why you were better at academia than me." He exhales a laugh, opening one of the files and reading the cover sheet. "I could never bury myself in research this way."

"Don't be so sure." I stand, closing my computer and slipping it into my case. "Let somebody threaten Mariska, and we'll see how much you like research."

A light flashes in his hazel eyes, and he spins his keys. "Somebody threatens Mariska, that'll be the last fuck-up he ever makes."

Gripping his shoulder, I follow him out the door. "Good answer. Keep in mind we're supposed to uphold the law."

"I never took any oaths." He glances back as the elevator doors open. "Even if I had, it didn't make a difference to you."

"I'm paying for that now."

"This story isn't over." His face turns serious. "Not by a longshot."

* * *

The girls are camped out in Stuart's condo playing Boggle when we arrive. Mariska has Cammie on her hip, and Star's hastily scribbling words as the egg timer counts down.

I'm feeling mildly better after spending a concentrated day tracking down potential connections to Sloan. It's not getting me closer to Melissa, but I have to believe with every passing day, she's softening. She loves me. She belongs to me. I'll report my progress to her tonight, and even if she doesn't reply, she'll get the message. I heard her, and I'm serious about giving her what she needs.

"This looks fun," Stuart, quips, walking over to Mariska and kissing her. Cammie lifts her head and pats his face. "Scoot."

"Yes!" Mariska coos to the little girl. "Stuart!"

I can't help a laugh. "Sounds like she's trying to get rid of you."

He grins, and the way his eyes glow at the two of them, I'm surprised he hasn't already proposed. He's clearly ready to procreate.

"Did you look into transferring to Princeton like I asked you?" His voice is low, and Mariska's brow lines.

"I told you, I'm not letting you pay for my college. It's not your place."

"How about I make it my place." He catches her around the hips and pulls her to him, and I realize I'm not as recovered from the pain as I thought.

Leaning forward, I read Star's list. *Toe, roast, leaf, leap, leer...* "Doing okay?" I ask, and she shakes her head, holding up a hand.

"I've got to win this time!"

"It's Boggle."

"Mariska's won every time!"

"Sorry, I didn't know you were playing for blood. I'm stepping across to my place," I say, heading to the door.

Mariska looks over her shoulder. "We're ordering Thai food tonight. You'll come back and join us, okay?"

I give her a little wave, unsure what I'll do tonight. Now that I'm outside my office, back in the world of couples and families, I remember the gaping hole in my life where mine should be. I head to my bedroom, slip off my shoes, and loosen my tie. The picture of Melissa and Dex is on the dresser, and I lift it, enduring the pain radiating through my midsection and focusing on my love for them.

"I'm not going anywhere, babe," I say softly. "I'm waiting right here for you."

My phone buzzes, and I see Patrick's face. Touching the screen, I lower the picture. "Hey, man, what's up?"

"Nothing," he says, blowing air into my ear. "Abso-fuckin-lutely nothing. I swear, I feel like I'm beating my head against a brick wall. That fucker hid everything."

"You're talking about Sloan?" Stepping over to my closet, I hit speaker on the phone and put it on the end table.

"Who else? I've spent the last two days shaking every tree I can think of, and nothing falls out. That prick was tighter than Fort Knox."

Nodding, I know he's running into the same thing I faced back when I first tried to investigate Sloan Reynolds. I realize my frustration probably fueled the rage I felt at not being able to keep him from Melissa. It's probably why I killed him. My legitimate options had run out.

"He was a piece of work," I breathe, slipping into relaxed jeans and a navy tee. "Have you gotten anywhere with Star's guy?"

"Until he makes another move, we're just waiting. Since he went directly to her, I don't have a lot of background. She tossed all the envelopes, so I have no postmarks, no DNA, no potential fingerprints..."

"Hang in there, partner. These assholes always screw up." I scoop up my phone and head back to the kitchen. "They're not as smart as they think they are."

"Fucking Sloan Reynolds was one smart motherfucker."

"He wasn't so smart. He had money and great handlers." Patrick and I've worked together a while, and I realize this is the first time I've seen him facing a dead end.

The line is silent a beat before he speaks again. "How are you doing?"

It's a question I'm not ready to delve into. I take down the half-empty bottle of Belvedere from last night and grab a tumbler off the drying rack. "I've gone through everything I collected on him the last two years. Nothing stands out."

"That's not what I meant." He pauses again. I know it wasn't. "You going to be okay?"

I've got a nice full glass of vodka, and I take a long drink. Pausing to let the burn pass, I nod. "I'll make it one more day."

"I'm watching her for you. She's safe."

Gratitude warms my chest. Or maybe it's the alcohol. Either way, "Thanks, partner."

"She won't talk to me either if that makes you feel any better. Apparently, I'm in the dog house, too."

Another sip and I rub my forehead with the back of my hand. "It doesn't make me feel worse."

"I think it's a good sign. She's mad, and being mad means she loves you. If she didn't, she wouldn't give a shit."

It's a good theory. Of course, then I remember her face at the birthday party, the tears in her eyes and the words she kept saying. Leaning back against the sink, I take another long pull. "I hope you're right."

* * *

The light of a few lamps casts a dim glow across my dark wood floors. My eyes trace the lines of my mahogany furniture. Stainless accents dot the interior, and an enormous flat screen television hangs dark on the wall in front of me.

When I bought this place, I was alone. Allison had died, taking with her my dreams of a home and a family. I was broken and empty, dark and angry. I had plenty of money to buy the ultimate bachelor pad, yet I had no intention of doing anything with it. I chose to be alone.

Then Melissa came. Then Dex. My life became so much more than I ever imagined when I moved in here. I had another chance at my dreams.

Now I'm back in this elegant cave by myself. Dex's cries are still in my ears, and the sight of Melissa refusing to look at me as she demands her key back...

I haven't eaten since breakfast, and even then, I didn't have much. An empty bottle of vodka is beside me, and anger twists in my chest. My fingers tighten around the crystal tumbler I'm holding, and I want to break it. I'm ready to smash every piece of elegant glass in the whole goddamn place.

The front door opens, momentarily interrupting my internal firestorm, and Star walks in with Cammie. The little girl is crashed out on her shoulder, and my thoughts travel to Dex. He'd be asleep on Melissa's shoulder right now.

Star deposits her daughter in Cammie's sleeping quarters then goes to the kitchen. I hear her digging in a crinkly plastic bag, and she's headed my way.

"Mariska said Walt knows all the best take-out places in a ten-mile radius." Her voice is too cheerful for how I feel. "I'm convinced. This is the best Thai I've had in… possibly ever!"

She sits on the coffee table in front of me, a plate of noodles in her lap. "You need to eat something."

My head is heavy, and I take in her appearance. Tonight, she's wearing tight jeans and a fitted, white long-sleeved sweater with thin black lines across it. Her long light-brown hair is loose and swept over one shoulder, and her face is more natural than I've ever seen it.

"What made you stick with this?" I say, lifting my hand to gesture to her outfit. "I thought you preferred rocker chic."

"I don't know," she smiles and glances up through dark lashes. "I guess I feel prettier this way?"

Nodding, I sit forward. "You look like Melissa."

She doesn't reply. Instead, she takes the glass from my hand, replacing it with a plate. I lift the fork and take a bite of pad Thai. It's good, so I take another.

"You've been driving a lot. Do you feel stiff?" She stands in front of me.

"I feel like shit." Instead of going back across the hall this evening, I'd sent my full-disclosure text to Melissa. As per usual, she didn't reply. All the vodka later, I'm twisted in my thoughts, trying to find any way back inside, through the wall she's built around her heart. It's killing me.

Star is on her knees, climbing behind me on the couch. "Mariska knows massage therapy." I feel her hands on my shoulders. "She showed me some touches. That's what they call them. *Touches*."

She pushes and squeezes my muscles, and warm relaxation moves through my neck, into my arms. "Feels good," I say, leaning forward to put the plate on the table, resting my elbows on my thighs.

"It does, right?" Star climbs around me and scoots the plate aside, sitting in front of me. "Check this out."

Her voice is soft, but my insides are toast. All I want is one thing... one thing 850 miles away. My head is right at her chest, and she slides cool palms to my temples. Slim fingers go behind my ears into my hair. Gentle but intense pressure on my scalp, her thumbs move to my forehead, and the pain eases.

Her voice is different, lower. "Like that?"

"Mm. It's nice."

My eyes blink open, and her slim torso is right in front of me, swaying gently. Long, chestnut waves move over her breasts, covered in that white sweater. She stops massaging my scalp and her hands move down to my cheeks, lifting my face gently.

"Beautiful man." Her thumb lightly touches my lips. "You're tired and you're hurting. Let me comfort you tonight."

For a whole half-second in the dim light, her lips are fuller, begging for a kiss. Her long, brown waves distract me with how much they look like Melissa's. I imagine them falling around me as she straddles my lap. My hands grip her small waist, and as she leans forward, I catch the scent of honeysuckle.

I'm on my feet as my brain's still working out a response. "I'll be across the hall," is as good as it gets.

The next moment, Stuart's at his door in boxers and no shirt, squinting at me in the light of the hallway. "What the fuck?"

"I'm sleeping here tonight." I push past him into the dark condo when I realize I've brought nothing with me. "Can I borrow a shirt? And a toothbrush?"

He stands for a moment, brow furrowed. A quick sweep of my appearance and he shrugs. "You should be able to find whatever you need in the guest room. Nobody ever sleeps there, but I use it for overflow."

"Thanks." I start for the door, but Mariska's with us, wrapped in a silk robe, her hair messy.

"Are you spending the night?" she whispers. "Let me move my art supplies."

I step back and let her pass, catching Stuart's eyes on her ass.

"Art," I say, since we're momentarily stuck facing each other.

"She's taking a class in nudes this semester." An expression flickers in his eyes.

My brow lowers. "If I see you nude, I'll kick your ass."

"Grow up." But he can't stop his grin. "It's art.

"As if your ego could get any bigger."

Mariska's back with us. "It should be safe now." She smiles up at me. "We almost never have overnight guests."

"Yeah," I clear my throat. "Got a little crowded at my place. Cammie or something."

"But you have Dex…?" Her eyes crinkle.

Stuart touches her back. "I figured this was coming. Let's turn in."

Thankfully, they take off. I step into the room and close the door. In view of my new full-disclosure policy, I decide in my next text to note that Star has my place to herself while I crash with Stuart and Mariska.

Stretching across the king-sized bed, I rub my forehead. I must've drunk more vodka than I realized. My body misses Melissa so much, it was ready to go for a cheap substitute to stop the pain. My stomach turns at the thought. Nothing is as good as Melissa. Closing my eyes, I picture her beautiful sapphire eyes, her long, dark waves over her ivory skin, her ocean-touched roses scent. I love her so much.

Even if she's thrown me out. Even if we're in a place where she won't talk to me. We'll get it back. I have to believe that, and when we do, I'll have no secrets from her, nothing to come between us. I won't betray her trust.

CHAPTER 9: MOVING FORWARD

Melissa

Work... work... work. I've done everything to bury myself in my marketing business, fighting with all I have to escape the pain of this gaping hole in my chest. A local strip mall is hosting a spring promo event, and several of the businesses have combined forces to do an inflatable playground for children with a bounce house and games, balloons and a tiny petting "zoo," consisting of rabbits, a few goats, a pot-bellied pig, and litter of kittens they hope to give away.

It's a solid week of work, collecting the various logos and nailing down exactly what type of promotion or event each shop will be hosting, locations and times, alternate arrangements for bad weather.

Sitting at my laptop, typing out the various press releases and newsletter templates for the stores, my eyes drift to the pin board of wedding ideas still lurking on my desktop. One pin is an ivory satin dress with large lace panels forming the bodice. Another is a white, strapless chiffon with lots of layers and movement in the skirt. Perfect for a beach wedding...

"I hadn't chosen my dress." Heat fills my eyes, and I lean my head heavily on my hand.

The board also includes cake ideas, and I realize I've got to stop Aunt Bea working on the wedding cake. "Oh, god." Another twist of pain.

Our engagement photograph is there, and the sight of me in his arms, soft lips touching my cheek, his dark hair moving in the breeze is almost too much. *He doesn't want this,* my mind shouts. *You don't want this.*

Standing I go to the kitchen for a glass of water. My mother has taken care of cancelling the roses, talking to the minister, the caterer, the musicians... Since we'd planned a beach wedding, we didn't lose any deposits. All I lost was my heart.

On the counter is a flier design I worked up for Aunt Bea. She wants to try decorated cake doughnuts in her shop. As old fashioned and out of touch with technology as she is, she still keeps up with the latest cooking trends. She's also addicted to the cooking channel.

Glancing at my calendar, I see it's Thursday. Has it been a whole week since Dex's party? Since that crushing day? Derek did not leave his key. He also did not take my necklace. It's back around my neck, actually, and every night I get a lengthy text from him detailing everything he did that day.

It's pretty routine info, and the only one I found interesting was when he made a point of telling me he was crashing with Stuart and Mariska while Star and her daughter stayed in his condo alone.

My hand instinctively moves to my midsection as I try to rub the cramp away. He knew I'd care about that. More heat in my eyes. All this information, all this thoughtful consideration... Why did it have to take such extremes to get us here?

An idea filters through my mind, and I pick up my phone.

Mom's gentle voice greets me. "Are you doing okay, honey?"

"Yeah, I need to go to Baltimore." The flier is in my hand, and I turn it over, thinking about what I'm doing. "Aunt Bea is starting a new product line, and I want to take pictures for her website. I'd also like to tell her in person about the wedding cakes. She's done so much, I feel like I owe her a visit."

"Oh, Melissa," she sighs, and I want to hang up immediately. Every wedding detail has been reluctantly cancelled by my mother, and all with repeating "are you sures" the entire time.

I power on. "I'll only be gone overnight. Would you mind keeping Dex?"

"You don't even have to ask." She's smiling now. "I love keeping my grandson."

Nodding, I slide my laptop into its sleeve. "He has Mom's Day Out in the morning. I'll let Hannah know you'll pick him up."

"Drive safe."

We disconnect, and I place a quick call to Bea. Of course, she'll be in the shop tomorrow. It's a fantastic idea for me to drive up and take pictures for the website. She can't wait to see me and show me her ideas for the groom's cake, and when is Derek going to make up his mind? I dodge that last question and tell her I'll be there by early afternoon. All that's left is getting through another night alone.

Evening used to be my favorite time of day. Derek would be home, the three of us would be together. Now the prospect of sleeping in that king-sized bed, surrounded by his warm, lingering scent, with no strong arms to hold me… It's become a little slice of hell for me to endure. Lately my endurance has moved to the couch.

Tonight, at least, I have something to focus on: packing.

* * *

Aunt Bea's shop is located a block off the main foot-traffic route in downtown Baltimore. We'd had to work to get customers to make the detour for her pastries and gifts, but a few well-timed samples and surprise office freebies combined with her talent in the kitchen and my ability to spread the word paid off.

Her shop is full of customers when I arrive, and parking in front of the store, I think of how different coming to the city from this angle feels compared to how it was when I lived alone in the Reynolds mansion.

A dark thought tightens my stomach, the empty Reynolds mansion. Sloan is dead. Derek killed him, and somewhere, someone knows about it. Whoever that person is could be anywhere. Glancing over my shoulder, an involuntary shiver moves down my spine.

Derek's nightly check in said they'd had a breakthrough in the case. It was unexpected, and he wasn't sure he believed it. Apparently, the harasser sent a letter to Star at the condo. He'd said it was too long to text, but he'd know more tonight.

As much as I want to be indifferent, I'm on edge waiting to hear what's happening, and hoping it doesn't make his situation worse. My thoughts are distracted as I enter the store, and I make my way past the waiting customers to a side table.

"I've got your special cupcake! " Aunt Bea nods to a little pastry on a small plate. It's a tradition she started before I moved home, and even after I was in Wilmington, she would still send me special deliveries at the holidays. "Drunken buttered rum."

Distractions vanish, my eyes widen as I check out the dark cake topped with white frosting and shaves of coconut flakes and pecans. "It looks amazing."

A male customer curiously inspects my treat as I peel back the wrapper.

"It's something new I'm trying," she says, assembling a pink and white polka-dotted cardboard box. "Cooking channel."

I grin and take a small bite. Rich buttery rum and spicy cinnamon fill my mouth. A hint of nutmeg, and I have to work to suppress a groan.

"How do I get some of that?" The man in the navy pin-stripe suit nods toward me with a wink.

His question is a bit vague, but Bea is on it. "Be my marketing genius and favorite customer." She winks back at him. "Her fiancé is a very lucky man."

His expression drops, and he orders red velvet. I wait until she's finished with him and helped the nanny and kids behind him, and once they're done, we're momentarily alone.

"Good?" The petite, round baker hustles over to me. Her apron is stained with pink frosting, and I can't resist teasing her.

"They think I'm so lucky, but they don't know I'm your test subject."

Leaning back, she crosses plump arms over her ample bosom. "As if I'd ever give you anything bad."

I lunge forward to hug her. "You give me sinfully delicious treats."

"Speaking of sinfully delicious, how's Derek?" A nudge and a grin, and I glance down.

"He's, umm… doing great."

Her face turns serious, and she goes to the door. In a flash, she turns the "Back in ten minutes" sign around, flips the lock, and pulls down the shades.

"What happened?"

Damn. I'm stunned by both her quick response and her question. "We sort of had a... well..." Tears flood my eyes. *I can't believe I'm still crying like this.* Grasping for control, I clear my throat. "We broke up."

Concern lines her face, and she leads me to one of the small tables. "I can't believe it," handing me a napkin, "I saw you together. How is this possible? What did he say?"

Dotting my eyes, I look down at the paper cloth trying not to cry more. "It was me, actually. I broke it off."

"What!?" Her voice is too high, and she collapses into the chair across from me. "Melissa, honey, you have got to explain this to me."

My gaze stays fixed on my hands. "We wanted different things." *No, that's not right.* I shake my head and try again. "We have different ideas about what a relationship means. To me it's a partnership, sharing, including each other. No secrets. To him it's... not."

"Can't you find a compromise?" Her voice is urgent but gentle. "You've been married before. You know men... well... I mean —"

"That's just it!" My eyes flash to hers. "I *have* been married before. It's the whole reason I had to end it."

Her grey eyebrows pull together. "You broke it off because of Sloan?"

"Because of what happened with Sloan. All the lies, the secrets. The double life. I married a man I thought I knew, and then it turned out... I didn't know him at all." I pause for breath then quietly add. "I won't make that mistake again."

Bea studies the table in front of me a few moments before taking my hand. "Then why do you still wear this?" The dark blue sapphire ring is on the third finger of my left hand.

My lips tremble as tears threaten, and I move it under my thigh. "I don't know."

It's a lie. I haven't been able to take it off because no matter how my insides twist and fight, it's the last piece of evidence holding me together. I'm afraid if it's removed, all my insides will bleed out.

We don't speak, but I can feel her studying me. I can feel myself unraveling in front of her, and I wish she'd say something.

"Sloan Reynolds was a sneaky young man." She leans back in her chair, and her tone grows thoughtful. "Very slick and always smiling, but always being naughty when no one was looking. I don't know where he got it. His father was a good man. His mother was a bit... materialistic, but she wasn't cruel or vindictive. Still, for whatever reason, their son was attracted to the darkness more than the light."

Slowly, my eyes move up to hers. I need to hear this. "You know, I caught him stealing from my register when he was about fifteen." She nods, hands across her midsection. "Why the son of the town's richest family would need to steal, I don't know. He saw me catch him, too, and I'll never forget his wicked grin. Slipped that money in his pocket and walked right out the door as if daring me to call him on it."

"Did you?" I whisper.

"Of course I did! I called Jackson right away and told him his boy had taken forty dollars right out of my cash register."

"What happened?"

Exhaling, she shakes her head. "His father thought it was funny, a boyish prank. He apologized for Sloan and said he'd send the money right around, and sure enough, his driver came by before the end of the day with the money and a little gift."

"What are you saying?" I wait for her next words as if they're the key to some incredible mystery.

"The average male is not born ready to share every thought in his head." She smiles at me now. "Half of them aren't even sure what to make of the thoughts in their heads beyond food and sex."

"Derek's not like that," I say under my breath, leaning back.

"Derek was alone for how long after his wife died?"

"Six years." Reaching out, I trace the wood grain with my fingernail.

"And he works in the security business. Investigations. Things that require the utmost secrecy."

My jaw tightens. "Yes."

"Derek Alexander is a war hero, am I right? A commanding officer? His friends and coworkers trust him? Vouch for his trustworthiness?"

"Of course." Pressure is building inside me, pushing upward in my chest.

"Honey," she exhales a chuckle. "Give the man a chance to mess up once before you throw him out of your life. Especially one as handsome and clearly devoted to you as that one."

"You don't understand. It was more than once, and the secrets he kept were…" I can't tell her the whole story. "They were huge."

"Another woman?"

"No!" The very idea burns in my stomach.

Bea's lips curl at my response. "Have you heard from him?"

"He texts me every night… telling me everything."

"Oh, sweetie." Her warm tone moves through me like a wave, and I know what has to happen. The truth is clear as a bell. I don't know why I didn't see it sooner.

"Love is a risk," she says. "Putting your heart out, making yourself vulnerable again is scary. I can only imagine how gun-shy you must feel after your last experience. But trust me, you picked the right man this time. Everyone can see it."

I'm on my feet and at her counter collecting my things before her last words are even uttered. "Do you mind if I reschedule our meeting?"

"Only if it's for the reason I hope it is."

"I'll call you next week."

* * *

Baltimore is two and a half hours southwest of Princeton. Somehow I manage to make the drive in two, my mind racing through everything Aunt Bea said to me the entire way. I don't call, I don't think or even give myself a chance to second-guess. Her words seared through my fears and doubts, making even my anger seem incredibly silly. If my mother were in the room, I know what her diagnosis would be: projection.

Fear, gun-shyness, whatever was going on, it's over, and now I'm sitting in my car looking up at the Alexander-Knight office building. My heart beats so fast it hurts. A quick glance at the clock tells me it's five-thirty.

"Please be here," I whisper.

Hopping out, I run inside and press the elevator button. It takes an eternity to finally open at the bottom floor. Dashing inside, I repeatedly press the button for the top floor. Finally the doors close, and another eternity as it slowly starts to rise.

Tapping my foot, I pace the small box. "Come on!" I growl, until finally the movement stops. A pause and the doors slowly open.

Running out into the breezeway, I head straight for the glass double-doors and push through. Nikki's not at her desk, and I only briefly wonder if she's even still working here. I'm headed straight for his office, but before I turn the handle, I stop. I'm breathing fast, and I'm actually trembling.

Wiping my palms down the sides of my jeans, I scrub my hair with my fingertips, hoping it looks pretty and not smashed from riding in the car all day. I'm wearing a red sweater, which is a relief. His favorite color. Hand on my twisting stomach, I take a deep breath and open the door.

The sight of him hits me like a freight train. He's behind his desk in his usual charcoal suit and tie. Elbows bent, his forehead is lined. A dark brown wave has fallen on one eye, and his lips are in a firm line making his square jaw stand out attractively. I wonder for a half-second what's got him so focused. His phone is in his hand, and he appears to be texting.

I don't know what to say, so I clear my throat softly. Steel blue eyes snap up to mine, and a rush of energy floods my body.

"Hi," I say softly. "I hope I'm not disturbing you."

Phone down, he's out of his chair and crossing the room to me at once. Just before he reaches me, he stops, hesitating. We're so close, his delicious scent teases my nose, his warmth hints at my skin.

"You never disturb me." The low ripple of his voice squeezes my heart, and I'm so light I'm either going to lift off the ground or faint. "I was just texting you… What are you doing here?"

He's holding back. I see his palm twitch, and I can tell he's trying to decide if it's okay to touch me.

"I needed to see you. I needed to tell you I was wrong. I'm sorry. I want you to please come home."

With every word, his brow relaxes more, the shine of love grows stronger in his eyes. I've barely said the word *home* when I'm swept up in his embrace. The strong arms I've been craving for weeks hold me tight, secure, and exactly where I'm supposed to be.

"Melissa," he breathes, kissing my temple, my cheek, until at last our lips crash together, tongues find each other and desire tickles low in my stomach.

A little noise, somewhere between a laugh and a moan slips out, and I'm grasping his shoulders, his hair, his face, trying to pull him to me as hard as I can. I want our bodies touching. I want every cell melting together. I want to be so wrapped up in him, we're like he said, *it's impossible to know where I begin and you end.*

"You're back," he breathes, kissing me again and again.

"I didn't hold out very long." I'm in heaven as his soft lips, that lovely, scratchy beard trace a line into my hair, behind my ear, until he stops and takes a long, deep inhale.

"It felt like a lifetime." Chills skate across my body. "I want to take you home and make love to you."

"Let's go." I grip his arms smiling. "Or here is good…"

My back is against the wall of his office, and he kisses me roughly. Heat floods between my thighs, and the only thing left is for our bodies to be reunited. I ache for it.

He pulls away, and our eyes meet. His are so full of love, but there's something else, something breaking. As we hold each other, his expression looks like he's being torn apart, and I'm instantly afraid.

"Derek, what's wrong?"

"Like I said, I was sending you a text to tell you…" His arms surround me, pulling me tight against him. His head is against my shoulder, and he only holds me. "Oh, god, Melissa."

I grasp his broad shoulders, trying to move him back so I can see his face. "Baby, what is it?"

"Just let me hold you. I need to hold you right now." His voice is muffled, and I swallow the knot in my throat. His lips move to my jaw as I hear noises from outside the office. They're loud and pushy, almost as if a team of individuals is forcing their way inside.

"What's this about?" Stuart's voice is stern.

"Derek Alexander?" A male snaps back.

I feel him tense in my arms. His head lifts, and he looks deep into my eyes. "Listen to me. I love you so much. You're my home and my family. You're all that's ever mattered to me—"

The office door slams open, and men in dark blue uniforms surround us. Stuart's voice follows them, demanding answers. Derek's arms are ripped from my body and pulled behind his back, but his eyes never leave mine. One of the men begins to speak.

"Derek Alexander, you are under arrest for the first-degree murder of Sloan Reynolds. You have the right to remain silent. Anything you say or do can and will be used against you in a court of law—"

"NO!" I scream, grabbing his arm. "Stop it! STOP!"

"Miss, I need you to step back." A sharp voice orders me. "You have the right to an attorney. If you cannot afford an attorney, one will be appointed to you."

Tears blind me. "Leave him ALONE!" I shout, and my hands shake as my fingers fumble to the cold metal on his wrists.

"Melissa," Derek's voice is in my ear, his face at my temple. "I have to go."

Pulling back, I find his eyes. Heartbreak is in them, and tears spill onto my cheeks. "I can't…" My voice trembles and breaks. "I can't let this happen…"

"Stay with Stuart."

Stuart is behind me holding my shoulders as the officer finishes. "Do you understand these rights as they have been read to you?"

"Yes," Derek answers, and my knees give out.

Stuart catches me. "Hang on," he says, and I grab him, trying to find my balance.

"Take care of her," Derek says.

Stuart nods. "I'll get her to Mariska and be right down."

It's the last they're able to say before the group of cops escorts him out of the building.

CHAPTER 10: UNMASKED

Derek

It's been a week since Dex's party, and nothing has changed. It's driving me crazy. I keep texting Melissa, debriefing her on my days. She continues not responding. I keep digging through these records, looking for any clue as to who's behind the letters. We continue coming back with nothing. It's starting to feel pointless, and the strain is wearing on all of us. Patrick's ready to set a trap, and for the first time since I've known him, Stuart agrees with his brother.

I'm turning over the details of their plan when my phone buzzes. One glance, and I'm surprised to see it's Star. Ever since that night in my condo, I've given her a wide berth. I sleep at Stuart's place and spend most of my time there or here. When we do speak, it's very basic: the latest on the case, if she needs anything, how Cammie is adjusting.

Snatching up my phone, I slide a finger across the face. "Derek here."

Panic fills my ear. "It's over! He knows we're here! Oh god!"

I'm out of my seat, snatching my blazer off my chair and heading for the door as she's still speaking. "Calm down. Where's Cammie?"

"I'm holding her." Sounds of movement, and the little girl makes a fussy noise.

"Are you in my condo?" Waving at Nikki, I'm out the double-glass doors.

"Yes. We're in the condo, alone—"

"Go across the hall and stay with Mariska until I get there. Can you do that? Is Mariska home?"

"I-I think so?" Her voice cracks, and I hear the tears coming.

"Star, listen to me."

A sniff. "Hm?"

"Don't cry. Think of Cammie. She doesn't know what's going on. You need to stay calm." Fishing in my pocket, I pull out the keys to the Audi.

"Okay..."

"I'll stay on the phone with you until you get to Stuart's place. Go ahead."

More rustling noises, another little fuss from Cammie. I hear a door opening and closing followed by soft tapping. Mariska's high voice greets her in the background.

"Are you in?" I'm on the road, making my way through traffic.

"I'm at Stuart's." She already sounds calmer. "We're here together."

"Good. Ask Mariska to lock the door and don't let anyone in until I get there. I'm five minutes away."

"Okay." She speaks to Mariska, but I cut in.

"I'm hanging up now."

"Derek!" She's back to panicky.

My stomach tightens. "What is it?"

"I'm just..." Hesitation. "You'll be right here?"

"Less than five minutes now. Don't be afraid. Walt's downstairs."

"Right."

"Hanging up now."

We disconnect, and my teeth clench. This is the break we've been waiting for. If this asshole was stupid enough to send mail to my condo, we can track it all the way back to his doorstep. *Shit!* Snatching up the phone again, I call Star right back.

"What is it!" Her voice is a gasp.

"Everything's fine," I say, trying to ease her back down. "Don't throw away the envelope. Don't touch it any more than you have to."

"I left it in your condo!" she cries.

God dammit. Keeping my voice calm. "We've got to have that envelope, Star. I'll stay on the phone with you. Go back across the hall and get it."

"Hang on… Cammie, stay with Aunt Mare Mare. I'll be right back." Door opens, door closes, noise of frantic movement… more frantic movement… I'm gripping the steering wheel as I wait. Finally, a loud exhale of relief. "It's here! I have it."

"Pick it up carefully by the edges and put it in a plastic bag." I'm pulling into the parking garage. "I'm in the building. I'll be up in less than a minute."

We disconnect, and my next call is to the office.

* * *

Stuart has the closure flap on the envelope and the stamp in his hands, and frustration lines his brow. "They're all stickers. None of this requires saliva."

"So whoever it is knows better than to leave behind traces of DNA."

We both sit back and stare at the brown envelope and the white sheet of paper. I pick up the letter and read it again.

Ms. Durango,

The time has come, the walrus said, for us to end our game. You've done everything exactly as I expected. Give these instructions to the Big Guy:

Meet me at the Palomino Bar, martini room, tonight at nine. I'll be the one with the Gibson and the gat. If he brings any helpers, my accomplice will turn your photograph, your underwear, and your exact location over to the MSPD.

I look forward to our meeting.

Signed,
A Friend

Tossing the paper back on the table, I exhale and stand. "Fuck it. I'll meet him tonight, and I'll go alone. I'm not worried about any of this. I'm ready to unmask this asshole."

Stuart's eyes flick to the clock then back to me. "That gives us two hours to work out a Plan B."

"I don't need a Plan B. We'll follow his Plan A. I've handled rats like this before. I'm happy to do it again."

"At least wear my Kevlar." He heads to the master bedroom, and I wait, turning his instructions over in my mind. An accomplice.

Star has Cammie in the living room, and we decided they should stay with Stuart and Mariska the rest of the night in case it's a setup.

My partner's back with his black vest in hand. "The perfect double-cross would be to pretend he's after you in order to pull us all away from covering her. Or to lead you out in the open alone."

"You read my mind, partner." I pull my black sweater over my head and take the vest from him. Once it's securely fastened, I restore my top layer and add a lightweight grey blazer.

"I'd feel better having you covered." Stuart hands me a small pistol I slip in my boot. "I don't need a gun to end this."

"You never know how he'll come at you." He steps to the door and opens it, and I follow him back to the kitchen. "This fucker didn't give us any time. If Patrick were closer, we'd have at least one more set of eyes."

"I give our *friend* credit. He's bringing you two together in a way I never could."

"Extra muscle is always helpful in situations like this. Regardless of whether I agree with him."

Clapping Stuart on the shoulder, I head for the exit. "Don't worry. I'll be back in a few hours."

* * *

The Palomino bar is adjacent to one of the nicer steak houses in town. The main bar is large and traditional. Wooden booths line the perimeter and a matching bar is located in the center of the room. A layer of tall tables with high chairs ring the space between the two, and it's all shiny brass and low lighting. Off to the side is the dim-lit martini bar where I'm looking for an asshole with a Gibson. And a gat.

It takes a few seconds for my eyes to adjust to the change in lighting. For a Thursday night, it's pretty deserted, but it's early.

A couple sits in one corner leaning close together. The female holds a pink martini, a cosmopolitan, I'd bet. Her date has something with a curled lemon peel slivered in it. Lemon drop. A table of three women is across from them, but again, pink drinks. Finally my eyes land on a patron in the very back, dead center of the room. I can't make out the face. Whoever it is has leaned out of the light, but on the table directly in front of him or her is a martini glass containing clear alcohol. In the bottom middle of the crystal is a small, white onion on a toothpick. Our "Friend."

Without hesitation, I walk straight to where he or she is sitting and stop, waiting for the snake to slither into the light. When it finally does, I'm momentarily winded. I have to take a step back.

"Bennett?" Confusion lines my face as I recognize the contract private investigator I've worked with for years. I've trusted him on several cases, and he's been my right hand tracking subjects in remote locations. The last time we worked together was... last year. He kept an eye on Sloan for me in Baltimore when I was in Wilmington with Melissa. Anger mixed with betrayal fires in my chest. I'm ready to kill this guy, but for the moment, he has the upper hand.

"Derek Alexander." He leans forward, placing his elbows on the table and giving me a sick grin.

"Robert." I pull out the chair across from him and sit. "I confess, I'm surprised. You're better at your job than I gave you credit for."

His eyes narrow before they travel over my torso. "Credit is hard to come by in your business, Mr. Alexander."

"The bird in the hand is always preferable to theories and promises."

He exhales a short laugh. "You're so fucking smooth. You with your suit and tie, your fancy car, your ultimate bachelor pad, and sexy-assed fiancée."

My fist tightens. "A smart guy would keep his thoughts about Melissa to himself."

"Or what?" He leans back and really laughs. "You'll kick my ass? She's not even yours anymore."

I meet his ice-blue stare. "I'll break your neck."

He takes a long sip of the Gibson in front of him. "Your preferred method of disposal." A pause as he evaluates my response. "Such a rookie mistake, losing control like that. You honestly thought no one would find out? I'm disappointed."

"The feeling is mutual." The waitress puts a short glass of scotch in front of me and sashays off again.

Lifting the toothpick, he slips the tiny onion into his mouth. "Even more disappointing. I gave you the perfect setup. That hot piece of ass right in your condo. You never even fucked her, and I hear she gives a hell of a hummer."

"You're talking about Star?" My eyes narrow. "Is she in on this?"

He shakes his head and frowns. "I'm no amateur. All she could talk about in Baltimore was how you believed in her. It was pathetic, and I fucking thought after the way she played your partner—"

"You asked her to help you?"

His cold gaze lands on mine. "Of course not. I knew she'd never turn on you. She's too in love with you." A disgusted noise, and he takes another sip.

I've heard enough. "What do you want, Bennett?"

"My letter was perfectly clear," he says with a smirk. "I want you, big guy."

Leaning back, I shove my drink forward. "What the fuck? I'm not gay."

"HA!" He says loudly, leaning forward in mock laughter. "Your ego is only outsized by your stupidity." Straightening, all traces of his smile disappear. "I want you taking a dose of your own medicine."

"What the hell does that mean?"

"Let's see... You're *Mister* Alexander, fucking American hero, fucking top in your field, fucking paragon of truth and virtue. Am I right? Or do I exaggerate?"

"You exaggerate."

"Maybe, but you do blaze in like the scales of justice ready to put anyone away, ruin his life, without a shred of mercy."

Studying his face, I remember the last letter. *Revenge is a dish best served cold.* "You said you wanted revenge. What have I ever done to you?"

He's collected again, running his finger around the lip of his now-empty martini glass. "Do you happen to remember a young man named Shane?"

Filtering through my memory, I come back with nothing. "No."

His head moves slowly side to side. "You wouldn't. You only knew him as Slayer. Slayer Bennett."

Lightning flashes behind my eyes, but I remain cool. "You're related to Slayde?"

"You might say that." He exhales a chuckle and signals the waitress. "You might say I'm the reason he exists."

Another Gibson is placed in front of him, and we both wait until the young, tattooed lady is gone again.

More than any other, that court case is etched in my memory. I remember what they said about Slayde's father.

"Are you pretending to care?" I evaluate the fucker sitting before me. "The court psychiatrist said you beat him regularly within an inch of his life."

"I didn't know about that." Staring into the drink, his voice drops, and for the first time, he doesn't come off as a raving fucking lunatic. "Shane doesn't know I'm his real dad." Bennett's eyes slide closed. "His mother was the most beautiful woman…"

"So you abandoned him." My empathy for this guy evaporates as quickly as it tried to appear.

"It wasn't like that. Mary pushed me away." He shakes his head. "When she got sick, she said it was God's judgment for violating her marriage bed."

"Sounds like Slayde's had a lot of crazy to overcome in his life." I take a long drink of scotch.

"But you knew the hell he survived. You had all the evidence. The psychiatrist said he had intermittent explosive disorder. They tried to reduce his sentence. But you wouldn't let them. You had no mercy."

Glancing away, I can't help admitting I still have a problem with that diagnosis. At the same time, I can relate to a father's concern for his son. I have Dex, after all. "So what? You want revenge because I did my job?"

His crazy returns with his rage. "You wouldn't stop until you finished him. He was destined to be a boxing legend, and you took it all away." His voice is a breathy growl. "Look at you. You're no better than him. You fucking hypocrite."

Quiet settles over the table. I think about his words, that case. "I was a lot harder then. I'd just lost Allison—"

"Save the sob story. It's time for payback, and you know the saying. She's a bitch."

"You want money?"

"Fuck no!" A spate of real laughter erupts from him now. "I want you to lose everything. I want your ass in prison, rotting away just like my kid's."

My brow lines. "You know he's out, right?"

"He's a fucking janitor. A nobody living in a shit town."

With an exhale, I lean back. "I don't know what to tell you. It was the right thing to do at the time. Slayde's paid his debt, and from what I understand, he's happy now."

"What the fuck do you know about his happiness?" Bennett shoves his glass forward. "I've been watching, waiting for the great Derek Alexander to slip up, and boy, did you ever."

"You want me to go to prison." I nod, looking at my glass. "What's your plan for making that happen?"

"Easy. You have two choices. The whore goes to prison or you do." He leans back, a calm smile crossing his lips. "What's it going to be, hero?"

Ice settles in my stomach. He's prepared for this. He's crazy like a fox, and he's left me no options. "That will satisfy you?"

"Watching you clean shit off of fucking toilets just like my boy had to? You bet your ass." He leans forward and his voice becomes a hiss. "I'll be fucking jerking all over your fucking photograph."

———

150

The image forces a grimace. "Turn myself in."

"You've got twenty-four hours, Big Guy." The smile on his face is testing my ability to not snap him like a toothpick. "I know that look. You touch me, you seal her fate. My accomplice has everything she needs to put Star away for life should anything happen to me."

Standing, he shoves his chair in. "I'm listening to the wire. By this time tomorrow, your ass had better be in a cell."

Sitting back, I watch him walk out of the bar. For the moment, it appears my former PI has the upper hand. I'm not sure how we're going to resolve this, but I have to talk with Stuart and Patrick. Then I have to call the Maryland State Police Department.

CHAPTER 11: OLD FRIENDS

Melissa

Stuart paces the office, his fists clenched as hard as his jaw as he shouts into the phone. "Derek is not a fucking flight risk. He turned himself in for Chrissake. I can't believe this bullshit."

I'd spent a restless night at the condo, sleeping alone in Derek's king sized bed, worrying, praying for his safety in Baltimore central lockup. Star was in the guest room with her daughter Camille. It was the first time we'd ever met, but she was demure. Shy and apologetic. Her daughter was beautiful.

Now I'm back at the office with Stuart, and the two of us are trying to think of any way to shorten Derek's stay, to prevent this from going any further. I watch Stuart talking to Patrick.

"We need your ass here now." Silence as he listens to his brother. "Because I can't fucking keep my eye on everyone alone."

My eyebrows rise. I can't help wondering what might happen with these two in the same room and Derek gone. Bolt down the furniture.

Stuart ends the call and turns to me. "How you holding up? Need anything?"

Shaking my head, I look down at Derek's desk. "I need him home."

"We all need that," he says through an exhale.

Just then, Nikki scampers into the room. Her eyes are red as if she's been crying, and she holds a brown envelope. I smile at her, glad she's stuck around. Having to find and train a new assistant would not be ideal at the moment.

"I'm sorry to interrupt." Her voice is high and quiet.

"It's okay," I say. "What do you need, hun?"

"I just wondered if Mr. Alexander... If Derek still needs me to mail these files for him."

"What files?" Stuart growls and doesn't make eye contact.

She's flustered and holds them out. I notice the tremor in her hand. "Bennett? His old PI said it was for a case he handled. He said it should go to the police department in Maryland."

"What the *FUCK*?" Stuart explodes at her, and her eyes widen suddenly before she drops the papers on Derek's desk and runs out the door.

He's right behind her. "You're Bennett's accomplice?"

I jump out of the chair and run after them. Nikki's behind her desk, tears streaming from her eyes in black lines. "I don't know what you mean!" She wails, but Stuart's not stopping.

He rounds the desk and grabs her by the upper arms, shouting in her face. "How long have you been working with that fucker?"

"I don't know!" She's crying harder, her face an ugly red mask. "Two years? H-however long Mr... Derek's used him!"

Stuart's face is flushed, and I jump between them. "Hang on!" I shout. "Stuart, *stop*! Let her go!"

He shoves her back, and I catch her arms. "Nikki, what do you know about Robert Bennett?"

She's shaking and grabbing fistfuls of tissues out of the box on her desk. "He's a contract PI," she sniffs, hands shaking as she wipes her face. "He does jobs for Derek here in town. Not as much in the last year, but—"

"Oh my god," I exhale, leaning heavily against her desk. "He knew all our weaknesses. His accomplice was right under our nose and didn't even know it."

Stuart's still fuming, but I can see he's slowly getting on the same page as me. "You didn't know what was in that envelope?"

Nikki's white-blonde head shakes rapidly. "I never look in his files. Derek said they were confidential. I only type up the reports he specifically gives me."

Going back to Derek's office, I scoop up the sealed brown envelope and rip it open. Out drops a photograph and a pair of black lace panties. Digging inside, I pull out the letter that details who Star is, her connection to the murder of Sloan Reynolds, and the address to Derek's condo in Princeton.

"God… freaking… Stuart!" I shout, and in less than a moment he's back with me. "He knew Nikki would mail this without question. She only asked because of the arrest."

Stuart picks up the letter and reads it briefly before glancing at the photograph and the panties. "Are those—?"

"Only one person can say for sure." I pick up the black thong by an edge of lace and drop it back in the envelope. "It's probably got both their DNA all over it."

"A pleasant thought."

"Tell me about it." We exchange a glance, but it's cut short by both the reality of what's happening and the immediacy of what's out front.

Nikki is crying at her desk, and I spin on my heel, heading for the reception area. When I get there, she's packing her stuff.

"Nikki!" I round the corner and catch her hands. "Wait. Please."

"I can't stay another day here." She shakes her head, tears streaming down her face. "It's all spoiled. I'm nothing but a problem now."

"It's not true," I urge, trying to find the words. "We need you right now, Nikki. It's a crisis situation. We don't have time to find a new receptionist."

"No," she sniffs, touching her face with a tissue. "I'm constantly fucking up everything. I'm a weakness just like you said."

"Patrick will be here tomorrow. Won't you at least wait and see him?"

Another sniff, and she considers what I've said.

"Patrick's your friend," I continue. "Why don't you take off this afternoon, and come in Monday when he's back."

She blinks up at me, and I smile. Leaning forward, I give her a hug. "We need you Nik. You're part of the team."

"The weakest link," she sniffs.

"Not true. You care about Derek, right?"

She nods but doesn't answer. I watch her dab her eyes more.

"That's what matters most. We're all here for him now." Smiling, I hold her hand. "Now you know to be extra vigilant. Anything unusual, run it past Stuart, okay?"

Her eyes flicker to the office where he remained behind. "I'd rather not," she says quietly.

"Okay, then run it past Patrick. He's your guy. Right?"

A wobbly breath and she nods. "Okay."

Releasing her arms, I head back into the office where Stuart is. I'm not crying, and I'm not fainting. I'm ready to find a solution. My Macbook is on Derek's desk now, and I stare at the screen thinking.

"What are we going to do?" I say.

He walks over to the bookshelf and pulls out a thick textbook. "We have to think like a lawyer. Our biggest problem is he confessed to the crime. We have to build a defense, find some precedent we can use..."

My mind immediately goes to a person I haven't seen in years. "I've got this." Sliding my finger across the touch pad, I log into my airline account. "I'm flying to Chicago."

Stuart doesn't even question. "I'll see if there's any way to sway the prosecution. I've been out of the game a while, but maybe I still know somebody in the Maryland PD."

"Go for it. Patrick will be here tomorrow." Looking up, I see Nikki preparing to leave. "Nikki! Would you set up the phones before you go? We're closing the office for the rest of the day."

She nods and circles her desk. Stuart's lips tighten, and he narrows his eyes at me. "You should've let her quit."

I'm flicking through flights trying to find the next one I can catch. "I don't know what's between you two, but you need to put it on hold until we get Derek back."

"Her incompetence makes us vulnerable."

My eyes flash to his. "Bennett won. He got what he wanted. Derek's behind bars..." My throat tightens, and I have to pause as despair tries to choke me. *Deep breaths.* "We don't have anything left to lose."

Two more clicks, and I've booked a flight. Powering down my laptop, I dig my phone out of my bag to call my mom. Dex will need to stay with her a few days longer.

"Damn, I hate research," Stuart mutters, flipping through the book I now see is a legal text.

"Your brother will be in the office Monday." My eyebrows rise. "I thought you were headed to Maryland?"

He exhales a laugh. "Are you suggesting I pass the buck?"

"Two heads are better than one."

"Travel safe."

* * *

The law offices of Merritt, Hampton, and Donnelly are located on the thirty-first floor in an office building on Chicago's East Loop. Stuart called his mother during my flight, and by the time I made it in last night, she'd sent a car to pick me up. I hadn't seen Sylvia since Patrick and Elaine's Christmas wedding in Montana, but she had only been back in the city a few days herself. We'd agreed to have dinner tomorrow night, and I crashed — after taking an unexpected call from Derek.

"What's in Chicago?" his voice is warm, and hearing him, knowing where he is, I can hardly keep the tears away.

"Not what. *Who,*" I say with a sniff, working for control. "Elaine's older brother Marcus. He's one of the best criminal defense lawyers in the country."

"That's right. Elaine was supposed to be a lawyer when she grew up."

"Edward was such a jerk about that. You'd think she said she wanted to be a stripper instead of a teacher."

He laughs, and I close my eyes. "I miss you so much. Are you doing okay?"

"As well as can be expected, considering." He pauses a moment, and I hear shouts behind him. "I'm not a fan of orange jumpsuits."

"You're much sexier in Gucci. Oh, god! I'm sorry."

He exhales a laugh. "My level of sexiness isn't a problem yet. I have my own cell, so for now —"

"How did you manage that?"

"A guy I did police training with is one of the guards. He pulled some strings."

Slipping my fingers over my mouth, I inhale quietly. "I can't stand thinking of you in jail. Baltimore is horrible."

"It was the right thing to do. We couldn't go on with this hanging over our heads."

"I'm afraid for you."

Quiet moments pass. "I'm a little worried myself," he says. "I'd just gotten you back in my arms, and now…"

"Bennett is such a bastard. I want to kill him."

"Hey, don't say things like that on a police line."

"And I can't believe the judge refused to set bail. You're not a flight risk."

"He might not've made the wrong call." His warm exhale feels so close. I hold the phone as if it's his cheek. "I'm not sure I'll get out of this one, and I've heard the French Riviera is beautiful year-round."

"Don't say that." A tone sounds in our ears, and I know our time is ending. "We're going to get you out." I speak fast. "Stuart's headed your way to meet with the prosecutor. I'm meeting Marc tomorrow, and Patrick will be in the Princeton office Monday-"

"I love you, babe."

"I love you more."

It's our last words before we're cut off. My head drops on my arms, and I can't fight anymore. My shoulders shake, and I dissolve into tears.

* * *

The foot traffic is light on Michigan Avenue this morning. Lifting my chin, I let the warm sun shine on my face as I take a deep breath of sweet spring air. I'm glad Sylvia's condo is close enough for me to walk. I need to think about what I'm going to say to Marcus. I'm ready to tell him everything, whatever it takes to save Derek. Nothing in my past is more important than getting him back home with his family.

I haven't seen Marcus Merritt in almost ten years—before I graduated from college or even knew Sloan Reynolds. I'm not sure how much Elaine keeps her brother in the loop on my life. When we were kids growing up together in Wilmington, our parents used to hint that Marcus and I might eventually get married. We dated off and on, but he was always a ladies' man. And as much as I loved him dearly, I was always looking for someone "more mature."

Pushing through the revolving glass doors, I shake my head. "Years ago and water under the bridge."

I cross the grey marble foyer leading to the elevators. Stepping out on the thirty-first floor, I quickly scan the polished surfaces of the waiting room. The décor is very traditional. Dark, cherry-wood paneling, stained oak floors, and built in bookshelves surround me. It's Sunday, so the office is closed. The receptionist's desk sits empty.

Unsure what to do, I step across the luxurious waiting area. Wooden doors with glass panes lead to a small conference room. I'm just peeking through when I hear my name and turn.

Marcus is stunningly handsome as ever. He's a bit darker than Elaine, with caramel-brown hair and hazel eyes. He's dressed in grey slacks and a light blue dress shirt with a navy tie. At six foot, he's so fit and polished, I can't help a laugh.

"When did you start moonlighting at *GQ*?"

He smiles, revealing straight white teeth, before kissing my cheek. "And how is it possible you're more beautiful now than you were in college?"

I hadn't packed for this trip, so I'd had to stick with my dark skinny jeans and red tunic sweater. "Hmm, I think you're winning this morning."

"Come on," he touches my elbow. I follow him through the opposite glass doors down a short wood-paneled hallway to a large, corner office.

"Nice place." My eyes roam the arched built-in bookshelves lining the walls. The coffered ceiling and gold accents create a stunning space. "How do you ever get anything done in here? I'd be staring at the ceiling all day."

He laughs, and the familiar sound comforts me. "Have a seat and tell me what I can do for you."

"Thanks for meeting me on short notice. And on a Sunday." He waves my thanks away, and I drop into a tan leather chair across from him. "I don't know how much you know about my life now."

He leans back and props his foot over his knee. "Seems my little sister said you were happily engaged with a baby on the way." His eyes scan my body. "I guess that last bit is old news. You look amazing."

I smile. "Dex is a year old now."

"He was in a picture she sent me of Lane. Cute kid. He has your eyes."

"Thanks. They play together pretty regularly. We're all back in Wilmington now."

"And your fiancé is the *Alexander* my new brother-in-law works with?"

"Right. Derek."

He only smiles briefly. "I can't say I'm sorry it didn't work out with Reynolds."

My bottom lip catches in my teeth, but I hesitate. "He wasn't the man I thought he was."

"You were too young when you married him."

I'm unsure whether to charge right into our situation or continue catching up. It's been so long since we've seen each other. I decide to ask one more question I actually want to know the answer to.

"How come you never got married? What's wrong with these Chicago girls, anyway?"

He grins and sits forward, leaning his forearms on his desk. "You know marriage isn't my thing. You're the only girl I *might've* considered settling down with."

"Oh, you *might've*."

"It did take me a while to get over you." His eyes twinkle, and I can't resist.

"No, it didn't. You were dating Jules Ashton the next week."

"Was I?" His brow lines, and I can't help remembering the attractive playboy Marcus has always been. It seems not much has changed. "Regardless, when we were together, I was all yours."

"We had a lot of fun," I say with a nod. "But I did have to go to college."

"Who's idea was that again?"

"College? Or educating women in general?"

He laughs loudly. "God, you always made me laugh. I miss that."

I give his enormous office another glance. "Say what you will. I know you want a little future lawyer running around this place. Pulling all your important papers off your desk and drooling on your furniture."

"Yes. You know me so well."

"I do know you well. That's why I'm here, Marcus." Our eyes meet, and I'm ready to get to the reason for my visit. "I need you. It's a matter of life and death, and you're the best lawyer I know."

He's immediately serious. "Are you in trouble?"

"Not me." Scooting forward in the chair, I glance over my shoulder. "What do we need to do for this to be confidential? Attorney-client privilege and all?"

"You agree to hire me as your attorney."

"I'd like to hire you as Derek's attorney."

His jaw moves, and I watch as he thinks, as his glance moves to my left hand. "You're not married?"

"We were planning our wedding next month. I'd love it if you could be there."

A brief smile, and he's back to business. "I'm not going to write down anything you say. Whatever

163

you tell me could be used by the prosecution against us."

Fear clenches my stomach. "This is so serious, Marc."

"What happened?"

Closing my eyes, I go all the way back, knowing what this is going to do to my old friend to hear the truth. "After Sloan and I were married a few years, his parents died, and we had to move back to Baltimore."

He nods, watching me closely.

"Our marriage grew more and more distant. Months would pass and I'd never see him. We stopped having..." I took a deep breath, swallowing my embarrassment. "We stopped sleeping together."

Silence. I forge on.

"I thought maybe it was his age? I didn't know what to think until I found that first receipt." I pause, cringing inside. "Then I found the next one and the next one." My chin drops, and I tell him everything. "He had escorts all over the country, apartments where some of them stayed. I was so humiliated."

I didn't dare glance up at Marc's face. If I saw anything in his eyes—rage, vengeance—I'd never finish.

"I moved to the other side of his mansion. I wouldn't see him. I insisted on marriage counseling, but really, I wanted a divorce. I wanted out." Taking a deep breath, I go for it. "Until the night he decided he was tired of my bullshit. He wanted to sleep with his wife. I fought him... I hated him. But I wasn't strong enough. He beat me and almost raped me."

Marcus is out of his chair and pacing his office. "What the fuck..." His voice is a low growl. "What the fucking fuck, Melissa? Why didn't I know about this?"

Looking up at him now, I can't stop my emotions. I'm not sobbing, but warm tears line my cheeks. "I begged Elaine not to tell anyone."

His face is pained, hazel eyes intense. "Why? Why wouldn't you let her tell me? I would've buried that fucker."

Shaking my head. "I was so ashamed." He hands me a cloth handkerchief, and I touch my face with it. "I didn't want anyone to know. I just wanted to be rid of him."

"So you left him?"

"We were divorced, and Derek and I got together." The memory of that floods my chest with so much warmth, I actually smile through my tears. "He was so good for me. I love him so much."

Marcus is in front of me now, leaning against his desk. "I like him already."

"That brings us to now." My brow lines as I study the double Ms monogrammed on his handkerchief. "He was working on a case last year, and he crossed paths with Sloan again. He was convinced Sloan was coming for me."

"Abusers never give up on their victims." Marcus's voice is matter of fact. "You belonged to him, regardless of whether you'd moved on."

Nodding, I continue. "Derek and Patrick and this woman… Star, an escort—they were going to set a trap to catch him, to put him away for good."

The room is tense. I can tell Marcus is waiting for me to say the worst. I don't prolong his anticipation.

"Derek killed Sloan. He said Sloan was strangling Star, that she was about to die, and he killed him."

"With a gun?" Marc's voice is quiet.

"With his bare hands."

The tick of his desk clock is the only noise in the room for one... two... three... seconds.

"I don't blame him," he says. "I'd have shot him in the face."

Blinking up at him, I know the desperation is clear in my expression. "He's been arrested for first-degree murder. He's in jail in Baltimore, and we've got to get him out."

My friend's jaw clenches as he rounds the desk. "What's his bail?"

"The judge wouldn't set bail. Said he was a flight risk."

"Fuck yeah, he's a flight risk. If it were me, I'd have your pretty ass and my little boy with me on the first flight to Nice. One-way tickets."

"The French Riviera," I say with a smile. "I've always been a bit partial to Monaco."

"Not sure of their extradition policy, princess. France is safer." He gives me a tense smile. A pause, then he starts moving quickly. "I need you to send me everything, and I mean *everything* you have about this case, everything you have on Sloan and his past, his crimes, all the information about Derek's past, any military honors he's received, recognitions..."

"As soon as I get back to Princeton." I'm out of my chair and heading to the door. He's right behind me. "I'll leave today."

"Melissa?" I look up at him and he touches my chin. Marcus has such a beautiful smile. "It's not going to be easy, but I'll do everything I can. I want to be at your wedding next month."

"I knew I could count on you."

A kiss on the cheek, and I'm gone.

CHAPTER 12: MAKING A PLAN

Stuart

Mariska's eyes hold mine as she moves on my lap. Her long, chestnut waves fall over her shoulders in a rippling curtain, and I'm doing my best to hold on, not finish before her.

We've been together four months, and I'm only scratching the surface of making love to this woman. She's sensual and elemental. She likes to feel every emotion, every sensation. It's fucking amazing and impossible all at once.

"Oh, Stuart," she whispers. Her eyes slide closed and she cups my cheek with one slim hand as her movements quicken. Leaning forward, she presses her soft lips to mine and exhales a little moan. *Fuck*, I'm on the edge. She arches back, and I catch a tight nipple in my mouth, giving it a strong pull. I feel her clenching around me as I'm buried deep inside her.

"Yes," she whispers, holding my neck as I kiss a trail across to her other breast and do the same, catching that tight dark bud between my teeth. Her body shudders, and she's almost there.

Again, she leans down and pulls my face to hers, roughly consuming my mouth. I'm right there to meet her. It's her pattern when she's getting close. Her kisses grow more desperate, her little noises wild. She's riding my lap like it's a fucking pony, and dammit it's the hottest thing I've ever known. Tracing my fingers across her ass, she groans, rising up on her knees and slamming back down.

The pressure in my pelvis is building, and I've got to stop thinking about how gorgeous she is.

"Come on, baby," I growl against her shoulder, giving her a little bite. "Come for me." That does it. One more rise and fall, her knees scrub against my hips and her insides break into spasms massaging me deep inside her.

"Oh, god!" Her arms are around my shoulders, and she finishes so beautifully. I lean my head back and let go. The force of my orgasm nearly pulls me out of my skin it's so intense.

"Fuck," I hiss, gripping her ass and moving her up and forward on me as she cries out more. Rolling us to the side, she's on her back, and I hold the inside of her knee, spreading her thighs as I drive deeper, harder, finishing those final, blinding thrusts as her fingers clutch my shoulders.

I'm holding the last one, trying to find my way back to Earth, and my eyes blink open. There she is, lying on her back, her hair spread out around her, smiling at me. Those sunset hazel eyes, golden and gorgeous, are filled with more love than I deserve.

I drop onto my elbows above her and kiss the base of her neck. "You are the fucking sexiest woman I've ever known."

Everything about being with this beautiful girl is new for me. I've never done the whole "making love" bullshit. In the past, it went along with my "no relationships" lifestyle. If I needed a release, it was pretty easy to find a willing partner. The women I'd been with liked it fast and dirty—bend over the desk, take it from behind, slap that ass, and we're done. Everyone was happy. Until now.

She laughs, and her fingers curl in the sides of my hair. I feel her lips against my brow, and I hold her as I find my bearings again.

"I'm not sure how I feel about that compliment, Stuart William." Her voice vibrates against my cheek as she teases me. "It makes it sound like you've known a lot of women."

One more kiss to that fabulous neck, and I lift my head. "Not all of them biblically."

Her nose wrinkles as her eyes roll, and I swear, I could take her again on the spot. Instead, I go back to the question that got us in this position. "You never answered me. Did you fill out the transfer application today?"

She exhales a growling sound and twists in my arms. My hug tightens over her. I'm not about to let her wiggle out of answering this question.

"Let me go, Stuart." Blinking up at me, her resistance is so adorable, I kiss her lips, long and soft. Then I swipe my tongue inside, finding hers for good measure.

When I lean up again, she blinks slowly. "You fight dirty."

"You give me dirty thoughts." Our eyes meet, and I continue. "Princeton is one of the top schools in the country. You might have heard of it."

"It's too expensive, and I have a scholarship at Ocean County College. I like it there."

"You'd rather go to a state school than live with me here."

She starts to struggle again, and this time I do release her.

"I have a job in Bayville. Kenny, my best friend is there. Remember her?" She sits up, wrapping the sheet over her beautiful body. I resist the urge to pull it away. "I won't drop my life to move here and live with you and let you pay for everything like I'm some... some..."

Her chin drops, but I catch it and lift her face. "You're here almost every day as it is. How would it be different?"

"You know how it would be different." Fire is in those beautiful eyes. I love it. "I'm here because it's an easy drive back and forth, and I like spending my free time with my boyfriend."

"Is that so?" A smile pulls at the corner of my mouth, but I hold on. We're leading up to a question I've been ready to ask since December.

"Besides, it sets a bad precedent if I let you win every argument by sleeping with me."

"Aren't we supposed to fight it out in bed?"

A little nose twitch, a teasing glance, and I can't take it anymore. Snatching the sheet away, I catch her around the waist and pull her body flush with mine. She squeals with laughter, and I cover her mouth, kissing her deeply until her struggling relaxes and her arms slide around my neck slow and easy.

Pulling back, I hold her body and her gaze a moment. Then I say it. "I want you to marry me, Mariska. I want you to transfer to Princeton and live here with me as my wife. Fuck this boyfriend-girlfriend shit."

Her eyes blink fast, and her brows pull together. For a second, my chest tightens. Sick hits the pit of my stomach when her tears spill over, down her temples and into her hair.

"Baby, what's wrong?"

Her body jerks with a sniff, and she cries more. She pulls herself up to me in a hug, burying her face in my neck, and I'm going crazy until she finally speaks.

"Stuart," it's cut off by another sniff. "Oh, Stuart, I want that so much."

Relief blasts through me, anxiety gone. I wrap her in my arms, holding her close. Her face is still at my neck, and I feel her tears on my skin. I feel all of her against my skin, shoulders to stomach to thigh to knee, and I think about that old idea of becoming one. She's the part of me that's been missing for so long. Inhaling deeply, luscious jasmine fills my senses.

After a few moments, I slide my hands over her bare back, from her soft shoulders to her soft ass. "So is that a yes?" My voice is low and gentle.

She nods against me, squeezing me in her arms.

"Mariska?" I'm smiling now, holding my wife in my arms. Everything has changed. "Look at me."

She takes a moment before pulling back, those beautiful eyes shining with her tears. "Will you please call about transferring to Princeton tomorrow?"

A laugh explodes from her lips, and she pulls up, hugging our faces together. "I guess if you put it that way."

Kissing her jaw, her cheek, I roll her onto her back and prop myself on my elbows. "Thank you for agreeing to be my wife."

Her eyes roll and she shakes her head. "As if you ever had any doubt."

"You are a very strong, independent lady, Mariska Renee." I pause to scoop her lips in another brief kiss. "I wasn't sure you'd say yes so easily. I worried you might think it was too soon."

"With as well as I know you?" Her cat eyes slant.

"I thought you might have some old-fashioned notion about finishing school or us needing to date for a year or something ridiculous."

"Don't give me any ideas."

My brow lowers. "Is that something you want to do?"

"Is that something I should want to do?" How she manages to go from sassy to shy in the blink of an eye slays me. I can't believe how vulnerable she is. Like I didn't just ask her to fucking marry me.

"No." I don't even let that idea hang around five seconds. "I don't want you away from me any more. I'm getting your ring as soon as I get back from Baltimore. Give your landlord notice and start packing. You'll start Princeton this fall. Summer if you want to start earlier."

She laughs, and her body arches against mine. Her head falls back, and she lets out the most amazing happy squeal. I was above her, but she pushes me back against the pillows. I'm on my back watching her hold her brow and shake her head.

"It's like a dream," she says. Then she catches my face in both hands again and kisses me. I can't help laughing now. "Do you remember how awful you were in Montana?"

"Hang on," I try to act offended and fail. "You came at me out of nowhere."

"You are literally the man of my dreams, Stuart Knight."

"Don't forget," I say, smoothing both hands over her cheeks, sliding her brown hair back. "You're the woman in mine, too."

174

"Would you make love to me again?" Her lips curl as her hand moves down between us. Her fingers wrap around my cock, and my body immediately responds to her touch, hard and strong.

"With pleasure," I say, before kissing her lips, her chin, her neck, making my way down her torso to the place I know will have her screaming my name.

* * *

Kissing Mariska goodbye this morning was the hardest thing I've done since this nightmare with Derek began. She's dressed in only my white dress shirt, looking like the most beautiful sex kitten who's ever agreed to marry anybody.

"My goal is to hit the prosecutor strong," I say, grabbing my suitcase so I don't grab her.

"Take as long as you need, baby." Her eyes are round and serious, oblivious to how her words affect me. "I'll be here doing my assignments."

"Your assignments?"

"You gave me a list last night. Don't you remember?"

She smiles and my suitcase goes down. I pull her to me and kiss her one long, last time. "Yes. I want all of that done when I get back."

"Or what?" Her expression is coy. "You'll spank me?"

"Hell, no." I exhale a laugh before I kiss her again. "If I say that, you'll never do it."

"Hmm... I suppose you have a point."

"If I didn't have to be in Baltimore..." One more kiss, and I'm out the door, only pausing once to look back at the beautiful creature who belongs to me.

Damn, I'm ready to fast track this week's business and get us all home.

Patrick's in the office when I get there, and he's got three law books out on our shared desk.

"You could take the office down the hall," I quip, causing him to look up.

"You're freakishly happy," he turns back to the book he's studying. "Mariska's a fucking miracle worker."

It's true, and even my annoying little brother can't bring me down this morning.

"Anyway, you left." He's making notes on a yellow legal pad. "Derek gave me this office, and it has all my shit in it."

It's true. When I came back from Saudi, I was put in Derek's old office, but I never felt right about taking my CO's spot, even if he had moved to Wilmington full-time.

"Working behind a desk isn't my thing. What have you found out?"

"Not much." He straightens and tilts his head, stretching his neck. Patrick's five years younger than me, and no matter how much we age, he always seems like a kid. Our little sister Amy is a perennial baby.

"Hit me," I say, loading my briefcase with my pick of the worst reports from Derek's "Sloan files."

"I need to talk to Melissa. She's been pretty pissed at me, but her evidence against Sloan is going to be critical. She's got email receipts of his transactions with hookers, photographs of her face when... he beat her..."

He pauses to grimace, and I share his sentiment. Melissa's a beautiful, classy woman. She's Derek's fiancée, Dex's mom. The idea of some fucker hitting her makes us all a little crazy with rage.

Clearing his throat, he continues, looking guilty. "I hate to ask her for those things. I know how much she wants to put it behind her. But they'll pretty much make the case for Derek's taking him out."

"You're sure Sloan has no surviving relatives?"

He drops into the desk chair and starts clicking. "Only distant ones, and most of them are older, infirm."

Pausing, I lean against the doorway. "You realize, if this does go to trial, you're an accessory to murder."

His lips tighten and he nods. "I've never been a more willing accessory."

"Tell me what happened that night. How exactly it went down."

My brother's hazel meet mine. His are more green than brown. "It was pretty fast. We were in a small conference room with a tech booth off the side."

"Why?"

"Star was the bait, but Derek didn't want her to be too far from where we could help her if things got ugly." He looks down at his hand and slowly makes a fist. "That asshole manhandled her pretty good. Slammed her head against the wall, then he had her pinned, his forearm against her neck."

"Shit," I exhale, stepping forward into my old office, thinking. I've only known Star about a week. She's a little rough around the edges, but she's sweet with her kid. Despite her painfully obvious crush on Derek, she seems like a smart girl. "So he was killing her?"

"I think so." He's still looking at his hands, remembering. "He had a reputation for liking it rough, and I was pretty preoccupied while it was happening."

For a moment, I'm stumped trying to figure out what my little brother might've been doing besides keeping his eyes on his target.

"Derek fought me to get out there. I held him back as much as I could, but he's fucking strong."

Shaking my head, I can't even imagine. "I'm surprised you could hold him."

"When she said the safe word, I let him go. We both rushed out, but when I went to Star, Derek went straight and finished things."

"So that's how it happened."

I take a step back, turning to face the female voice addressing us. Melissa is standing in the doorway. Her dark brow is furrowed and her lips are tight.

"Hey, you're back." Patrick's out of his seat and headed toward her.

She steps into the office and meets him, giving him a warm hug. "I forgive you for not keeping your promise," she says, leaning back and mussing his hair. "But I don't forgive you for not telling me."

"None of this was supposed to happen." He follows her back to the desk. She steps over to where I'm looking out the window at the highway.

"Marcus is going to help us. He said he'd fly to Baltimore to meet you. He's scheduled a meeting with the prosecutor, but he needs us to send him everything we've got on Sloan and Derek."

Putting the case down, I snap it open and pull out the files I'm taking with me. "Fax these to him now. I want to have them with me when I get there."

———

She nods and takes them from me, but she stops to speak to Patrick. "Is there any chance Elaine can come here today or tomorrow?"

"She was planning to drive up with Lane on Thursday. Her school's spring break is next week."

"We're going to need her sooner than that."

"What are you thinking?" Patrick sits on the edge of the desk facing her."

"My photograph, the email receipts I printed off... I'd say she could FedEx them, but I don't want to take any chances of them being lost."

He nods and pulls out his phone. "She'll do that for you. I need to ask her now so she can find a substitute."

Melissa rubs her eyes. "I wish I could have Dex here with me. I miss him so much."

"She could bring him with her. Lane needs the company."

Shaking her head, she drops her hand with a sigh. "He'd better stay with Mom in case I have to go to Baltimore. I want to be free to do whatever Derek needs on a moment's notice."

God, I hate hustling her right now. I'm concerned as well about the possibility of a long, messy trial. None of us want that.

"I need to get on the road," I say, nodding to the papers.

"I'll fax these now," she says, heading down the hall.

Patrick walks back around the desk and drops into his chair. "Bennett cooked us good forcing Derek to confess like that."

"Let me know if you find anything else useful." He nods, and it hits me he arrived last night. "Why

179

aren't you sleeping at Derek's place? There's no reason for you to be in a hotel."

He glances down and manages to look embarrassed. "Star and I have sort of a past. I don't want to make Elaine uncomfortable."

"That's pretty mature of you, brother."

"Yeah, well, I tested Elaine enough in the beginning to last a lifetime." He glances over his shoulder, out the office window as he says the last bit. "She's the best thing that's ever happened to me."

I'm feeling pretty generous, considering my recent developments with Mariska. "I hear that." We pause a moment. "Stay at my place. Melissa's here now, and Mariska will probably be back and forth to Bayville."

His lips poke out and he nods. "It's a good idea." Turning back, we exchange what is possibly the first warm greeting in our lives. "Thanks, bro."

"No worries."

The door opens and Melissa breezes back in. She hands me the papers. "I'll fax my evidence as soon as Elaine gets here with it."

"She texted she could probably be here tonight," Patrick says, reading from his phone.

"Perfect," she's focused, all business. "Marcus needs everything we have on Derek—medals, service awards..."

"I can personally vouch for his conduct in the line of duty," I say.

Melissa's brow relaxes, and her eyes glisten with tears. "Bring him home, Stuart."

I touch the salty drop off her cheek. "I'll do everything in my power."

CHAPTER 13: INSIDE

Derek

My lunch tray has just touched the long cafeteria-style table when I feel him standing over me. So far it's been pretty quiet, but I knew it was a matter of time before the population would start to feel me out. Without lifting my eyes I wait as the large form takes a seat across from me.

The food is shit. A flat sandwich, bologna on stale white bread, sits in front of me. A banana and a plastic cup of juice complete the meal.

"We've had two new guys since you got here." My lunch guest pauses, but I don't look up. "You still have your own cell."

Silence.

I pick up one half of my sandwich and inspect it. Mayonnaise and what I can only assume is fake cheese join the flat processed meat. My stomach turns and I put it back down.

"You a mole?" The enormous guy isn't deterred.

"No," I say, acknowledging him.

"A snitch?"

"No." My expression is flat. I appear calm, but my adrenaline is ticking up slowly.

His dark eyes inspect me. "You're white collar." A beat, another quick scan. "What you in for?"

"Murder." Returning to the food, I decide it's probably wise to keep my strength up, even if it's crap, and take a bite. The meat is salty and the bread sticks inside my mouth.

The fellow across from me bends a dark eyebrow. "How'd you do it?"

Reaching for the plastic cup of orange juice, I pull the foil off and take a sip trying to get the crap food off my teeth. It takes a moment, and in the meantime, I turn my right hand over, palm up.

His eyes flicker down to it then back up to me. "Strangled?"

Shaking my head, I'm able to speak. "Broke his neck."

Silence falls between us again. He's studying me. "You Italian?" I shake my head no. "Latino?" Another no. "Irish?"

That makes me almost laugh. "No."

"Biracial?"

Lifting my blue eyes, I smirk. "What do you think?"

He watches me a beat. "You're military."

"Good guess," I say, trying the banana. Peel off, I break a piece and put it in my mouth. Mealy.

"I can smell that shit a mile away," he says.

I don't answer. I break off another piece of fruit.

"Okay, soldier," he continues. The reference makes me flinch, but I let it go. "You can call me Chairman. I'm your welcoming committee."

My brow is lowered as my eyes return to his. "I'm not interested in a welcome."

"Shut the fuck up and listen." I'm pissed, but his brow lowers as well. I notice he's expanded a few inches in size, and I decide I'll check out that weight room after all.

Sitting a little straighter, I decide to hear him out. "I'm all ears."

"We do things a little different here. You're not in the joint. You're only in a holding pattern. We don't do white versus black, Dago versus Polack, Mick versus Spick." I resist asking if he writes greeting cards. He leans forward, and his tone turns sinister. "We do bad-asses versus pussies. Looks like you might be one of the bad-asses."

"You're smarter than I thought."

"You want to survive Phase one of your incarceration? Sit at the head table with us." He nods in a direction behind me, over my right shoulder. "We'll protect you."

"If I'm one of the bad-asses, why do I need protection?"

"Because if you're not sitting with us, you're one of the pussies. We don't truck with pussies. Somebody needs to blow off steam…"

Our eyes clash, black iron against blue steel. I guess it's time to get affiliated. Glancing over my shoulder, I see the table in question.

Another, equally large black guy is sitting hunched over his plate of shit. Beside him is a skinhead white fellow just as big as he is. In the next seat is a smaller, wiry guy with sallow skin and a black buzz cut.

"Who's the little guy?" I say, turning back.

"Reverend Moon. Rev for short." Chairman leans back and a look of admiration passes over his face. "Don't cross that little fucker or you'll end up in a sling. Or worse."

Taking another sip of OJ, I look at the man in front of me then I look around the room where we're sitting. "This is central lockup. We're not in prison, there's no culture here. How do you know so much?"

He's off defense, and his chest deflates slightly. "You're a rookie." Shaking his head, he acts so wise. "You'll see when you've been around a while, it's one big circle. Maybe you get out... Well, you're never getting out, but maybe Rev gets out. He's just a habitual drug offender. He'll be back. After a while, we know you. And you know us."

His eyes laser into mine, and I nod. "Badass."

"Or pussy."

Without another word, he stands and takes the tray off the table in front of him. I watch as he goes, thinking this is my life now. I might not like it, but I'd better get ready.

* * *

Stuart sits across the glass from me, holding a phone. My partner's dressed in a brown tweed blazer over a white shirt, no tie. He's also wearing jeans. I mentally wonder what it is with the Knight brothers and suits.

"How you holding up?" His brown-hazel eyes assess me through the glass.

"Apparently I'm a badass."

A short laugh, and he shakes his head. "I could've told you that. Anybody giving you trouble?"

"Nah, just the usual shit you'd expect."

He doesn't say anything for a moment. "I'm sorry you're in here, brother. You killed a worthless piece of shit. You did the world a favor."

Shaking my head, I don't let that continue. "I broke the law. Now it's a matter of whether I'll find mercy or whether I'll stay here for the duration."

184

"I'm meeting with the prosecution tomorrow morning," he says. "They're going to try and make the case for why you should stay, but we're ready to fight it. Melissa got you one of the best lawyers in the country, from what she claims…"

"Elaine's brother."

"Right. Do you know him?"

Shaking my head, I look down at my hand. "Only by reputation."

"He's flying out here tonight. We've collected everything you put together on Sloan—good work, by the way—and with Melissa's evidence, we should be able to build a strong case for 'defense of others.'"

My eyebrows rise. "I hadn't considered that."

"You can thank my little brother," he laughs. "Seems you're not the only college graduate in the office."

"If you weren't so busy playing soldier, you'd have finished college."

"Somebody's got to defend our country."

It's our old banter, and it takes my mind off the shit I'm living with now. The America private citizens wonder if we should worry about defending. The America they'd rather kill. My mind drifts to the nighttime. The things I miss most.

"Can you get me a picture of Melissa?" I ask, looking down at my hands. "When they arrested me, I only had my phone, which they confiscated."

"Of course." He nods. "You got it."

"And one of Dex."

"I'll get them to you tomorrow. Tonight if I can."

We're quiet a moment, and I can't help saying what's on my mind. "She has to go on record with what happened to her." Wincing, I look down at the

Formica space between us. "She never wanted anyone to know. She wanted to put it behind us."

"Look at me." Stuart's voice is sharp, and when I glance up, his brow is lowered. "Melissa is more determined than I've ever seen any woman. She's not angry or backing down. She's doing whatever it takes to get her man home."

"Yeah," I say through an exhale. "Because of what I did."

"You did what you had to do." His tone is more emphatic, and I can't stop the label that floats across my brain: *Badass*. "We're doing what we have to do. Keep your spirits up. It won't be long."

* * *

Dinner. I'm in the line, holding my tray as a blob of what appears to be pulled pork is dumped on it. Turning away, I'm faced with a cafeteria full of men waiting to be convicted, sentenced, and either let back out into the population or sent to prison.

Two young guys who should be in college joke and laugh as they take their seats. An old man who looks too weak to do anything significant passes. He's probably the worst offender of all, preying on those weaker than him. Then my eyes land on the table in the back, the group of thugs waiting to see if I'll join them.

I was a Marine. I took an oath. Now I'm one of these guys, a convict trapped in a holding pen while the system either succeeds or fails. Clenching my jaw, I start toward the same spot where I had my lunch earlier, where I've had every meal here alone. I'm not a pussy, but I'm not a thug. I might be a badass, but I'm not joining the ranks of the repeat offenders.

Nobody speaks as I take my seat, but I feel Chairman's eyes follow me. Regardless of what happens outside with Stuart and the rest, I'm on the inside, and I have to establish my identity. Here it is.

CHAPTER 14: THE CASE

Stuart

Pacing my hotel room, I study the photographs I printed off at the drugstore earlier. One is Melissa looking up from where she's sitting on the beach and smiling. The breeze is swirling her long hair back, and her sunglasses are pushed up on her head. I nod. It's a good one.

Flipping it back, I have one of Dex. Melissa texted it to me. It's from his birthday party, and he's hugging Derek, climbing into his lap with a big smile. The last is the one from his condo. I've seen it in a frame there dozens of times. Melissa, again, forwarded it to me. They're perfect—loving and sweet—they'll keep his spirits up, remind him of home, help him remember why he has to get out.

It's late or I would take them over tonight. Instead, I'll run them by first thing in the morning before I meet with the prosecutor. My phone buzzes, and I slide my finger across the face.

"Stuart here."

"It's Marcus," the male voice says. "Just checking in about tomorrow. I'm pretty sure we have all we need."

"Did you get Melissa's evidence."

"It was on my computer when I got to the hotel." He pauses, and I hear him struggling for words.

I help him out. "It's tough stuff."

"I've never met Derek Alexander." His tone is serious. "I don't usually take cases where I haven't met the client. Her photograph changed my mind."

"We've got a pretty sound case for defense of others."

"If we can get around the premeditation and entrapment allegations."

"Entrapment would be stronger if it'd happened on the first night. In terms of when it happened, Sloan propositioned her. He was offering her a job, giving her a trial run."

Marcus exhales a laugh in my ear. "You'd make a good lawyer."

"I just know my friend." My stomach is tight, determination burning in my chest. "He doesn't belong in prison. If he made the executive decision to take this guy out, it was the right call."

"Only he wasn't at war. He was at home, a civilian, committing a crime against another civilian."

"Defense of others."

"If that fails, we can go with objective reasonableness." I hear pages flip in the background. "Derek was licensed to use deadly force. He didn't work as a cop, but he was trained as one. He was also a decorated commanding officer, responsible for leading troops. His judgment should be without question."

"It's not the most popular defense right now."

"Still, it should gain more sympathy than an abusive suspected murderer who was in the process of trying to kill an escort while Derek was in the next room."

Adrenaline surges in my veins. "I feel like we've got a strong argument."

"I was going to suggest bringing Patrick in to testify, but at the moment, they have Derek acting alone."

"He'll do whatever it takes to help get Derek out."

"I'm thinking of my little sister. If this doesn't go well, I'd rather not be the asshole who put her husband behind bars."

My fist clenches, and I look at the clock. It's after ten. "They did the right thing. I'm holding onto that fact."

"I'll meet you in jail."

Hanging up, I pace the room again. Bennett had better keep his ass far away from here. If I ever cross paths with that traitorous sonofabitch, I'll kill him.

* * *

A suit isn't my dress code of choice, but today's business calls for a professional image. Tough, no bullshit. I skip the tie in favor of a black dress shirt unbuttoned at the top. Sliding the cuffs forward, I fasten the top button on my grey herringbone two-piece. I'm shaved, and my hair is brushed neat. I look like I'm in fucking *Oceans 11*.

It's a far cry from jeans and Carhartt jackets, breaking horses on my uncle's ranch in Montana, sleeping by a campfire under an endless sky, holding Mariska's body next to mine as the winter wind rages outside that small cabin on the plain. Damn, I miss that.

I give the king suite where I spent the night one final sweep. Marcus is bringing all the paperwork. I have the photographs I'll leave at the desk for Derek.

It appears I have everything I need. Door card in my pocket, I head out to face this day.

When I agreed to return to Alexander-Knight, I never expected my first case to be fighting a murder rap against my best friend. I came back unsure what direction I wanted to take. Derek said I could have some time to find what interested me. One week back, and I'm fighting to keep him out of prison, going head to head against a life-sentence for murder facing experienced prosecutors. I haven't been in a pre-trial conference in ten years. Turning my Silverado into the parking lot of the state correctional facility, I consider if this keeps up, I'll have to trade my truck in for a sedan. *Not happening.*

Marcus is at the jail when I arrive, and he's dressed in dark-grey sharkskin holding a black leather messenger-style satchel.

"Interesting," I say, nodding at his suit.

"It's my favorite for defending murderers," he says with a smile. "Classic Rat pack."

"Where the hell did you find sharkskin?"

"Brooks Brothers." He nods at me. "Armani?"

I shrug. "Louis Vuitton." I didn't grow up on a horse ranch. I just prefer it to this.

I pass over the envelope containing the photographs Derek requested while Marc fills out the check-in form. I'm next, then we empty our pockets before going through the metal detector. On the other side, Marcus holds his arms up as the security guard pats him down. It's like going through airport security, but worse. No cell phones in jail, no devices of any kind. If something goes down, we're stuck here just like every other criminal in the joint.

"I spent half the night going over all we've got," he says under his breath, as we follow the guard down the corridor. "Sloan Reynolds has no family, no dependents, and his company doesn't want his shit coming out." His eyes meet mine, and he nods.

I smile and nod back. "You're the best, right?"

"That's what I hear." We pause outside the door before facing the prosecution.

* * *

We enter the small conference room and each shake the hand of the prosecutor, a solemn-looking African-American gentleman.

"Earl Mason," he says, taking a seat across the table from us, files spread out before him. "I've reviewed the case against Derek Alexander, and I have to say, it looks pretty open and shut."

Dark eyes glance up at us, and I can tell he's not finished. "Your client willfully and of sound mind murdered Sloan Reynolds. He said so right here in his confession. As far as I can tell, we have every reason to expect a conviction for first-degree murder."

Marcus places his satchel on the table beside him. "Quite a bit is left out of that confession, which is why we're here today." I watch as he pulls out three thick files.

"And you are?" A salt and pepper brow lowers over Earl's eyes.

"Marcus Merritt, attorney for the defendant."

"I haven't seen you around the courthouse before." He scrutinizes the man beside me, but I don't even sense a tremor from Marc. "Are you licensed to practice in the state of Maryland?"

"If necessary, I will associate local counsel for trial, but we don't think a trial will be necessary." Marcus answers with a swagger that makes me wince. This old man is not one to fuck with.

The prosecutor holds his gaze a beat longer before returning to the documents in front of him. "We're here to informally discuss resolution of the pending charges against Mr. Alexander before pretrial discovery and trial preparation begins. I've told you what I have. What do you have?"

Sliding the first folder across the table, Marcus begins. "My client is, and was, engaged to the ex-wife of the deceased."

"That doesn't exactly help you."

Marcus pauses, and his expression grows stony. "Until you see what's in that folder."

We wait as Earl opens it, watch his brow line as he peruses Melissa's evidence. "What is this?" he finally asks.

"Miss Jones divorced Sloan Reynolds after he beat her to the point documented in that photograph." A pause, and I feel my partner collecting himself. "That battery followed her discovery of his penchant for prostitutes."

A slow inhale, and our opponent closes the folder. "Was this incident reported to the police?"

"No." Marcus's voice is grave. "But she has a witness that can corroborate her story."

"It's weak, but I'm still listening. You're describing a conviction for second-degree murder, a crime committed in the heat of passion. It carries a ten-year sentence with at least five to be served. Do you have anything else?"

Another manila folder crosses the divide. "The defendant was in the process of building a case against Sloan Reynolds when the crime occurred. In this folder you will see evidence, including photographs almost identical to Miss Jones's, of a woman Reynolds assaulted, Jessica Black. My client had reason to believe Reynolds murdered Miss Black."

Again we wait while the prosecutor evaluates the files in front of him. His lips tighten as he turns page after page. "Is any of this on the record?"

"Miss Black did file a police report for battery, which is how we obtained that photograph of her beaten face." Marcus's fingers cross as he folds his hands. "She later backed down from pressing charges. She didn't name Reynolds in her case, but we have evidence that she was in Baltimore as his escort when the crime occurred."

A few moments pass, and the attorney across from us puckers his lips as he thinks. "So Mr. Alexander took the law into his own hands. Voluntary manslaughter."

No one speaks for a moment.

"So there's more. Okay, Mr. Merritt. What's behind Door Number Three?" His eyes are on the last folder Marcus holds.

"It's the heart of our defense of others argument." He slides it across, and the older man takes it. "Inside you see a photograph of the victim dead, and in his pocket is a pair of thong underwear."

"I hope this is relevant."

"We are in possession of that undergarment and believe if it's tested, you will find Reynolds's DNA on it."

"And?"

"You will also see photographic evidence of one Star Brandon, a high-class hooker Reynolds was... servicing at the time my client acted in defense."

The prosecutor seems bored at this point. "How is this evidence?"

"As you can further see in the photograph, Ms. Brandon's neck and torso are bruised and battered. Reynolds was in the process of strangling Brandon to the point of death when my client was compelled to use deadly force to rescue her."

"Sloan Reynolds was unarmed at the time of death. Deadly force was not required. Three to five years, one year in prison less time served, the rest on probation."

In that instant, Marcus's tone changes, and I hear why he's the best. "We're not letting our client spend one more night behind bars. We want him out now. He's a decorated veteran, a former commanding officer, a member of law enforcement, respected Ivy League professor, and a leader in the security field. He had objective reason to believe the only way to stop Sloan Reynolds's pattern of abusive murder was to take him out in the line of duty. Sloan Reynolds was a low life using his family's money to fund his lifestyle of abuse and cruelty to women. I think we've got as solid a case as we need, sir."

Silence falls over the conference room. The clock ticks slowly, and mentally I'm standing, spiking the ball, and doing the Harlem Shuffle all at once. On the outside, we're as cool as the minute we walked in.

Earl sits back and sighs. "As you may know, no one has come forward to press these charges on behalf of Mr. Reynolds' family or friends. Only one party seems genuinely interested in the possibility of a conviction."

My insides are tense, and I sense Marcus preparing to hear him out. I can't believe anybody would have anything good to say about Sloan.

"Mr. Reynolds' company took out a sizable life insurance policy on him. The insurance company has been reluctant to pay because of the appearance that Mr. Reynolds might have somehow committed suicide, since he was alone and there was no recorded cause of death. In which case they do not have to pay."

"Makes a difference," Marcus says with a nod.

"On the other hand, if Mr. Reynolds were murdered, the company stands to get a double recovery under the policy."

"Double indemnity." Our attorney half-smiles.

"What is this?" I say.

"Don't you know your classic movies, Stuart?" Marcus turns to me. "If Reynolds is murdered, his company gets double their money under the life insurance policy."

"Correct," Earl replies. "And I've got a company accountant looking to turn a zero-value policy into double recovery if I can get a murder conviction."

"How much is the policy?" I ask.

"Two million dollars."

"Listen," I flash, "I can guarantee you if this case goes to trial, that company is going to get ten million dollars' worth of bad publicity. We'll show the world its CEO was a wife-beating rapist who was killed in the act of choking a prostitute to death. You can't buy enough insurance to protect the company from that level of damage."

Earl seems to notice me for the first time. "What's your say in all of this?"

Sitting forward, I'm glad to have a say. "I'm here both to confirm everything Marcus has said, but also to stand in the place of Derek... Mr. Alexander."

"You are?"

"Stuart Knight, founding partner of Alexander-Knight, LLC, and retired Marine. I was under the direct command of the defendant. He's a good man of high character."

"Semper fi," Earl says, glancing down.

"Yes," I agree, meaning every word.

"Well, gentlemen, I'm not interested in going out on a limb for a rich degenerate, who has no one particularly interested in his murder. Especially when it's only to help a company that stands to profit from his death. Speaking of publicity, that's frankly the kind of publicity that gets district attorneys unelected and prosecutors fired." He pushes back from the table and stands, reaching across to shake our hands. "If Mr. Alexander will plead guilty to the misdemeanor charge of failure to timely report a homicide and pay a one-thousand dollar fine, I am inclined to dismiss the charges. I'll speak to the judge and see if we can get the paperwork going to get him home today."

For a moment, I feel like I'm back in a PTSD dream. I'm unsure if what just happened is real or if I imagined it.

Marcus is the epitome of smooth. "Thank you, Mr. Mason—"

"Earl," the prosecutor corrects him.

"Earl," he nods. "I knew once you'd had a chance to see what was at stake, it would be a pretty simple decision."

"Nothing is simple." Earl's expression goes immediately serious. "Murder, vigilante justice, these are not things I take lightly by any means."

"Of course not," Marcus says. "I didn't mean to imply—"

"However, there are also situations in which reasonable, thoughtful men are compelled to act." He pauses as if for emphasis. "In my considered opinion, this was one of those situations."

Rising from my chair, I reach across the table, holding out my hand. Earl seems surprised, but then he takes it, giving me a firm shake back.

"I can assure you," I say, infusing my words with as much sincerity as possible. "This was one of those situations."

Earl nods and smiles for the first time since we've seen him. "Let's get Mr. Alexander back home to his family."

Chapter 15: Badass

Derek

Breakfast is over, and I'm facing free time. I know my defiance of Chairman and his band of "badasses" at dinner won't go unanswered. What I don't know is when or how the answer will come. I decide to make my way to the weight room in the interim. It's been years since I've faced the prospect of hand-to-hand combat. I was trained to do it in the Middle East. I never dreamed I'd face it behind bars in my own country.

The prospect of Rev and a shiv flickers through my mind. It could get a whole lot worse than hand-to-hand. It doesn't scare me. It pisses me off. Adrenaline surges in my veins, and I feel myself getting ready. I'm running on three weeks of uninterrupted frustration here, starting the day Melissa put me out of the house. My only break lasted all of five minutes in my office when I held her in my arms again. When she'd asked me to make love to her, and the fucking cops walked in. Maybe a good fight is exactly what I need.

Last night, I'd stood at the bars of my cell. My forearms rested on the door and I looked out at the peeling white paint, the center space filled with round tables bathed in the blue light of the dark hours. None of us would be here for long. Jail was a constant stream of in and out, depending on what happened with the courts. I wondered how much longer I'd have before moving either to prison or being allowed to walk.

Stuart had said he would bring me pictures of Melissa and Dex, but I can only guess he wasn't able to make it happen before visiting hours ended. Closing my eyes, I tried to conjure the scent of ocean roses. I couldn't, but I could remember how it felt to smell them. My body craved hers. Standing in the darkness, I considered the worst—a lifetime of separation. It clenched my insides, and even if I wasn't afraid of the inmates or the horrors of life inside, I didn't know how I'd get through the years of this separation. *Would I ask her to wait for me? Could I be that selfish?*

"Melissa," I whispered into the darkness.

I hadn't been given many breaks since this nightmare began, but the greatest one had been encountering Benjamin Lance at check-in.

Ben is from New Orleans just like me, and even though he's from one of the rougher, African-American neighborhoods while I grew up in the Garden District, we'd bonded over our hometown connection when we did our police training. I can only imagine his shock at seeing me booked for murder. He'd managed to get me my own cell and kept it that way for the several days I'd been in hock. If nothing changed, it'd be the last kindness I could expect.

My thoughts drifted to Slayde Bennett. I could still see him sitting in that courtroom, ice blue eyes full of hate and rage. He was deadly calm as his judgment was handed down. He walked out of the room with a life sentence and never looked back. I never thought I'd see him again. He was a murderer and he could rot in prison for all I cared. It only shows how you never know the moments that will alter your life.

Remembering him last year, standing in that corridor with Kenny, he had changed. I was too angry at the time. The idea of a murderer walking free, getting out of the judgment I'd spent so much effort to secure, hit too close to home. It smacked too much of Sloan's ability to slip out of every charge I'd tried to make stick. All I could see was the system failing again.

Yet now, looking back, I have a different view. He still had the body of a fighter. He still moved like he could take anyone out with one hit. He still had the ink, and he projected aggression. Only the eyes had changed. My first sight of him stands out, the way he looked at Kenny, the tenderness and love. I didn't want to see it that day. I only wanted justice, and I took everything from him again.

Exhaling, I turn and walk into the darkness at the back of my cell. I demanded justice in all things. Why should I escape it?

Melissa's beautiful smile fills my memories, her soft body in my arms and her beautiful hair spilling around us. Closing my eyes, I feel her lips against mine. Placing my fists against the cinder-block wall, I remember her legs around my waist, her soft sighs and little moans as I move inside her, plunging into her depths. Again, the prospect of a life sentence twists my stomach.

She needs to understand why I did this and why I didn't tell her. It's something I could never say before, but now that I'm facing a future without her, I want her to know. I couldn't let it go. I couldn't put it behind me. As much as I love her, it went against my nature to allow him to walk. Jessica Black or no

Jessica Black. Star or no Star, none of it mattered. He'd touched her in a way that couldn't be forgiven or forgotten.

It went beyond our beginning—his lying to me about her. It went beyond me not knowing what a loser he'd become when I'd agreed to track her for him. It went beyond her showing up in my office that day she'd learned the truth and shooting all my dreams to hell with one word.

After all I'd lost and all I'd found, the idea of him being alive in the world after what he'd done to her was abhorrent to me. She'd shown me that picture of her battered face, and it was indelibly marked on my soul. The mere fact of it was an underlying driving force I couldn't deny. As much as Melissa was mine, his unanswered crime was like the distant hum of a freight train growing louder and louder until it blasted through everything.

Inevitably, inexorably, as long as I lived on this planet, my future would lead to that moment in a small conference room in Baltimore when I got revenge. The darkness of what he'd done to her overcame me, and somewhere in that darkness I lost myself. No matter how honorable or law-abiding I might be, nothing would satisfy the blood lust in me. Sloan Reynolds had to die.

And now, justice continues its journey. Now I have to pay.

All the thoughts keeping me awake last night press against my brain as I enter the empty gym. I sit on the vinyl-covered bench and the low throb of pain sticks in my chest. *Melissa*... my soul cries her name. I want her. I need her. How will I survive if I'm in this place until I die, separated from her forever? *Fuck.*

I grip the weight bar and push up, feeling the burn in the pit of my biceps. I haven't worked out in almost a month. I've been away from home, dealing with the separation, dealing with this situation. Bennett's manipulation was clever. It showed how well he knew me. I wouldn't let Star pay for my crimes. I couldn't value my family above hers, even if she insisted her life was worth less than mine. Who makes those kinds of decisions?

The question has only entered my mind when I realize I'm not alone. I return the five hundred pound load to the rack, and my peripheral vision counts five men in the room with me. Lowering my arms, I sit up, not quite ready to make contact.

A deep inhale. I allow the battle I fought all night to flood my veins with anger. I focus all my frustrations over Melissa, Sloan, my future, to compress into one raging need for expression. I need an outlet. Looks like I have five.

"I got your message, boy." Chairman stands at the head of the bench. "You're a pussy. You'll do real good inside. Lots of cocks to suck."

I don't answer. I only sit up slowly allowing the gates I've opened to flood me with rage. What's about to happen will be sweet release. I can feel the strength building in my fists in anticipation.

"He's a pretty boy." The voice came from behind me, but my eyes are locked on Chairman's. "Hold him. I want him to be my pussy."

Try it, fucknut. The thought tickles in my brain before it closes in like a steel trap. A touch on my shoulder, and my hand snaps over it, clasping the wrist and flipping it around in a move so fast, everyone jumps back. It's the big white guy. He's on his knees with a broken wrist. A scream starts, but I punch him in the face and he drops. One down, four to go.

Only, they're ready now. I might have gotten lucky with the first one, but now two mountains of black flesh have me by each arm. Chairman stands back and watches. Rev is in front of me, and his black eyes narrow like a snake. I don't think, I only respond. A swift kick to the face, and he flies back to the wall.

"You've got to be faster than that, little man," I growl, but the hulks holding my arms aren't finished.

"It's about to get rough, pussy," the one on my left snarls.

My arm is jerked up behind my back, bending me forward, and the asshole on my right grabs my face. I know what's coming when I see him shift his balance to the other leg. I only have one chance. A loud groan scrapes from my throat as I throw everything I've got to the right. His knee flies past my head making contact with the fucker behind me. It's not a hard hit, but it stuns him. His grip loosens a fraction, and I spin around, out of his control.

"Oh, I like this one," Fucker to my left smiles.

Chairman moves his back to the wall and is making his way around the perimeter. I don't have time to wonder why he isn't getting involved. The two are slowly approaching me again, both smiling. What happens next is so fast, the specifics are fuzzy.

One guy lunges at my torso while the other takes a shot at my face. His fist makes contact with my cheekbone, and a flash of white explodes behind my eyes. I was already in the process of shooting a roundhouse kick to the right while driving a punch to the left. The punch misses but my foot makes contact with the other guy's face. I feel the crunch of his jaw in my bones, and I know he's out of commission.

He goes down, but so do I. Puncher is over me ready to start raining blows. A fist like a concrete block slams into my kidney, and I can't stop a groan of agony as pain blasts through my torso. His next punch is right to my gut, and my wind disappears.

I reach out and grab the metal leg of a weight stand near my head. Pulling with all my strength, I drag my body out of the line of his next, finishing blow.

His fist makes contact with a metal rack, and a howl of pain fills my ears. I only have one chance to get the upper hand. Pushing off the floor with both arms, I shoot my leg back, making contact with the soft flesh of his throat. A sick gulp, and he drops like a tree. I don't have time to check, but I hope I haven't added a second murder to my rap.

Panting, I face Chairman. Rev is on his feet against the wall, but he's not making a move yet. Keeping him in my view, I step back until I've got a wall behind me as well.

"Not bad, soldier," Chairman says, nodding. "Maybe you are a badass, but you crossed me. Can't let that pass."

I'm breathing hard, and my eyes move from him to Rev. "Bring it."

A flick of his wrist, and both men lunge for me at the same time. I see the glint of light off the weapon in Rev's hand, but I don't have time to block it before Chairman has my arms. Flexing my muscles, I twist away, but Rev is ready. He stabs me deep in the left side.

"FUCK!" I shout, struggling to get my arms free before he's able to do it again.

I'm too late. He's driving it into me again as I try to shift my weight so I can kick him into next week. Chairman anticipates my plan and jerks my body to the side, knocking me off balance. The movement drives the knife between my ribs. All at once, I can't breathe.

I go down gasping. I'm suffocating. Hot, sticky liquid is flooding around me on the floor. It's my blood. The room is receding... moving out from my vision. I feel the clock ticking as my muscles go weak. I can't get air.

Commotion fills the space around me, and I register two things before I blackout—Rev is slammed against the wall, and Chairman's arms are jerked behind him.

"Captain!" The word echoes in my ears, and I remember it was Ben's nickname for me when we were in training.

"You're a cop." Chairman's says, hatred dripping in his tone.

It's the last thing I hear before the curtain falls.

CHAPTER 16: THE WORST

Melissa

Lane is on his knees at Derek's long dining room table eating mac and cheese while Elaine sits beside him holding a glass of white wine.

"I hate waiting," she grumbles, picking up a stray noodle that escaped onto the mahogany surface.

I can't help smiling at how a child changes the tone of Derek's single-male penthouse condo. A line of trucks is on the floor in the living room in front of the gigantic flat-screen television that's paused on a little-boy building show.

"At least we're all together," I exhale, wishing Dex were here instead of with my mom back in Wilmington. "If you hadn't made the drive, I'd be bouncing off the walls."

"You could've gone to the office to wait with Patrick."

"Even worse!" I cry, dropping into one of the leather armless chairs arranged around the dark-wood table. "It's nothing but reminders of what's happening."

"Did Kenny say she was driving up?" Leaning forward, I pick up the wine bottle and pour myself a glass.

"She and Slayde had to finish with clients at the gym, and then they were picking up Mariska at her place." She glances up at the clock. "It only takes half an hour to drive here from Bayville."

I resist the urge to chug my glass of wine, and instead, I'm out of my chair again, pacing the room. "What can we do, Lainey? I'm about to go crazy."

"Want to watch a movie?"

"Not really." Chewing my lip, I walk to the windows and look out on the spring afternoon.

Stuart and Marcus had an eleven o'clock meeting with the prosecutor this morning, and from there they said they'd know if Derek would have to go to trial or if they would commute the charges and sentence him to time served. We've only heard once from Stuart, who said their meeting with the prosecutor was very productive. All that's left is a judge to sign off on their agreement.

"My chest is so tight, I feel like I'm having a heart attack," I laugh. "It's like we've won, but we haven't. One person stands between us and the future."

My best friend is out of her chair and crossing the room as I'm still speaking. Standing beside me looking out, she hugs me, putting her chin on my shoulder. "I don't know a whole lot about this process," she says, "but I think if the prosecutor is on our side, the judge will go with his advice."

"Even in a murder case? What if they get one of those hanging judges?"

"Oh my god, stop!" She cries, shaking her light-blonde head. "Now you're making me nervous."

A sudden knock on the door actually makes me scream. "Jesus!" Rubbing my stomach, I dash across the room to answer. "I'm so nervous, I'm screaming at the drop of a hat."

Star is outside with Cammie on her hip. "Is it okay if we hang out with you guys?"

"Of course!" Holding the door wide, I let them both in.

Star's involvement in the case is over. Bennett played his hand, and for now he seems to be winning. Still, none of us can return to normal life while Derek is in jail.

"I can hardly stand this," Star says, putting her baby girl down. The little girl immediately crawls to where Lane is driving his truck up and down the lines in the rug. "I wish he'd waited. I wish he'd talked to me about Bennett's ultimatum."

She wrings her hands, and I grab another wine glass. "Wine?"

"God, please," she exhales. "I'm about to start smoking again."

"I might join you!" Elaine says, joining us around the table. "Cheers." She holds her glass up, and we tap our three glasses together.

I take another long pull and walk to where the babies are playing, oblivious to our adult concerns.

"She's so close to walking," I say, as Star's dark-haired beauty pulls up on the coffee table. "I remember when Dex was that age."

With a sigh, I drop my head in my hands. Derek has to come home. He can't miss being with Dex, teaching him to play football, helping him learn to ride a bike. The thought of him getting a life sentence makes my entire body shake.

"How much longer before we know something?" Star asks.

"No idea," Elaine says, taking another drink. "Stuart will call Patrick first, I'm sure. They're just waiting to get an appointment with the judge."

"That time I went to court, it took four hours before I saw the judge," she said, sitting on the floor by her daughter.

My brow lines. "Why did you have to go to court?"

Looking down, she clears her throat. "Just some… misunderstanding in Myrtle Beach."

"Oh my god," I say, remembering Star's former occupation. "I'm such an idiot. I'm sorry."

Seeming to read my mind, she shakes her head. "No! It wasn't anything like that. I just… it was sort of a wardrobe malfunction, you might say."

Blinking around, I try to place what that might mean. "Oh…" is all I can manage.

"They're stricter than I realized on the public beaches."

"Ohhh!" It's clicking into place when another knock on the door makes me jump. Nodding at Elaine I head to open it. "I didn't scream that time."

"It's the wine," my best friend calls after me.

She's right. I'm feeling warm and less panicky for the first time all day. Last night all I did was roll around in Derek's king-sized bed missing him and wishing I could call him. We'd already used our one phone call, so I was left with my stomach twisted and aching, hoping he still had his own cell, praying that he wasn't being targeted. I'd heard stories of prison justice. At the same time, Derek wasn't in prison yet, and Sloan wasn't a helpless victim who needed avenging. Stuart had texted yesterday asking for pictures of me and Dex to send to him, and the request made me simultaneously happy and miserable. Happy that he was thinking about us; miserable at the thought of him needing pictures to get through extended periods of separation.

Kenny, Slayde, and Mariska are at the door, and when I open it, Mariska pulls me into a hug.

"How are you holding up?" She studies me, her golden-brown eyes full of concern.

"It's possible this is the worst thing I've ever had to endure," I confess.

"That's saying a lot," Elaine mutters, taking another sip of wine. "Anybody need a glass?"

"I'll have some," Mariska goes over to her, smiling.

Kenny goes straight to Lane on the carpet, and he's in her lap at once, hugging her and sliding his fingers in her violet hair. "Mommy purple," he says.

"How's my big boy?" She kisses his cheek. Slayde sits on the leather sofa beside her, and watching them makes me want Dex here even more.

"I should have Dex," I say mostly to myself.

Elaine's beside me. "It's better he's with your mom." She slides my hair back from my shoulder. "He'd be fussy if he were here. You're stressed, and we need to know what's going to happen first."

Dropping my chin, I rub my forehead hard. I know what she's not saying. If the outcome is not what we're all straining for, I'd rather not come apart in front of my little boy.

"Oh, Lainey," I say as she hugs me again.

Slayde's deep voice cuts through the tension. It's so calm, I welcome the change. "I know this isn't the most correct thing to say, but why didn't he... not get arrested?"

For a moment, I consider the attractive young man sitting in Derek's living room. He's dressed in jeans and a navy tee with a matching navy windbreaker on top. We've only met once before at Elaine and Patrick's wedding. He's the love of Kenny's life, and his past is so mixed into what's happening here, it's hard to fathom.

As he waits for my answer, his dark brow lines, and Kenny looks up at him then at me. I can tell she's thinking the same thing, wondering why I'm hesitating.

Star jumps in from where she sits across from them on the floor, Cammie pulling up in her lap.

"It's my fault," she says, pulling her face away from the baby's grasp. "He was protecting me... or us."

"I don't understand," Kenny says, and her large blue eyes flicker from Star to me. "How was he protecting you if he killed Melissa's ex?"

My eyes go to Elaine's, and her expression is worried. I'm not sure how much Stuart's told Mariska, but Kenny and Slayde know nothing about this story. I'm not sure how much Derek wants Slayde to know.

I'm about to answer, but Star continues. "A guy that used to work for him... Bennett? He started blackmailing me, saying he was going to turn me in for the murder. But when Derek met with him, he was really after revenge. Derek put his son away for life... I think for the same thing."

"Star!" I say, trying to head her off, but it's too late. The words are out before I can distract her.

Slayde's face changes at once. His ice blue eyes cut to me. "Who is this Bennett?"

"I-I've never met him," I say, truthfully, wishing at least Patrick were here to help me explain.

Slayde is on his feet, walking to where I stand, as Lainey pours us another glass of wine. "I need you to tell me," he says.

Kenny follows, standing behind him, one hand on his waist the other holding his hand. She's so tiny, but Slayde's not quite six foot. He's slim and muscular, and everything about him, from the way he moves to the way he stands, underscores his past as a fighter.

"You should probably hear this from Derek," I say, holding his gaze. "I don't know the whole story, and I'm afraid I'll get the details wrong."

"Just... try." His expression is so intense, my chest clenches.

"Derek didn't actually tell me," I hedge. "He didn't have time before... I got the story second-hand from Patrick."

"Patrick knows?" Kenny's brow lines, but Slayde cuts in.

"Melissa," his voice urges. "Please."

I take a breath and tell him what I know. "Bennett is a contract PI Derek used for cases here after he moved to Wilmington with me."

"He's from Princeton?" Slayde asks.

"I'm not sure. If not, he's from somewhere near here."

Slayde's eyes wince. "Go on."

"Derek didn't know about this. Patrick was floored telling me the connection..." I try to remember the exact details. "Derek helped build the case against his son, who he called Shane." Slayde's eyes wince again, and my heart beats painfully hard. "He said Derek put him away with no mercy and he wanted Derek to suffer the same fate."

Slayde exhales a long breath, and covers Kenny's slim arm with his hand. I can't help noticing the bold 21 inked near his thumb.

"Where is this Bennett?" he says.

"I don't know." Looking up at Elaine, she shakes her head. "It's possible Patrick might be able to find him."

Star and Mariska have slowly walked to where we're standing, and now they join us.

"What's going on?" Star says softly. "Do you know Bennett?"

"No," he says not breaking eye contact with me. "Only one man ever claimed to be my father. He was the worst kind of lowlife." His voice trails off, and Kenny's arm tightens around his waist.

Turning back, a phone rings, and Elaine's out of her chair, dashing to the guest bedroom. "It's mine! It's got to be Patrick."

My head feels light, and I pull out a chair to sit. Mariska runs over behind me, placing her slim hands on my shoulders.

"Hey, babe, what's the news?" We all lean forward listening. Elaine's voice is unbelievably calm. "Okay," she says. She frowns, and the room starts to blur. "Oh shit, Patrick, talk to Melissa. She can tell me what you say." My best friend rushes toward me. "What?" She pauses. "Oh, right! Speakerphone!"

She pulls the phone away, touches its face, and sets it on the table in front of me. Then she drops to her knees beside me, taking both my hands in hers and holding them tightly. I can't breathe waiting for what Patrick will say. Everyone in the room is huddled around my chair. Only the babies play on the carpet in the living room.

"I have great news and then... not so great news."

I'm sure I'm going to throw up until Mariska shouts. "Good god, Patrick! Just tell us if Derek is free!"

"Yes—he is! The judge agreed with the prosecutor." We all exhale in a united noise. Tears flood my eyes, spilling over onto my cheeks. I'm shaking as waves of relief rattle my insides.

Mariska and Elaine hug each other, and then we realize Patrick is shouting over the noise of our celebration.

"Hang on!" Elaine says, "Hang on, guys. What, Patrick?"

We all grow quiet, and Patrick continues. "While the meeting was happening... well... it seems a fight broke out in the jail where Derek was located."

Fear clenches my insides. "Is he okay?" I manage to choke out.

"No... he's not. One of the guys had a shiv, a makeshift knife, and he stabbed Derek twice."

A strangled cry, and Mariska's on her knees at my side, wiping my hair from my face. I don't even see her. My vision is blinded, and all I can see is Derek slipping away, needing me. I try to force my brain to understand what he's saying.

"I think I'm in shock," I whisper. Everybody is frozen, staring at the small device on the table, waiting for more.

"Patrick, what's going on?" Elaine shouts again.

"He's in the ICU at Johns Hopkins. I'm in the car headed your way. Can Melissa come down and meet me? I'll drive her to Baltimore."

Pain causes me to bend at the waist. I turn to the side and grasp the chair next to me. I can't breathe. "Lainey," I whisper. "I can't breathe."

"Oh my god, Patrick, you have to tell us if Derek's going to be okay."

"It's still a bit touch and go, but he's at the best hospital in the country. I have to believe he'll be fine."

"She'll be ready," Elaine picks up the phone and switches it off speaker. "I'll ride with you. Text me when you're out front. We'll come down when you get here."

* * *

The drive to Baltimore passes in a blur. I sit looking out the back window as Elaine and Patrick discuss what happened up front.

"Marcus convinced the prosecutor Derek didn't deserve to go to prison?" My best friend says.

"Mmm... More like nobody would come forward to defend Sloan Reynolds, so why did he want to send a decorated Marine to prison for defending someone against attack."

"Your 'defense of others' suggestion?" Elaine is proud — possibly even a little smug.

Patrick grins. "As much as I want to support you in this Us versus Them thing you're doing. Your brother was pretty vital to the case."

She exhales and leans back in the passenger's seat. "Why can't you take credit for doing a great job? Why does everyone have to be a member of the damn bar association?"

"I think you mean the state bar."

"Whatever! You helped. Did he even acknowledge that?"

"He didn't get a chance." Patrick smiles at her, and glancing back, I see so much adoration on his face. "Hey, look at me. I only talked to Captain Asshat, and he was so relieved, he was fucking nice to me. I can only imagine they were shitting bricks waiting for that judge to decide."

My best friend looks out the window. "They should have been. We were all counting on them."

We ride in silence as the music plays on the radio. Patrick finally speaks. "I know your dad and brothers were shitheads when you told them you wanted to be a teacher instead of a lawyer—"

"They still are," she quietly grumbles.

He lifts her hand and kisses it. "I'm not. I think you're an amazing teacher. And I'm really glad you're related to one of the top lawyers in the country."

Her eyes slant at him, and for a moment, I'm not sure if my bestie will make a quip or kiss her new husband. She does the latter, and despite my growing anxiety, I smile.

I might have been mad at Patrick for encouraging Derek not to tell me about Sloan, but I can never be mad for long. He's made my friend one of the happiest people I know. Their love is so strong. Chewing my lip, fear tightens in my chest. I can only hope our love is strong enough to pull Derek through.

* * *

We're practically running down the polished corridor. Stuart and Marcus are in the waiting room, and the minute we see each other, they stand and head in our direction. Marcus gives me a hug.

"Melissa," he exhales. "We were so sure he was in the clear and now this."

"What happened?" Elaine says from behind me.

I turn and her older brother leans forward to kiss her cheek. "Hey, sis."

219

Stuart's entire body is tense. "Ben said it looked like they jumped him in the weight room. By the time he got there, Derek had been stabbed twice."

My hand flies to my mouth. Tears blur my vision, and another set of arms embrace me. Elaine hugs me on top of her brother, and for a moment, I take comfort from my childhood friends.

I only give it a moment, however, straightening up and wiping the tears away. "He's going to be okay." My voice is wobbly, and I have to force myself to believe it. I won't give up on him. Not after how far we've come.

"Mrs. Alexander?" A soft voice speaks from behind us, and I turn.

"Here," Patrick says, gesturing to me. I don't correct him.

The doctor joins us in the waiting area, grim-faced. "May I speak to you in private?"

My knees try to go out, and Stuart catches my arm. Blinking up to him, I hold his hand. *Be strong, Melissa.*

"It's okay," I manage. "These are his closest friends… and his lawyer."

A tight smile doesn't soften the doctor's expression. His eyes travel over the five of us before he continues. "We moved him to a private room. He's heavily sedated, but he's not intubated. He won't require surgery, since the lung didn't fully collapse. Luckily the wound wasn't very deep or jagged. I took him off the ventilator, and once I see how he responds to treatment, we'll bring him around."

"So he's okay?" Stuart cuts to the chase in his usual, direct way.

"He's developed an infection around the second stab wound that we're monitoring. His fever spiked, and we've started antibiotics in his drip. I'm concerned about sepsis."

The white threatens again, and I'm sure I'll faint.

"Mrs. Alexander," the doctor catches my arm. "I didn't mean to be insensitive. Can I get you something?"

"No," shaking my head, I blink down as tears fall. "So he's… not okay?"

His voice softens. "Your husband is healthy and fit. I'd rather be overly cautious. He had some minor contusions, and his body needs rest."

"Can I see him?"

"I'm limiting visitors—as much for exposure as anything else."

My chest squeezes. The tears won't stop flowing, and Elaine passes me a handful of tissues.

The doctor observes me a moment. "Still… He might benefit from having you beside him."

Without hesitation or even a look back, I go to Derek's hospital room. I can't see him from the small window. A screen stands between the bed and the door, and inside, the steady beep of monitors fills the air.

Stepping around the screen, a fresh flood of tears spills down my cheeks. He's so pale. Lying on his back, his shirt is off and wide bands of gauze are wrapped around his chest. I can see the thick pads where his injuries are. I can't bear the thought of what happened to him. Stabbed, beaten, jumped by five men…

The IV bag hangs near his head. His dark hair is pushed back, and his eyes are closed. That lovely scruff is still on his cheeks, and I want to press my face to his, kiss his lips gently, tell him it's going to be okay. *I'm here. I'll never leave him again.*

The doctor's concern for infection is on my mind, so instead I pull up a chair at his bedside and sit, sliding my cool hand under his large one. I kiss the top before lowering my face to put my damp cheek against it.

"You're so warm," I say, swallowing the thickness in my throat. "The doctor is giving you something for that. He says it will fight the infection."

No change. The beeping continues, and I continue to stroke his hand, making my way slowly up his forearm. His skin feels so good to touch. I have him with me again. It feels like years have gone by since he held me in his arms. Looking back, I realize how precious our love is, how much I have to fight for it. He doesn't tell me important things. He protects me too much. We can work through these non-problems.

"I'm so sorry we fought," I whisper, smoothing the dark hairs on his forearm. "I'm sorry I was angry. I love you."

Movement behind the screen, and I look up to see a nurse entering. She has dark hair touched with silver, and when she smiles, lines form around her brown eyes.

"How about we wake him up?"

"Is it time?"

"His fever is down, and the antibiotics have been going several hours."

I stand quickly, moving out of her way. "Do you need me to wait outside?"

"Nope. I'm just changing out his bag, reducing the medication. When he comes around, he'll

222

probably want to see a familiar face. He might be a little disoriented."

My chest clenches. "Thank you," is all I can say.

I watch as she works around him. The doctor enters holding a metal clipboard with papers on top. He steps over to one of the large monitors and makes notes. "Oxygen levels are good," he says quietly. "Let me know if anything changes."

The monitor beeps, and I wait. Nothing seems to be happening.

"Mr. Alexander?" The nurse touches his shoulder.

No response.

Her expression changes, and fear cramps my stomach. "Is something wrong?"

"Not necessarily." She steps over to the monitors again and makes a few notes. "I want you to call me when his eyes open. I'll be back to check on you in a little while."

She goes around the screen, and it's just the two of us. I'm on edge near his pillow waiting, straining for him to wake up. A round clock above the small television mounted on the wall says it's almost nine. I hadn't asked if I could stay overnight, but the doctor didn't seem interested in making me leave.

My mind drifts back to when Dex was born. I'd decided to have a drug-free delivery, and my groans and screaming as I worked to get our little son into the world nearly drove Derek out of the hospital. I'll never forget how helpless he looked. A bit like he looks now. Once it was over, he never left my bedside. At one point he climbed in beside me, putting one arm over my head and the other across my waist and around our new baby nestled in my side. It was one of the happiest moments of my life.

Quickly assessing the position of the tubes and monitors to his left, I sit on the bedside in the small space to his right. Slipping off my shoes, I stretch my legs down his. The arm I was just caressing is between us, and I'm careful not to disturb his injured torso. The beeps continue steadily, without interruption, as I place my cheek against his shoulder and wrap my arm across his chest.

For a little while I only hold him, feeling the warmth of his body soothing the fear in my chest. Several moments pass, and my muscles begin to relax. I feel his calm breathing, in and out, and it calms mine. My body melts into his, and for the first time in three weeks, I feel whole again.

"I won't leave until you're back with me," I say, sliding my palm carefully over his shoulder.

CHAPTER 17: FINISHED BUSINESS

Derek

An irritating beeping noise is in my ears. It's dark, and I'm sluggish. My limbs are so heavy, I can't lift them. Confused, I blink up at the ceiling, trying to remember where the hell I am and how I got here. The last thing I recall is lying on the floor of the jail, blood pooling around my midsection.

Clearly, someone called help. Wait. Ben was there. He called me Captain... Something is across my shoulders. I try to lift up, but pain sears my left side, and I remember the knife going between my ribs, gasping for air. *Shit*. That fucker must've punctured a lung. So I'm in the hospital? Another beep, and I try to move again, but the slim band across my shoulders prevents me.

Turning my head, everything changes. I realize what's holding me. Melissa. Her soft hair is against my shoulder. I try to lift my arm again, but it feels weighted down. I want to hold her. Straining my neck in her direction, I take a deep inhale... ocean roses. Warmth swells in my chest. She's in the hospital bed beside me.

"Derek?" Her voice is thick with sleep, and the sound is so lovely. Lifting her face, her dark brow pulls over those beautiful sapphire eyes. "Are you awake?"

I try to answer, but my mouth is so dry. "Yes." It comes out a scratched whisper.

"Oh!" She's on her feet at once. "Are you thirsty? Here, let me get you a drink." She runs around the foot to my other side. A plastic cup is on a rolling tray. She grabs it and is back at my bedside just as fast.

"Take a sip." Her hand lightly touches my chin as she holds the straw to my lips.

Fuck the water. I want to drink in her lovely form, standing over me. Her eyes are a little swollen, and I realize she's been crying. My lips part, and I pull the tepid water into my mouth. It's not very good, but it soothes my throat.

"You're here." I whisper. It's all I can think. She's here. After all those nights apart when my body ached for hers, she's right here in this room with me. Then she's up on the bedside again, leaning closer, but holding herself off my torso.

"I'm here," she repeats with a smile, her eyes glistening with more tears.

"Don't cry," I say, but my voice cracks again. She quickly holds the straw to my lips, and I take another sip.

More tears are in her eyes, but she's smiling now. She sniffs as they stream down her cheeks, and she leans forward, pressing her forehead to mine.

"I'm so happy you're awake. I've been waiting to tell you how much I love you. I want you to come home. I want us to never be separated again."

I tilt my chin to kiss her cheek. She lifts up, but hesitates before kissing my mouth. "The doctor is worried about infection..."

"Kiss me." My voice cracks, but the order is clear. Her lips press together, and she hesitates. "Melissa," I say a bit stronger. "I'm not worried about infection. Kiss me, dammit."

She breaks into a smile before lightly cupping my cheeks and leaning forward. Her soft lips press against mine, and I curse my inability to hold her. Lightly pulling my lips with hers, it's just a tease of a kiss. I growl and lift my head, kissing her more forcefully, but the movement sends a stab of pain into my ribs.

"Ugh," I gasp, falling back against the pillow.

"Oh my god!" She hops up. "I'll call the nurse!"

"Melissa," I growl. "Get over here and give me a real kiss before I fucking hurt myself."

My words freeze her on the spot. She blinks back at me then exhales a laugh. With a shake of her beautiful head, she's at my side again in the same spot as before.

"You're the most stubborn man," she whispers in that low, sultry voice I love.

"What do I have to do to make you listen to me?"

Her eyes sparkle as she cups my cheek. "I'm listening to you." She touches my lips softly with hers and pulls back. I let out a frustrated growl, and she speaks again. "I hear every word you say."

This time her lips crash against mine with all the longing we both feel. Mouths open, my tongue finds hers and curls with it. Desire floods my veins, and I manage to lift my right arm. It's heavy, but I hold the back of her neck, drawing her body closer to mine. She lets out a little sigh and lifts her chin. Pulling her closer, I press my mouth to her soft throat.

"You have to be careful," she whispers, threading her fingers into the sides of my hair.

"I'll let you know if anything hurts."

Slipping off the bed, she's again beside me. My arm falls and she catches it, moving it under the blanket. "You've had some pretty serious injuries. Let me call the nurse."

All I want is to hold her. I've waited so long for this moment. "Only because I don't want to stay in this bed longer than I have to."

She smiles and leans forward to kiss my forehead. I make a move to catch her and she laughs, dancing back. "Your recovery might be extensive."

"Don't worry. I'm not finished with you."

* * *

Three weeks, and I'm back in the Alexander-Knight office in Princeton, collecting the files I'd brought up from Wilmington and sorting through the files I'd dug out while I was here away from Melissa.

The doctor in Baltimore released me a few days after I came around, once my infection cleared up. I had to check in with my doctor here, who put me on bed rest. I still get winded, and at times I feel like an infant learning to walk again.

Speaking of infants, Melissa brought Dex from Wilmington to stay with us, and my ultimate bachelor pad looks more like a nursery than ever. It's exactly the way I like it after those nights alone, hating the sterile single-ness of the place. Today, they're in Baltimore meeting with Bea. Our wedding plans have been restored, and Melissa is taking pictures of doughnuts. I didn't even question her.

"These are the last of the files," Nikki says, taking a stack of accordion folders off my desk. "You want them in the back filing cabinet?"

"We should probably think about scanning them and saving them on the hard drive." I open my

MacBook and click on the main directory folder. "As a leader in online security, it's pretty ridiculous for us to keep paper files in the office."

Her chin drops and she pauses at my door. "I'm not planning to stick around and help with that. I've sent my resume to a few offices, and I have an interview with one tomorrow."

Stopping what I'm doing, I push back against the desk and slowly stand. "I guess we never finished talking about that."

"There's nothing to talk about. I don't belong here anymore."

Patrick has returned to Wilmington with Elaine and Lane, and I briefly glance in the direction of Stuart's empty office. He hasn't made it in yet this morning.

"I understand how you feel," I say. "If you need a reference, I'll be happy to give you one."

"I won't make you lie for me," she says with a bitter shake of her head. "I slept with Mr. Knight, I helped a blackmailer trap Mr. Alexander in a murder rap—"

"To be fair, it was an honest mistake." I'm not holding it against her.

"Yes, because I'm such a god-awful secretary, you didn't let me open your mail."

I don't have a good answer for that because it's true. I'm standing in the office trying to think of a nice send-off when the glass doors open, and a face I never expected to see here emerges.

Slayde pauses in the doorway when he sees Nikki and me standing there. "Hi," his voice hesitates. "Hope I'm not interrupting anything."

"I was just taking these files away for Derek." Nikki takes off toward the back office, and I'm left facing the son of my nemesis.

"Would it be okay if we talked in your office?" He steps forward, and his expression is conflicted. "Star told me what happened. I just... I need to ask you some questions."

"Of course." I step to the side and motion for him to enter.

He walks in, but doesn't take a seat. Instead, he steps to the bookshelves and puts his hands in his front pockets as he studies my photographs of Melissa and Dex. I step around my desk and take a seat.

"You hired this guy Bennett to be your private investigator?" He asks, turning to me. "You didn't know anything about him?"

"I knew his work history," I say. "I needed someone to work cases here when I moved to Wilmington. He came highly recommended, and Bennett is a common enough name. I'm sorry, but you never entered my mind."

The young man nods and paces to the other side of my office. "No, *I'm* sorry." He stops and faces me, those ice blue eyes burning with intensity. "I'm sorry for what he did to you, the blackmailing and the forcing you to turn yourself in. I'd never have wanted him to do that. I'm not about revenge."

Nodding, I lift the Montblanc pen off my desk. "I believe you."

"It sounds like a line, but I'm not sorry I went to prison. I was a waste of space, an ungrateful killer." He pauses and rubs an inked hand over his mouth, glancing down. "Doc changed my life. I'd never have met him if it weren't for what you did."

I knew a little of Slayde's story. Patrick had explained his transformation to me when we

230

debated whether Lane should spend time with Kenny now that she was dating an ex-con. Based on how I knew him, the answer was an automatic No. However, since leaving prison, Slayde had started over, taken control of his life. He rescued Kenny then he rescued his entire work crew and was named a hero. We'd decided he was one of the rare success stories of the penal system, and it was obvious Kenny couldn't be more in love.

He looks up at me. "Do you know where this Bennett is now?"

"I haven't had a chance to look into it," I say. "It's only my first day back in the office. But I'm sure I could find him for you."

"Would you?"

I'm just leaning forward to wake up my computer when a cold voice breaks through our conversation.

"No need to look," the man says. "I'm right here."

Slayde spins around just as my head snaps up to see none other than Robert Bennett in the entrance to my office. He's smiling, leaning against the doorjamb. His brown hair — the same color as his son's, I notice — is neatly trimmed, and he's dressed neatly in khakis and a short-sleeved shirt, as if he were just out taking a drive and stopped by the office.

Despite his casual appearance, I'm on high alert. He wanted revenge, and I'm not sure he's satisfied. Momentary silence fills the air as the three of us assess one another. My attitude is angry, defensive, but I can feel waves of rage rolling off of Slayde. His fists clench as does his jaw. I'm on guard against what he might do, at the same time, I recall his reputation for control.

"What do you want?" Slayde's tone is low.

"Shane?" The man says, pushing off and taking a step toward us. "I wasn't expecting you to be here."

"My name is Slayde," the young fighter replies. "Why are you here?"

An evil smirk crosses my former PI's face, and his dark eyes narrow. "I've been keeping tabs on my old employer, waiting for him to be strong enough to get back to work."

"That doesn't answer my question."

My brows rise. Slayde might be tamed, but a lot of his old ferocity still exists.

"Take it easy, son," Bennett says, stopping in his tracks. "This is for you. Everything I've done has been to avenge your honor."

"I'm not your son."

"Well, biologically speaking —"

"I don't have a father." Slayde's fists tighten again, and I remember his signature move. High-volume punching. "The man who raised me was a fucked up bastard, and you were nothing more than a sperm donor."

Robert frowns. "I wanted to be there for you. I followed all your fights, all your matches. I was so proud of you."

"Once I was an adult. Where were you when I needed you? When I was seven years old being beaten for leaving a fucking Lego on the floor? When I was locked in a closet for hours for not knowing how to make breakfast?"

"My cousin was a fucked up loser," Robert snaps, and for a moment, I see a glimmer of the old

Slayde reflected in his face. "Trust me. If he hadn't died already—"

"He was an alcoholic who was broken after the love of his life died." Slayde's demeanor shifts like sand, and I can see how he's changed since I faced him in the courtroom. "At least now I understand why he hated me so much."

"It doesn't excuse what he did to you."

"I never said it did, but you knew about it. You knew who I was and what I was going through. You never did a thing to help me."

"How could I?" Robert holds his hands open in a plaintiff gesture that makes me sick. "I was in no position to raise a kid. I was alone and not in a good place myself when Megan died."

"You could've sent the cops. You could've done something to help me."

Bennett shakes his head, and I see the crazy rage spark in his eyes. "NO! This isn't about me. This is about HIM!" He waves his arm at me. "You survived. You made it out of there and made a name for yourself. You were a star, a rising legend!"

"I was a broken loser just like the drunk who raised me." Slayde's shoulders droop. "I was so full of rage. I went through money like it didn't matter. I went through women like they were worthless whores."

"Until Derek Alexander ended your life."

Slayde's head snaps up at that. "He didn't end my life. He started the chain of events that helped me find peace. It's more than you ever did."

Bennett lunges forward now. "How can you say that? You don't know him like I do!" Sneering in my direction, his level of hatred for me is stunning. "He struts around here like some fucking hotshot, like he's some king."

I would argue, but I'm feeling my injury. My wind is cut in half.

"You're just trying to assuage your own guilt," Slayde murmurs.

"It's time the king was dethroned."

"What are you talking about?" Slayde's voice is an echo in my ears. Bennett's hand is in his coat, and I see the gun as he pulls it from his pocket.

"You are fucking... NO!" Slayde shouts, making a lunge toward the man.

A *BLAST!* rings out, and I flinch, anticipating the bullet wound. In the hair's breath of a second, I know it could very well be more than my body could handle in my current state. Slayde is young and strong, but if it hits him in the chest, in the heart...

Gunfire is a sharp, staccato sound. It ends almost as fast as it begins, leaving you to wonder if it truly *was* a gun. *Could it have been fireworks? A car backfiring? No, cars don't backfire in these days of computer-controlled starters*

My first thought upon all these reflections is *I'm in shock.*

My second is *I haven't been hit.*

Looking up, I realize Slayde is standing in the center of my office as well, seeming stunned. On the floor in front of him, the man claiming to be his father is crumpled into a heap. A thick, blackish pool is forming around him, and I realize he didn't shoot at all. Bennett was the victim here.

Wresting control of my scattered thoughts, I look up, and in the hallway, I see her standing there. In her hand is the small pistol Stuart put in my boot the night he dressed me in Kevlar and sent me out to meet our unknown blackmailer. I'd given him the small gun back, and he'd put it in his desk, where for the first time since she'd been a part of our team, our weakest link took control of the situation and changed it for the better.

Nikki shot Bennett just as he was attempting to shoot me. Now he's on the floor at Slayde's feet, writhing in pain, and my secretary stands, blue eyes huge, shivering in the reception area.

* * *

The police have cleared out by ten. One of Nikki's friends drives her home, promising to stay with her, and Slayde heads back to Bayville. I send a quick text to Melissa, promising to tell her everything once I get home.

When I meet Stuart at the bar across from our office, he has Marcus on the line discussing the details of the shootout and whether he needs to come in town to represent Nikki. It's the same bar Patrick and I visited the night he decided to drive to Wilmington and take Elaine back, and I can't help remembering that night with a smile. We've come a long way since those days.

"I can't believe she fucking shot him," Stuart says, shaking his head.

"Does it ever calm down around there?" I hear Marcus laugh over the speaker on Stuart's phone. "I'm putting you assholes on a $250K retainer."

"I'm sure you are." I say, noting his Armani style as I take a sip of the Glenfiddich the bartender places in front of me. "You'd be happy letting us keep you on the dole."

"Depending on the timeline, I could probably handle this when I'm in town for the wedding. If it comes to that."

"I'll keep you in the loop. Slayde witnessed the whole thing, and I intend to press charges."

"We're becoming the poster office for 'defense of others,'" Stuart says, sipping his beer. "At least we're not in Baltimore this time."

"He's lucky she didn't kill him," I add. "She said she closed her eyes and pulled the trigger."

"Good god," Marcus says. "My fee just went up."

Stuart stands, polishing off his beer. "It's late. I'm headed home to Mariska."

"Yea, I've got to get back and tell Melissa what happened."

Marcus is right there to give us hassle. "It's a Thursday night, and you're going home at ten? You fuckers are so whipped."

"Famous last words," I say, finishing my scotch.

"Famous true words." I hear the grin in our attorney's voice.

"Just keep talking, friend," Stuart pays our bill and slips on his blazer. I shake my head, remembering the days when my partner was just as cocky.

"Don't get me wrong," Merritt continues. "I love pussy, but there is no way in hell I'm letting it order my life. I control my destiny."

Yeah, yeah. I've seen enough to know how this story ends. Taking the phone from Stuart, I turn it off speaker. "Hey, before you go, I wanted to thank you for helping me."

"Just doing my job," he says. Then as if remembering, he's back to teasing. "Thank me by paying your bill."

"Don't worry."

The slightest pause, and a serious tone enters his voice. "I'm glad you weren't hurt today. Melissa's a special lady, and she loves you. You're a lucky man."

"Thanks again."

"See you next month. Now I'm headed out for the night."

Disconnecting, I hand the phone back to Stuart. We decide to split a cab rather than driving. Sitting in the back, I look out the window at the passing lights.

"I'm thinking of offering Slayde a job," I say.

Stuart shifts in his seat. "Doing what?"

Shaking my head, I don't know why I feel the need to reach out to these kids. "I'm on the market for a new PI."

"It'll only work if Kenny will move here."

"We might make it work if he doesn't mind commuting." A few quiet moments, and I remember our other unfinished business.

"I was also thinking of asking Nikki to stay on." He looks out the window, and I keep going. "Since she saved my life and all. How would you feel about that?"

"I don't have a problem with Nikki," he says through an exhale. "All that shit is water under the bridge in my mind. She handled things wrong, but maybe I did, too."

Silence again. I'm not sure what to say. "That's pretty generous of you."

He glances at me, and a smile spreads across his face. I'm confused, but not for long. "I asked Mariska to marry me. She said yes."

"What?" Now I'm smiling. "Well, damn. Congratulations."

"Yeah." He leans back and looks out the window again, still smiling.

"None of that past shit matters anymore. It was stupid anyway."

We're at the condo, and my partner slaps my back before heading up the stairs. I'm feeling good as I go to the elevator. Marcus and his playboy swagger cross my mind, and I remember how Stuart was before Mariska came along. I wonder what girl's going to knock our hotshot attorney on his ass.

Jason is filling in for Walt again. He hits the elevator button and smiles, a wistful look in his dark eyes as the elevator comes down. "That little guy of yours is one cute kid. I used to dream of having one of my own."

"What's holding you back?" I glance at him as I wait.

His dark head bows. "You have to woo the fairer sex, and I'm financially challenged."

I can't help thinking his sallow complexion and oversized nose might also be challenges, although the right lady would overlook such things. "Money isn't a necessary evil. Be creative."

Shaking his head, his melodrama continues. "I'm not creative either, sir. It's my curse."

Clapping his shoulder as the elevator doors open, I'm ready to be upstairs wooing my own lady. "Only one person can change that situation, my friend."

"No truer words." He waits as I get inside and hit the button for the top floor "Have a good night, sir."

The condo is dim when I arrive. Dex, I'm sure is sleeping, and as I step through the kitchen area, I see Melissa sitting on the black leather couch in front of the gas log. A glass of white wine is in her hand.

I drop my keys on the oak table, and she looks over her shoulder. Our eyes meet, and hers are soft and full of love. "How are you feeling?" Her voice is a gentle wave in my direction.

I don't waste any time going to her. She's wearing only one of my white dress shirts, and I'm feeling awake in every part of my body, most of which are located below my belt. Leaning forward, she puts her glass on the table, but I don't want her to get up. I want to scoop her into my lap and hold her.

"I'm not used to feeling weak," I say, sitting beside her and loosening my tie. My eyes never leave hers, and her cheeks flush under my gaze. "I'm ready to be back to normal."

I lift my tie over my head, and she leans forward to unbutton my top button. "I know," she says and kisses my throat. "At least you're here with me."

Her movements give me a nice view down the front of the shirt loosely covering her body. She's bare underneath, and my thoughts are moving away from this conversation to the bedroom.

"We had some excitement at the office today."

"Is that so?" She shifts so she's straddling my lap. "Tell me about it."

My hands slide up her smooth thighs to her ass, and I tease the edge of her panties with my fingertips. "I'll give you the short version."

A little shiver, "Okay."

"Slayde came to see me. He apologized, but he also wanted to know if I could find his dad for him."

"I had a feeling he would want that." Her elbow rests on my shoulder, and her beautiful cheek is against her slim hand.

I can't help thinking the best part of my day is holding this woman in my arms, talking. I understand now she needs this, and damn if I'll give her any reason to put my shit on the doorstep again.

"I was ready to tell him I could when the asshole walked in the door."

Her head lifts, and her expression changes. I was sure she would've heard this from Elaine who heard it from Kenny by now, but I guess not.

"Derek!" she whispers. "Oh my god. What happened?"

Pulling her to me, I kiss her soft lips. They melt to my pressure, accepting my comfort. "Nothing to me, as you can see. Slayde had the confrontation I think he's always needed…"

Her brow lines. "And?"

"Bennett was pretty pissed I'd escaped a life sentence. He pulled out a gun." She slides back onto the couch, both hands cover her mouth. "Nikki shot him."

Jumping up, she paces my living room shaking her hands. "Oh my god, Derek. I don't think I can take any more of this."

Easing to my feet, I capture her in my arms and hold her close, smoothing her long dark hair as I kiss her temple. "He's not a threat to us anymore."

She tenses and pulls back to find my eyes. "He's… dead?"

"No, but he's under arrest. They've taken him to the hospital for treatment then I intend to press charges. Marcus said he'd help us ensure Bennett will never threaten us again."

Wiggling free of my embrace, she holds my arms, her eyes glistening with tears. "I'm not sorry." Her voice drops to a whisper. "I hoped he was dead. Does that make me horrible?"

I pull her to me again and she melts against my chest. "It makes you human. Bennett is a psychopath."

For a moment, her small body rests against mine. My hands slide down her waist to her hips, and I pull her closer.

"I have an idea," I say against her hair. "Let's do something to take our minds off the bad stuff." She exhales a little laugh and puts her arms around my neck.

I want to carry her to the bed, but this fucking lung injury prevents me. Instead, I take her hand and lead her to our dim-lit room. Her lacy red bra, pink nightgown, and emerald silk robe are scattered around the room... these delicate items break the dark mahogany furniture, stainless accents, and white linen of my male space. I love the change.

Stopping, I turn to face her, watching her beautiful eyes as I unbutton the shirt she's wearing. Sliding it open, I cup her breast in my hand, teasing a beaded nipple between my finger and thumb. Sapphire turns to navy as desire builds and tightens across my fly.

Leaning forward, I capture her mouth in a deep kiss. My tongue sweeps inside to hers, curling with it as my thumb circles the tip of her breast. I want to sweep her up, throw her on the bed, and climb after her, claiming her in whatever position we land.

Again, I have to be more deliberate. I kiss her slower, pulling her full bottom lip between my teeth. She rises on her tiptoes with a little squeal, tangling her fingers in the sides of my hair as she kisses me again. Her tongue plunges in my mouth, and I can feel the heat rising in her body as it presses against my chest.

Being more deliberate might not be as bad as I originally thought.

Breaking away, she gasps as she quickly unfastens the last of my buttons. I take the opportunity to touch the side of her neck with my tongue then cover it with my mouth, pulling her flesh in a hard suck.

"Oh, god, Derek," she gasps, ripping the last of my buttons free and jerking at the bottom of my undershirt.

A little chuckle rumbles from my throat as I remove them. Another little noise from her, and she spreads her palms flat over my chest, smoothing them up and curling her fingers so her nails scrape my skin. It's teasing and erotic, and I'm quickly unfastening my belt as her breasts press against me.

"You have to take it easy." Her voice is low and sultry. "Let me do all the work."

I can't help a grin. "Whatever you say, Miss Jones."

"Sit back against the headboard."

The remainder of my clothes are gone, and I comply, getting comfortable against the pillows. She stands at the foot of the bed a moment, letting her eyes travel over my body. Fire follows her gaze, and I'm ready to ditch the helpless act.

"You'd better do something or I will," I say with a rasp.

Her eyes widen a flicker and she's on her hands and knees, climbing up the length of my body. Along the way, she ducks her head to plant a kiss on my thigh. It's like a charge of electricity straight to my cock. Once there, she stops again, blue eyes flashing to mine. My stomach tenses, and she dips her head forward, pulling my tip into the hot space of her mouth.

"Melissa," I groan as she begins to suck. Her tongue flickers around the edge, and my head presses back against the pillows as my orgasm roars to life. Her hand grips my base, pumping my shaft, and her head bobs to meet it. Tension builds, and my eyes squeeze shut. I'm panting, but fuck if this doesn't feel like heaven.

"I'm close…" But she doesn't stop. I want to be inside her before this ends, so I sit up and catch her under the arms.

She comes off me with a pop, and I fall back, taking her naked torso with me. "Ride me," I groan as she reaches down, sliding my tip into her clenching, hot center. "Come on, baby."

I'm in. My whole shaft is engulfed in her. It's hot and tight, and she's on her knees facing me, rising and falling fast. "Oh, god," she moans, bucking against me.

I can barely take the sensations. "Melissa." My voice is hoarse, and I can't stop thrusting up into her. As hard as she's getting off on me, I'm unable to stop meeting her fuck for fuck.

"Oh, YES!" She cries as I grip her ass. I'll probably leave a mark, but damn if I can help it. She's flying over the edge, and I grab one of her bouncing tits in my mouth, giving it a hard pull followed by a little bite. She cries out again, and it's all I need.

My lung burns, and I don't care. I feel like I'm dying the most fantastic death possible. I close my eyes and hold her, letting my orgasm fill her, pressing up into her as her nails bite into my shoulders. A cough pushes through my moans, and I take a ragged breath.

"Fuck," I gasp. "I think that was the best yet."

She collapses against me, and I rock my hips once more, allowing the receding waves of pleasure to ripple through my pelvis. Her arms hang on my shoulders, and I feel the smile on her lips.

Then she starts to laugh. "You always say that."

Holding her waist, I roll her onto her back and prop on my elbow beside her. "I mean since I got home."

She arches her back and laughs more, and I catch a nipple in my mouth again, giving it a little pull. "Oh!" She squeals, curving the other way. "You're insatiable."

Nodding, I bend down to kiss the hollow of her neck, making my way up to her jaw. "I will never get enough of you."

"Mmm." Her hands cup my cheeks. "That goes double for me."

We hold each other a moment, looking into each other's eyes. I think about the recent past, our future… "Everything straight in Baltimore?"

"Yes," she nods. "And I've been able to restore all our previous arrangements. The only problem was with the caterer."

"No food?"

"It's okay. I talked to the manager of a hotel near our venue, and I was able to reserve their ballroom. Catering included."

My brows rise. "Seems like that was a lucky break."

"It really was." Her slim fingers thread into the side of my hair. "Now all you have to do is show up in your dress blues."

"Whites."

"Shit!" Her eyes blink close, and I laugh. "I always get it backwards."

"Doesn't matter." Leaning down, I kiss the side of her jaw. "I know what to do."

"Me too," her voice is warm. "And I can't wait to do it with you."

That makes me smile, and I capture her lips again. Our tongues touch, and love burns in my stomach, spreading upwards into my chest. We've endured so much, and in only a few short weeks, this woman will be mine forever.

She turns her face and whispers at my ear. "What are you thinking?"

The touch of her lips against my skin stirs other parts of my body. "I'm thinking of something else I'd like to do with you."

A little laugh, a little touch, and our bodies move together in a way I will never jeopardize again.

CHAPTER 18: THAT DAY

Melissa

Elaine stands behind me as I lift the delicate band over my hair. I opted for the flowing beige strapless chiffon dress. It's plain with only the tiniest seed pearls scattered across the bodice. A wide, grosgrain ribbon forms an empire waist, and the skirt flutters in rippling waves just like the ocean.

My dark hair is down, but I secured the sides at the back of my head in a barrette, and my best friend-matron of honor stands behind me attaching the veil to it.

"I love this veil so much," she whispers once it's in place.

Sheer tulle hangs from the top, but right at my shoulders, a band of floral lace ripples down and along the edge, curving back up the other side.

"I can't believe this is happening." Heat fills my eyes.

"Hang on!" Lainey cries, dashing for the tissues. "If you start crying, I will, and we don't want to look like raccoons on your wedding day."

That makes me laugh, and I look up at the ceiling, quickly doing some mental math problems to distract my overactive tear ducts. "Hand me a mimosa," I order, taking the tissue from her and blotting under my eyes.

"You're beautiful!" She says, eyes brimming.

"Now you're doing it!" I laugh, touching the tissue under my lashes again.

"One postponement, one cancellation, and we finally made it."

"Two months ago, I was pretty sure this was never going to happen." Standing, I press a hand against my sternum to calm the pain that memory provokes.

"Not me." My best friend's arm goes around my back. She leans her light-blonde head against my dark one. "I never gave up on you two. Derek is the perfect prince for your fairytale."

"He's more than a prince."

"You're right." Elaine smooths her hands down the front of her thigh-length sequined dress. "Patrick's my prince. Derek's more like... the king in this story."

I almost snort mimosa through my nose. "Oh my god," I laugh harder. "Don't tell him that!"

She breaks into laughter, and I look up to see Mariska and Kenny joining us looking fresh and pretty. We all spent the day having our hair and nails done. We got pedicures for my beach wedding, and I sprang for everyone to have massages. For the last few hours, we've been lounging and taking our time getting dressed. The wedding starts at six, and a quick glance to the clock says we're in the final countdown.

As matron of honor, Elaine wears a thigh-high, strapless sequined dress the color of sand. Kenny's dress is a one-shoulder sea-foam green chiffon. Mariska's is a strapless chiffon in ocean blue. We all have our hair down in loose, rolling waves like the ocean, and the effect is stunning. Perfectly blended with our location.

"You guys are laughing way too much," Kenny says, prancing forward in her champagne stilettos.

"Give me a mimosa."

"Oh!" I wave my hand at them and pull my skirt up so I can run across the room. Digging in my bag, I pull out a handful of tissue-wrapped parcels. "I have these for your feet. You can't wear heels in the sand."

Tossing them each a bundle, we rip into the packages to find lace-covered elastic foot-thongs.

Kenny's small nose wrinkles. "What is this?"

"It's 'shoes' for a beach wedding," I explain. "Look. Slipping off the Marine-blue heel I'm wearing, I fit the contraption over my foot. The thong portion goes between my toes and the lace overlay covers the top of my foot. I hook the back over my heel. "Isn't that pretty?"

Her face changes. "Yes…" she starts to laugh, "It actually is."

With the stiletto queen onboard, the rest of the girls ditch their shoes and start pulling on lace "thongs."

"Have you seen Derek's hair?" Mariska gushes to her friend. "I love it."

Standing up fast, "What did he do to his hair?"

"He cut it." Elaine is next to me and makes an excited face. "He looks amazing."

I'm not sure I'm happy about this. I love threading my fingers through his collar-length dark waves. "Why would he do that?"

"Probably because of the dress whites," Mariska continues, unaffected. "Stuart went with him and got even more taken off his."

"Stuart's hair was already short." I say, looking in the mirror and feeling concerned. I can't imagine Derek high and tight.

Elaine's right with me, placing her hands on my waist. "Trust me. You're going to love it."

"Love what?" My mother enters the room in her rose-colored, tea-length chiffon dress.

"Mom," I step over and hug her then pull back, nose wrinkled. "Where's Dex?"

"Star's watching him. He's having a ball, playing in the sand with Lane and Cammie." She leans toward the mirror and straightens her dark hair behind one ear. "If they weren't so cute, I'd make them stop."

"Is Star okay watching them?"

"She doesn't mind, and Amy's with them."

"Amy's here!" Elaine perks up at the mention of Patrick's little sister. "I'll be right back. I haven't seen her yet."

She runs out, and my mother gives me a serious look. "I have something for you."

"What is it?"

She holds out a cream-colored envelope with my name written on it in brown ink. It's fine linen stationary with a large *A* embossed on the outside, and I recognize Derek's handwriting. Taking it carefully, my lips press together. I look up at her.

"Take it behind the screen and read it," she says with a little smile.

Stepping around the wooden dressing screen, I do as she says.

At first, I only slide my hands over the smooth paper. His script is precise and blocky, controlled just like my man... except when he isn't. A tingle of love passes through my stomach, and I turn the envelope over. Lifting the seal, I pull the heavy paper out and open it. He's written me a letter.

Dear Melissa,
(Or should I say "Miss Jones"?)

I'm a bit older than you, so this might seem old-fashioned. I wanted to write you a letter to read on our wedding day. In the future, if you ever doubt me, you can read this and know my heart.

Before I met you, I was in a dark place. I thought this part of my life had ended, and I never expected to have a family or even to find love again. Then you appeared.

You changed my life in ways I can't explain. The weeks we were apart, the nights I thought our separation might last a lifetime… It was the worst time of my life.

I can't imagine me without you.

I'm sure I'll mess up again, but please know if I do, I'll be the first one to fix it, to find a way back to us.

I lost myself in the darkness of trying to protect you, but you're my light. In the worst time of my life, your true colors shined through, and you demonstrated how deep your love is. You saved me.

Thank you for being my life. Thank you for giving me a son. I dedicate myself to loving you, to your happiness, and to never letting you feel in the dark.

My love.
My life.
My family.
I'll be the one down front waiting to make you mine.

Love,
Derek
(Or should I say "Mr. Alexander"?)

I sniff a laugh, and it's way too late for tissues. My makeup is ruined. "Oh, Derek," I whisper. "You are full of surprises."

"What's going on?" Elaine is back, and when she rounds the screen, she squeals. "Oh no! We have to redo your eyes!"

"Just forget it," I say, waving my hand. "I'll put on some lipstick and go with it."

"Your veil doesn't cover your face!"

"It's okay. He'll know why I'm crying." My eyes drift to the window, and I share a secret smile. "It'll make him happy."

Elaine shakes her head as she smooths my hair back. "I'm not sure you're going to be happy with these wedding photos in a year."

"I'm already happier than I can ever say."

* * *

At the front of our line, Kenny holds Slayde's arm. He's in a dark blue suit that makes his eyes glow silver. Behind them, Mariska holds Stuart's arm. He's in his dress whites, which I now know means white pants, belt, and hat. The coat is the traditional deep navy with red piping. He looks amazing, and my breath catches in my throat imagining how my Marine will look.

Behind them, Elaine absolutely glows in her sparkling dress. Patrick is more formal than I've ever seen him in his Guard uniform. Navy coat and pants, gold stripes down the legs, gold crest on his sleeves and hat. Gorgeous.

Edward Merritt, my best friend's dad, takes my arm. "Your father would be very proud," he says, and I glance up at his salt and pepper hair, remembering a time when everyone imagined I'd be with Marcus.

"I appreciate you doing this," I say softly. "I can't imagine anyone else escorting me."

He gives me a warm smile that crinkles the corners of his green eyes. Elaine looks so much like him. "You're a beautiful, accomplished woman, Melissa. I'm proud to represent your father."

Squeezing his arm, I put my head briefly against his shoulder. "Thank you."

My cousin Ryan appears in a navy suit to escort Mom to her place in the front. He's a cute college guy with messy blonde hair. Mom takes his arm and kisses his cheek before the two head out toward the front.

The strains of Pachelbel's Canon drift to us, and it's time to move. Kenny and Slayde begin the procession, and my chest clenches. Mariska and Stuart are next. I don't miss the warm look that passes between them, and the idea they have a secret only briefly enters my mind before Elaine and Patrick start walking. Butterflies fill my stomach, and I feel like I'll laugh and cry at the same time.

The music gradually builds, but I can't see him yet. Our witnesses all stand by their small white chairs arranged in two sections on the sand. Friends and relatives smile as I pass. A few cover their mouths, and some dab their eyes.

Damn this flat sand. I grip Edward's arm, trying to see him when the procession opens before me. Dex is the first one I see in his little navy suit. He points at once and shouts, "May!" which makes everyone laugh. He starts to run to me, but Mom catches him in her arms. I blow him a little kiss before looking up again.

In a flash, I pan across the groomsmen—Slayde looking like a rockstar, Patrick looking like a model, of course he gives me a wink. Stuart is completely intimidating, but his eyes are on the beautiful girl in ocean-blue chiffon standing with my bridesmaids.

When at last I see Derek, my breath catches. Under the black brim of his white cap, his steel-grey eyes fix on mine. It's as if he sees all the way to my soul, and I feel it catch fire inside me. My vision tunnels. I don't even hear the words of Edward giving me away. I only know I'm drawn to this man watching me with such intensity.

A flash of timidity tightens my stomach as I reach out to take his white-gloved hand, but the moment he pulls me close, all fear melts away. We're facing each other, and I can only gaze at him with all the love expanding in my chest.

The minister leads us through our vows. Everything is very traditional.

For better or worse...

For richer or poorer...

In sickness and in health...

The words are a promise from the bottom of my heart. Derek removes his glove as we exchange rings. Shining, thick gold bands for each of us. Finally we've made it to the part I've been waiting for.

"I now pronounce you husband and wife," the man says. "You may kiss the bride."

My lip catches in my teeth, and Derek reaches up to touch it with his thumb. "That's for me to do," he whispers before sliding his hand behind my neck and covering my mouth with his.

Of all the times we've kissed each other, this kiss outshines every one. His warm lips move mine apart, and with the gentle taste of his tongue, my head grows light. I'm afraid I'll faint, but his strong arms hold me. It's amazing and passionate, and I never want to let him go. Until I realize our friends are clapping and a loud whistle slices the air.

He smiles against my mouth and lifts his head a fraction. "It seems we have an audience."

My dazed eyes open and I laugh, cupping his cheek. "I almost forgot."

We turn as the minister calls over the noise, "I present to you Mr. and Mrs. Derek Alexander."

The applause grows louder, and Stuart steps forward, giving a low command. He and their fellow Marines form a line of crossed swords, and we pass under the gleaming arch. Mom releases Dex, and he baby-runs to us. Derek catches him, lifting him on his arm. I turn and face my guys, and in that moment everything in my life is complete.

* * *

The hotel ballroom sparkles with white twinkle lights and dim lamps. At each table are bottles of champagne and small containers of bubbles. I haven't stopped dancing with Derek since we arrived.

"We should probably eat something." His low voice in my ear is a warm massage to my insides.

"I don't want to be out of your arms," I say, resting my temple against his cheek. I feel him smile.

"You never have to worry about that."

Glancing up, I kiss his lips briefly before letting him lead me off the dance floor to where our friends sit at a round table covered in white linens. Close by is the wedding cake, and Aunt Bea outdid herself making a four-layer round cake covered in white fondant. Each layer has a navy bow around its base, and the Marines emblem decorates them all the way to the cake topper — a Marine in dress whites holding a bride in his arms. I smile and rest my cheek against Derek's shoulder.

"Getting tired?" Elaine says to me, from where she's sitting on Patrick's lap.

I shake my head no just as Sylvia joins our group. "Derek," she steps around and gives him a brief squeeze. "The wedding was lovely, but I'm afraid it's late for me. Has anyone seen Amy?"

"We reserved a block of rooms if you'd like to spend the night here," he says, holding her hand.

"We have one at this lovely B&B in town," she says with a smile. "We already unpacked, or I'd stay. Now if I can just find my child."

"Hey, Mom," Stuart rounds the table to where Sylvia is standing. Mariska is right behind him, holding his hand.

"Since most everyone is here, we figured it's time to announce it."

"Announce what?" Kenny perks up, her dark brows clutched.

My eyes widen in anticipation. I had a feeling this was coming.

"Mariska has agreed to marry me."

"What!" Her friend is out of her seat and going to them fast. "When did this happen?"

Mariska beams as Kenny takes her hand. "I actually agreed about a month ago, but then he changed his mind."

Kenny's face snaps up, but Stuart grabs Mariska around the waist, pulling her to him and kissing her neck before nipping her ear.

She squeals a laugh. "I was teasing!"

"Mom had to bring me the ring," he corrects her. "It was our grandmother's."

"Oh! Let me see." We all crowd around to examine the delicate white-gold engagement ring. It's in the shape of a flower lying on its side with a large round diamond in the center.

"It's beautiful," I say with a smile, looking up at Stuart.

"I wanted it to be bigger—"

"That would've ruined the design!" Mariska argues.

"It's perfect for you," Elaine says, giving her a hug. "And now we'll be sisters."

"Speaking of sisters," Sylvia interjects. "If you see your other one, tell her I'm looking for her. Congratulations," She stretches up and kisses Stuart's cheek. Then she puts an arm around Mariska's shoulders. "Best wishes, although you don't need it. You are one impressive young lady."

"Thank you," Mariska laughs.

Stuart gives her another squeeze before answering Sylvia. "I spoke to Amy at the bar a few minutes ago. I'll try and find her if you want."

"Oh, I can wait a little longer," his mother pats his arm. "I'm glad to see my children so happy."

Derek's arms are around me again, and I can't help agreeing with her. So much has happened to get us here. Breakups, secrets, heartbreaking discoveries that turned into blessings or paths to forgiveness, and now the most resistant member of the group has found a home.

"This day couldn't get any better," I sigh, leaning my head back against his shoulder.

His lips touch the side of my neck, sending tingles through my stomach. "It's only the beginning."

I know he's right. We've each made it through the dark times, and we've found the one to hold, keep, love, and save. Another wedding to plan, more babies will arrive...

I'm so lucky to be with this man. He's risked his life for me again and again, and all I want to do is make that risk worth taking. When I see the love in his eyes and feel the love in my heart, I know it is. The future is wide open, and our love is strong. I can't wait to see what's next for all of us.

The end.

EPILOGUE: RUNAWAY

Amy

Returning from Paris, the last thing I'm in the mood for is a wedding. Still, Derek Alexander is the closest thing I have to a third brother. He's also my favorite of Stuart's friends—and Patrick's, I guess. Anyone who can get those two to put down their arms and stop fighting is a master in my book. Also, Mom insists I go with her so she doesn't have to go alone. I suspect she's hoping I'll meet someone as always. The woman is living for more grandchildren these days.

I've only been to Wilmington once, but it's a precious little beach community. Sylvia, being the way she is, has found an exclusively plush bed and breakfast for us to stay in. It's would be the perfect girls' getaway, and I love spending time with my mother—except for the wedding part.

"Melissa is the dearest thing," she says as she unpacks her black and white-patterned Vera Bradley luggage. "She's in marketing, so if you have a chance, let her know that's what you do."

"I doubt she'll want to discuss work on her wedding day." I watch as she fiddles with the navy and red-patterned silk scarf tied neatly at her throat.

She steps back and runs her hands down her sandy-blonde bob. For her age, Mom is still a beautiful woman. It helps that she's Coco Chanel-elegant in all things, the result of her upbringing. She survived the same elite childhood as my brothers and I. The nice thing is she's not cold-hearted, passive-aggressive, or a materialistic bitch like so many of my friends have for mothers. We had dear old Dad to fill that role.

"How much time before the wedding?" I assess my long blonde hair and decide I won't need to wash it. I would, however, like to freshen up.

"It starts at six, so we should probably leave in a half hour."

"I'll be ready."

I step into the large bathroom and close the door. I haven't had any time to come down from my sudden departure from Europe. I haven't even given myself a moment to consider what Armand is thinking. I honestly don't care to know.

Sinking into the warm bath, I close my eyes and allow the lavender-scented water to relax me. Armand made the fuck-up. I was always completely honest with him. It's probably the reason he hasn't called since I walked out, not that I really care for that to happen either. No, he knew before he even said the words how I would respond. Now here we are, and I'm not looking back.

Promptly half an hour later, I'm dressed and applying red lipstick as Sylvia fastens a chunky strand of pearls at her neck. She's dressed in a beige, sleeveless shift with black accents at the shoulders and hips. Classic Coco. I on the other hand, am wearing a long slip-dress with high slits above each leg. It's white with black leather accents, and I top it with a fluffy mohair vest. Very Valentino.

"You look fresh off the Paris catwalk," Mom says with a smile.

I shrug. "Not much point living in Paris if you don't indulge in the fashions."

We're out the door and headed to the beach in less than five.

* * *

The wedding is a stunning showcase of our nation's finest. I still can't believe both my older brothers are veterans. Patrick most of all. Stuart was always fighting his natural tendency to be exactly like our father, but my favorite brother is so playful and fun. It's still hard to imagine him carrying a rifle, much less actually using it to kill someone. Of course, I'm pretty sure his stint in the Guard was intended to satisfy our father's chauvinistic requirements while avoiding deployment. Poor darling. Talk about backfires.

"Looks like you came back from Europe a woman." The familiar male voice surprises me with its cheerfulness. I turn to see my oldest brother actually smiling for the first time in my life.

"Looks like you came back from Saudi a happy man."

He shakes his head. "I never went back to Saudi. That's what made me a happy man." I wait as he signals the bartender. A scotch neat for him, vodka rocks for me. "Have you met Mariska?" he watches me as he sips the amber liquid.

"I haven't, but she's very beautiful."

"I asked her to marry me."

That almost makes me drop my drink. *"Et tu, Brute?"*

"Yep," he grins again. "Me too."

"I go away and everything falls apart." Taking a long sip of vodka, I watch as he chuckles. He's so fucking happy, I can't believe it. Stuart does not chuckle. Only now it seems he does.

"So what brought you back? I thought you loved Paris."

"Oh, I do love Paris." I take another, longer drink, finishing off my vodka as my mind races to find a suitable answer. I can't say the truth: Armand asked me to move in with him, and I caught the first flight home.

"Even the City of Lights gets old after a while." It's not very good, and I can tell he doesn't buy it. "And Mom's not getting any younger."

Stuart accepts that lie a little better. "Well, I'm glad you're back. It's good to have the family together again." He pats my arm. "Come over and meet Mariska."

"Mmm," I nod, giving him a little wave. "Let me get a fresh drink."

He strolls away, and I turn and flag the bartender down. "Vodka rocks." I slide a tenner across the counter. It's an open bar, but tipping ensures better service. I'll need a few more of these if I have to deal with all the love going around.

Taking my drink, I turn my back to the bar and notice a tall, slender specimen of male waiting beside me. He orders a vodka rocks, and I quickly assess him. Dolce & Gabbana suit, fatigue-green and stainless Tag, light scruff on the cheeks. *Interesting.* Stepping back, he catches my inspection and pauses. I lift my chin and own it. After the house I grew up in, men don't intimidate me.

Apparently, I don't intimidate him either. *Even more interesting.*

He exhales a laugh, revealing nice white teeth. "Are you here for the bride or the groom?"

"Hmm..." I realize I'm not sure how to answer that question. I'm equally acquainted with both.

"Groom, I guess."

"You guess?"

"I'm friends with both, but I knew Derek first."

"Ah," he nods.

"You?"

"Bride." Then he hesitates, taking a sip of his drink. "Actually, no, that's not right. I guess my answer is the same as yours. Only in reverse."

He looks out at the dance floor where the happy couple hasn't stopped slow-dancing since they arrived. Something wistful is on his face, and I can't resist.

"You have a history with Melissa?"

Blinking hazel-green eyes back at me he seems to wake up. "We were childhood friends. It's unexpected to see them all married."

"I'm never getting married." *Good god, Amy, over-share much?* Looking down at my drink, I realize it's nearly empty. I'm more relaxed than I realized.

My companion doesn't skip a beat. "Is that so?" he chuckles. "And what are you? Eighteen?"

Irritation burns in my chest. Treating me like a baby is *not* a good idea. "I'm twenty five, and I guess that's a compliment?"

"Baby," he exhales, turning back to the bar.

"Old man," I say, waving at the bartender and ordering another.

"Old man?" The guy turns to the side and leans on his elbow facing me. "You think ordering another is a good idea?"

"I can outdrink you any day of the week." *No idea what I'm doing right now.*

He gives me a player's grin. "I'm a lawyer."

"So you're an asshole who's about to be outdrunk by a baby."

Something flickers in his eyes. It's a spark I've seen before, and it usually leads to naughty places. "I haven't played drinking games since college."

"Is that fear I'm hearing?"

"Line 'em up."

He slides a hand to his waist, moving his suit coat back to reveal a trim physique. Yes. Something naughty might be just what I need to get the funk of Paris off me. It is a wedding, after all. Isn't everyone supposed to hook up?

"I have a better idea," I say, waving to the bartender again. "We'll take the bottle."

The well-tipped server is happy to oblige, and I grab it, two glasses, and my black clutch. "This way, lawyer."

A small billiards room is off the main ballroom, and it's completely empty. The reception party is focused on the room where the food, drinks, and band are located. Striding into the cozy, dim-lit space, I place the full bottle of vodka and two slim glasses on a tall table with two bar stools.

"Do you play?" he asks, stepping over and sliding the cue ball across red felt.

"Not billiards." Cracking open the bottle, I pour two glasses mid-way. "You're up."

Stepping to the counter, he lifts one. "*Skal.*" With a clink, he slams the entire contents back.

"Swedish?" My eyes only pinch a little as I do the same.

"I figure if we're shooting vodka, we should keep it real."

I'm pouring another drink feeling looser than ever. "So if you're not Swedish," I glance up and give him a playful wink, "Where is home? Here in Wilmington?"

"Chicago." He takes the glass, openly letting his eyes run all over my body. A warm tingle follows his inspection.

"I don't believe it," I say, sliding the fur off my shoulders to give him a better view.

"How come." He moves a bit closer. "Too conventional?"

"Chicago is where I live now."

"Now?"

"I spent the last year in Paris."

His eyebrows rise. "The City of Love?"

"I prefer City of Lights."

"Right." He's even closer now. Close enough that I can smell the fresh linen scent of his cologne. "You don't do love."

"I do *other* things." It came out as more of a purr than I'd intended, but I'll go with it. I feel good, and I want to bury my face in his delicious scent while I tangle my fingers in those caramel-brown waves.

A pause. Our eyes hold each other's a moment. "What's your name?" I ask.

"Marcus." I like it. Marcus the lawyer. "What's yours?"

"Amy."

"Pretty." Unexpected warmth simmers in my stomach. "What's your game, Amy?"

The sound of his voice saying my name is a delicious vibration under my skin. *What's my game?* It could mean anything, but I go with the less provocative interpretation.

"International trade and finance." I push my lips out just a bit over the *S* sound, allowing my eyes to stay on his mouth. It's a nice mouth, and I love the feel of scruff against my bare skin. "I'll probably focus on PR now that I'm home."

He's not backing down, and a shimmer of excitement moves through my stomach. "Are you experienced at PR?"

"Why don't you find out?" My voice has gone a little lower. It's enough for him.

Another step forward, and our bodies are touching now. He's warm, and that crisp linen fills my senses. Large hands slide up my hips, and I close my eyes, dropping my head back for him to kiss me.

He trails his lips lightly up my skin, more taking in my scent than tasting me. It makes me wet. When he reaches my jaw, he pulls a little nibble in his teeth, and a noise comes from my throat.

"You're good at this," I whisper, finding his eyes.

"I like surprises."

"Surprises are one of my two favorite things."

His hands span my lower back, lifting me onto the stool, before his mouth covers mine. The slits in my skirt allow easy access to my center. His lips force mine open, and our tongues curl together. It's not frantic and grasping, it's controlled and confident. He tastes like cinnamon and expensive vodka, and I feel his erection pressing against my thigh. It's fantastic, strong and demanding. Another shiver moves through me as my fingers quickly unfasten the buttons of his shirt. I'm enjoying this too much for a random.

"Are you cold?" He breathes against my skin, tracing a burning trail to my ear. He pulls the top between his lips, and my insides clench.

When I reach the bottom button of his shirt, I slide my hands down the front of his pants between us. "I'm ready to know you better."

Stepping back, he loosens and removes his tie, tossing it on the table. His shirt is open and untucked, and his lined chest makes my mouth water. Eyes dark, he returns to me and pushes my sleeve down my shoulder. I shrug it off and allow him to unfasten my bra.

"Mmm," he rumbles, cupping my breast and rolling my nipple between his fingers. "You are a naughty girl."

"I think I'm a lucky girl." My voice cracks with desire as he pulls the dark bud between his lips giving it a hard suck that shoots electricity straight between my legs. More wetness. God, this is going to be good.

"I think I'm the lucky one." He kisses back up to my neck, scuffing my skin in a delicious way.

I've managed to get his pants unfastened, and I slide one hand down his cock, curling my fingers around it. *Damn, it's thick.* "Why don't you get lucky then?"

A rustle of pockets, and I help him open the foil wrapper. Our mouths reunite, and I push my breasts against him as he slides on the condom. Light chest hair tingles my nipples, and I'm heady with lust, anticipating the feel of him stretching me. Large hands return to my ass. I hold my breath a moment before he moves my thong and pushes inside.

"Oh," I exhale at the same time he mutters a "Fuck me."

Marcus lifts me off the seat and thrusts harder, going deeper. My legs are around his waist, and I arch so our moving bodies massage my clit. If we were controlled before, we've given in to flat-out carnal enjoyment now. It's crazy and reckless and wild.

267

He slams my back against the wall, and he's hitting me hard, rocking us both in perfect rhythm. Sizzling electricity vibrates my veins and pleasure snakes up my thighs.

Here it comes, my mind whispers. "Oh, god," I gasp as my orgasm grows hotter with each thrust.

"Harder," I beg, and he complies. Again and again, he pushes into me until he groans in my ear. He's coming, and the noise of his climax pushes me over the edge. All at once the tidal wave bursts, flooding me with ecstasy.

"Oh, yes!" I cry as the orgasm quivers in my thighs. It's one of the best I've had in a while.

"God, you feel good," he groans against my neck, giving me two more deep thrusts as I ride out the aftershocks of pleasure, my insides tensing around his cock. A few more movements, and we're on the way down.

He's still holding me securely in his strong arms and I like the way he feels.

My insides immediately recoil at that thought. "To the bride and groom," I laugh, pushing against his shoulders.

He eases back, holding the condom as he pulls out, lowering me to my feet. I avoid his eyes as I straighten my top. Protection trashed, he fastens his pants as I straighten my thong and grab my clutch. I don't have time to mess around. I've got to get the fuck out of here now.

"I'd like to have you for breakfast," he says, turning to me with a cocky smile. I'm annoyed that it thrills my insides.

"Tempting." I give him a wink.

"Are you staying in the hotel? I'm on the tenth floor."

"I'm actually here with my mother. She's at a B&B, so I need to be sure she has a way home."

I've made it to the exit, vodka bottle and glasses forgotten. He follows me into the ballroom and pauses. "Okay, check on her. I'll head up and order us some wine. See you in a few?"

"Sure." Stepping forward, I kiss his cheek. He captures my lips briefly, and I curse the damn flutter in my stomach.

"Room ten-sixteen." He holds my eyes then. His are deep hazel-green, and I refuse to acknowledge they're damn sexy. He is a *random*.

"Ten-sixteen," I nod. "Got it."

He heads toward the lobby, and I only briefly hesitate before turning on my heel and making my way to where Sylvia stands chatting with Stuart and Mariska. I'll meet them, say goodnight, and get back to the B&B. In the morning we'll be gone. No shitting where I live.

Surprises are nice, but my second favorite thing? Running.

* * *

Missed the story of what happened to Sloan? Keep turning for an Exclusive Sneak Peek at One to Protect!

Curious about Slayde? Check out the Exclusive Sneak Peek at One to Love, *and see he and Kenny changed each other's lives!*

Your opinion counts!

If you enjoyed *One to Save*, please leave a short, sweet review on Amazon or wherever you purchased your copy.

Reviews help your favorite authors find new readers and even get advertising opportunities.

Thank you so much!

* * *

"Follow" my Amazon Author Page, and get an email whenever I release a new book!

AND/OR

Get Exclusive Text Alerts and never miss a SALE or NEW RELEASE by Tia Louise!

Text "TiaLouise" to 77948 Now!

(Max 6 messages per month; **HELP for help; STOP to cancel**; Text and Data rates may apply. Privacy policy available, allnightreads@gmail.com)

AND/OR

Sign up for the New Release Mailing list today! (http://eepurl.com/Lcmv1)*

*Please add **allnightreads@gmail.com** to your contacts so it doesn't bounce to spam!

* * *

Thank you for reading!

Dear Reader,

I hope you enjoyed *One to Save!* Derek and Melissa are the center of the One to Hold world, and it's always fun to be back in their heads.

The idea for this book came after several readers noted their favorite Hero's tendency to keep secrets from his fiancée. Melissa has been through a lot, and I wondered if she would be strong enough to hold Derek's feet to the fire and make him treat her like a partner and not a child. Looks like she was!

I hope you enjoyed all the moments in their journey. I hope you were surprised, I hope you swooned, and I hope you even shed a tear. Most of all, I hope you felt the love between these two great characters.

Up next, I can't wait to dig into Amy and Marcus's tale. Amy is as playful as Patrick, but as resistant to settling down as Stuart. Marcus you already know. (#SexyLawyer) Crashing these two together promises to be FUN!—all around the city of Chicago. Be watching for it mid-June!

As always, let me know what you think of my books! Email me your thoughts, feedback, what you liked—even what you didn't like! I really like hearing from readers.

You can write to me at **allnightreads@gmail.com** or visit me on Facebook at **https://www.facebook.com/AuthorTiaLouise**!

Finally, if you enjoy my books, I hope you'll leave a short, sweet review on Amazon and/or wherever you purchased this book! Reviews help indie authors more than you know.

Thank you again for spending time with me. I hope to hear from you soon!

Stay sexy,
<3 Tia

BOOKS BY TIA LOUISE

Note: All are stand-alone novels. Adult Contemporary Romance: Due to strong language and sexual content, books are not intended for readers under the age of 18.

One to Hold
(Derek & Melissa)

Derek Alexander is a retired Marine, ex-cop, and the top investigator in his field. Melissa Jones is a small-town girl trying to escape her troubled past.

When the two intersect in a bar in Arizona, their sexual chemistry is off the charts. But what is revealed during their "one week stand" only complicates matters.

Because she'll do everything in her power to get away from the past, but he'll do everything he can to hold her.

Also available in audiobook format on Amazon, Audible, or Tantor.com.

* * *

One to Protect
(Derek & Melissa)

When Sloan Reynolds beats criminal charges, Melissa Jones stops believing her wealthy, connected ex-husband will ever pay for what he did to her.

Derek Alexander can't accept that—a tiny silver scar won't let him forget, and as a leader in the security business, he is determined to get the man who hurt his fiancée.

Then the body of a former call girl turns up dead. She's the breakthrough Derek's been waiting for, the link to Sloan's sordid past he needs. But as usual, legal paths to justice have been covered up or erased.

Derek's ready to do whatever it takes to protect his family when his partner Patrick Knight devises a plan that changes everything.

It's a plan that involves breaking rules and taking a walk on the dark side. It goes against everything on which Alexander-Knight, LLC, is based.

And it's a plan Derek's more than ready to follow.

Also available in audiobook format on Amazon, Audible, or Tantor.com.

* * *

One to Keep
(Patrick & Elaine)

There's a new guy in town...
"Patrick Knight, single, retired Guard-turned private investigator. I was a closer. A deal maker. I looked clients in the eye and told them I'd get their shit done. And I did..."

Patrick doesn't do "nice."

At least, not anymore.

After his fiancée cheats, he follows up with a one-night stand and a disastrous office hook-up. His business partner (Derek Alexander) sends him to the desert to get his head straight—and clean up the mess.

While there, Patrick meets Elaine, and blistering sparks fly, but she's not looking for any guy. Or a long-distance relationship.

Patrick's ready to do anything to keep her, but just when it seems he's changed her mind, the skeletons from his past life start coming back.

Also available in audiobook format on Amazon, Audible, or Tantor.com.

* * *

One to Love
(Kenny + Slayde)

Tattoos, bad boys, love…
Boxing, fame, fortune…
Loss.

It's the one thing Kenny and Slayde have in common. Until the night Fate throws them together and everything changes.

It's a story about fighting. It's about falling in love. And it's about losing everything only to find it again in the least likely place.

* * *

One to Leave
(Stuart & Mariska)

Some demons can't be shaken off.
Some wounds won't heal.

Until a pair of hazel eyes knocks you on your ass, and you realize it's time to stop running.

One to Save
(Derek & Melissa)

Some threats come at you as friendly fire.
Some threats take away everything.
Family won't let you go down without a fight.

The Secret isn't as secure as Derek's team originally thought it was, and a person on the inside of Alexander-Knight is set on exposing him, breaking him, and taking away all he holds dear.

Refusing to let anyone suffer for his crimes, Derek takes matters into his own hands. He's exposed, he's defenseless, but his friends are determined to save him.

* * *

One to Chase
(Amy & Marcus)

Amy Knight, meet Marcus Merritt.

Patrick's ambitious, over-achieving little sister is meeting with one of the top law firms in Chicago. The only problem is the sexy, high-powered attorney interviewing her is the same green-eyed player she hooked up with after a certain wedding in Wilmington.

He's also Elaine's older brother. *Is this even legal?!*

Complications everywhere, and the more they run, the less they're sure who's chasing whom.

Coming June 2015!

ACKNOWLEDGMENTS

Always, my deepest thanks goes to my sweet husband "Mr. TL" for his patience and support. In this story, he even provided his legal expertise. Thank you, babe, for rewriting that scene because, "No lawyer would ever say that." (LOL!) I love you.

Thanks to my sweet daughters, who are excited and supportive even when I tell you it's going to be another six years (at least) before you can read one of these.

BIG thanks to Lauren Perry for coming to me with her gorgeous photography. You were right—it IS Derek and Melissa! And to Steven Novak, my faithful cover designer. You ROCK!

Thanks to Natalie and Love Between the Sheets for always making my cover reveals and release days so successful. Thanks to Mandie "Google Queen" Jones for keeping me sane and being the greatest PA ever. Hugs to Chrissy Badder for loving my guys and helping me promote them. Squeezes to Ilona Knight-Townsel for running the Alexander-Knight Files. Every single one of you is an asset, and I appreciate you so much.

One of the great things about being a writer is meeting new reader friends. I've got so many great "Keepers," who see me through my moments of frustration, nerves, and fun brainstorming. (Yay!) Huge hugs and thanks to you guys. I love your comments, teasers, and feedback, but most of all your enthusiasm. You keep me going!

To all the bloggers who help me—enormous hugs and thanks. Indie authors would be hard-pressed to find new readers without you. You provide a real service, and I hope you know how much I appreciate every one of you, big and small.

Most of all, I have to thank my readers, new and old, who love this series, who love Derek and Melissa, and who send me sweet notes telling me how excited you are or how a story touched you or helped you. You are what it's all about.

Thank you. <3

* * *

Exclusive Sneak Peek

One to Protect
(Derek & Melissa)

"Special Skills"
Derek

Only two hours have passed since I told Melissa goodbye, and already that tightness is creeping across my chest. It's a mixture of anger and needing her in my sight where I know she's safe.

She didn't press the subject, but all weekend I could tell she wanted to know what I was working on, what was "bothering me."

Damn Nikki. If I weren't so pleased by the luscious surprise of finding Mel waiting for me half-nude in my condo Friday night, I'd reprimand her for keeping tabs on me. I don't need an office manager who doubles as my mother, or who reports my behavior back to my aunt — or my fiancée.

Now, sitting at my desk remembering, the only thing strong enough to spoil the afterglow of our weekend is this new case... and her old scar. That damn silver line, a constant reminder of what that fucker did to her. Even worse, it reminds me he's still out there walking around free.

In my line of work, I know how those assholes are. They all have some fucked up notion their victims belong to them — only them. My fist is clenched on the desktop, and I focus on relaxing it.

Sloan will pay for what he did to Mel. I intend to make sure of it, but she's right. Letting him spoil our present gives him too much power. I'd rather put that aside, in my "To Do" file, and focus on my weekend with my little family—sheer red lingerie, loads of sex, and nonstop affection—hell, I should have a shitty week more often.

Shitty week…

I turn to my computer and stare at the report on the screen. As much as Mel wants to know, I can't bring myself to tell her what I'm investigating. It's not that I want to hide my work from her. She could probably help solve half the cases on my desk. I don't want her to be afraid, and I don't have a reason to make her worry yet.

Patrick's in Wilmington watching over her for me, being the guard he is when I'm not there, and I've got tabs on Sloan. We'll know if he leaves the city or makes any threatening moves. Privately, I wish he would. Nothing would make me happier than taking him out in an act of self-defense. With his record, not a jury in the world would convict.

Nikki snaps me out of my reflections. "I'm headed to the coffee shop. Can I get you anything?" She's standing at the door in one of her usual, too-tight wrap-dresses.

It takes me back to her first day here, assigned by my aunt Sue's temp agency. I was still grieving Allison. Three years had passed since my first wife died, but time didn't matter. I didn't want a replacement wife or a girlfriend or an outlet or *anything*, and the idea that my aunt might've selected this woman for any of those reasons got under my skin like nothing else. I didn't need help getting over my wife. I had no intention of getting over her ever, and Nikki's appearance pissed me off.

The reality is, despite her former, inappropriate assertions that I needed to "get laid," she never once made a pass at me. She'd actually seemed more interested in Stuart, my first partner and Patrick's older brother.

I suppose after all this time I should put the past behind us. It doesn't make sense anymore now that I have Melissa. Everything has changed.

She's waiting, and I exhale. "No. Thank you." The departure from my usual, impatient tone makes her pause, and I continue. "You're always thoughtful, Nikki. I appreciate it."

Her mouth drops open and then quickly closes. "I'm… um… well." She stops stammering, pokes her lips out duck-face style, then nods. "Okay, then. You're welcome."

Turning on a stiletto heel, she heads out of the office, and I grin. That may be the first time I've had Nikki at a loss for words.

Back to my computer, I pull up the file I've been studying for ten days—the one that's had me so distracted. I keep telling Patrick we don't do domestic work, yet I always end up being the one old friends or acquaintances call when they need help.

That's how it started—a runaway case for a friend of a friend.

I was culling through mug shots of beat-up teens and file photos of dead girls. Patrick would say this is the worst part of our job, but truthfully, I don't mind it. I can see past the tragedy to my role here, giving people closure. I know what it's like to need it, and I don't mind helping people get it.

Then I saw *Jessica Black*. Dead.

The name was so familiar, but I couldn't place her at first. Staring at the photo, trying to think, I'd been struck by her appearance—fair complexion, petite frame, and long brunette waves. She looked a lot like Melissa — minus my fiancée's bright blue eyes.

I'd clicked on the thumbnail to read the report. Runaway. Missing five years. Arrested for prostitution several times. Found beaten once. Badly. Now deceased under mysterious circumstances.

Minutes passed as I stared at her photo. Why was she so familiar? She wasn't from Princeton. Her hometown was listed as Raleigh. Shaking my head and chalking it up to overprotectiveness spurred by her similarity to Mel, I closed the document and went back to searching for the runaway.

Nikki had interrupted me that day as well, stopping in with a BLT from the cafeteria.

"I know it's your favorite." She placed the thick sandwich in front of me with a smile. "You need to eat."

I only nodded. "Thanks."

She didn't leave. "Remember the last time I brought you lunch? It was the day Melissa showed up here so angry and unexpected. I was sure I'd never like her, but now she's the sweetest..."

Nikki continued talking, but I wasn't listening. Cold realization flashed in my brain like lightening striking a tree.

Jessica Black. It was the name on the email Melissa had put in front of me that day she visited our offices. The day she dropped a nuke on all my dreams of a life with her, when she revealed my former "mentor," her ex-husband Sloan Reynolds's secret double-life. He had high-end escorts all over the country, and Jessica Black was his first careless slip. Melissa had found it.

Nikki was still reminiscing as I spun around in my chair, shaking my computer awake. Fingers flying over the keys, I pulled up all the information I could find on the dead girl.

She'd been living in Baltimore for a year. I wondered if she followed him from wherever they'd hooked up the first time. *Why would she do that? Was it possible she was in*
love with him? Was it for the money? Had he promised her anything?

It didn't matter. She'd disappeared off the police blotter from the time she arrived there until now, when she'd turned up dead.

Reasons scrolled across my brain of all the possible causes of death, but looking at her beaten face, all I could see was the photo Melissa had put in front of me all those months ago.

My instincts were on high alert. Sloan was getting antsy, and I knew what he wanted. Jessica Black might look like the real thing, but she wasn't it.

Substitutes would never fill the possession he felt. I'd followed enough of these twisted fucks to know. He was coming for Melissa, and it was just a matter of when.

All last week, I'd tracked down every misstep I could find on him, looking for anything that would stick, that would get him off the streets or at least keep him in Baltimore. I hoped to find a recent paper trail linking him to Jessica, but every lead came up cold. He was either too slick, or his people buried everything.

Even the guy I had watching Sloan in Baltimore had nothing. Jessica disappeared a week before I'd hired him, a month after Sloan had broken into Mel's beach cottage and then gotten off with a slap on the wrist. Apparently I'd moved too quickly when he waltzed into her home threatening to rape her. We had to wait until he actually committed the crime for his money and position not to matter.

The thought clenched my jaw. It was the one thing above all that caused the "stress" Nikki kept texting Melissa about. Only "stress" wasn't what I felt. What I felt was flat-out fucking rage.

The best part was when he threatened me in court with police brutality charges. I'd nearly brutalized him on the spot, but Melissa held me back. I'll never forget her face. She went still as a stone, as if it was the ending she always expected. It was like a heel-kick straight to my gut. I couldn't let her down that way.

Now all she'll say is she wants those memories left in the past. *Just let it go*, she tells me.

Fuck that. That asshole is a threat to my family, and it's clear he's dangerous. Priority 1 is devising a plan to bring him in, and it has to be something that won't ooze off his slimy back.

Snatching my phone off its base, I hit the speed-dial button.

Patrick answers, cocky as always. "Don't tell me. You've come to your senses and realized life at the beach is the only way to live."

"I need you to up the watch on Melissa."

I appreciate how his tone becomes immediately serious. "What's going on?"

"I have to finish a few details for our new Houston client, and then I'm headed your way, possibly for a while."

"This can only mean one thing. Or one asshole."

"I'm emailing a report and mug shots to you now. The name's Jessica Black." Fingers clicking on the keys, I shoot everything I've found to him. "I've exhausted all my sources here. See if you can do anything from there with it."

"Sure." He's silent for a moment, reading. "Jessica Black... Raleigh? That's just down the road. I'll rattle a few cages."

"If you do find anything, I need to know why she moved to Baltimore. What she was doing there. If she was seeing anybody and who."

"Did you tell Melissa about this?"

Pressing my lips together, I rock back in my chair. "No."

"Think that's a good idea?"

"Not really, but I'll tell her when the time is right. I don't want her to be afraid."

Sitting forward again, I pull up the report for our Houston client and read over what's still outstanding. A full system analysis is due Friday. I lost a significant portion of last week searching all the police databases for information on Miss Black.

"If I pull some extra hours, I can have Houston wrapped up and out of here by Wednesday." I start a log on my desktop of what's still outstanding, what jobs are lined up next, and what I can handle from Wilmington in case I can't get back right away.

Nikki's thank you gift can be a week off with pay, maybe a Spa Finder mini-holiday. In the middle of planning my getaway, I realize Patrick is still on the line.

"Sorry to keep you in a holding pattern."

"No worries. I can tell this is serious. Somehow. Even though you haven't told me any details."

Patrick can turn any situation into a joke, and I alternate between being pissed and being glad about it. At the moment, I'm too focused on closing the office and getting to Wilmington to lose time on it.

"I'll tell you everything when I get there. Just keep your eyes on Mel."

"She'll be as protected as the crown jewels."

It doesn't satisfy the tightness in my chest. "Maybe Elaine could invite her to stay in your guest room til Thursday."

"You're joking, right? You know Mel won't leave that cottage without a mandatory evacuation order."

Studying my notes, I wonder how many boxes I'd have to pack if I left for Wilmington today. No, I have to wrap up this damn Houston case here, where I can focus.

Frustrated, I push the laptop back on my desk. "We're professionals, dammit. Get creative."

He laughs. "What would work if you were Melissa? I'd say we invite her over for dinner and mix her drinks too strong, but she's pregnant. And even if she were still drinking, we couldn't keep the party going for three nights. Just tell her what's up."

"If I can be there on Wednesday, I will."

"Fine, but will you at least tell me what's going on? Who is Jessica Black? Or who *was*, I guess..."

"Jessica Black was a high-end hooker, an escort. She was also one of Sloan's regulars. A few years ago, she was beaten pretty badly, but she wouldn't report the guy. Then she moved to Baltimore. I don't have anything concrete, but my gut says she fell in love with him. How, I can't imagine. Now she's dead."

Silence meets my ear for several moments. When Patrick speaks again, his voice is sober, all joking gone. "And she looks a helluva lot like Melissa."

"Right."

"I know what to do."

In that one sentence I hear my partner lock into closer mode, and it's right where I want him. Patrick can be a royal fuck up when it comes to women, but he's damn good at his job. And to her credit, Elaine seems to have put an end to his screwing around.

"I've got an idea," he continues. "It's something I floated past you a while back, but now with this... Raleigh... I might have a connection to what you need."

"I didn't expect anything less. See you in a few days, and Patrick? Thanks. I owe you one."

"It's nothing more than you'd do for me."

"You know it."

* * *

EXCLUSIVE SNEAK PEEK

One to Love
(Kenny + Slayde)

"The sun sets to rise again."
Slayde

How was it possible she was so amazing? I lay awake, staring at the ceiling, Kenny's soft body draped over me as she breathed quietly against my chest.

Lifting a long strand of dark violet hair, I slid it around my finger before holding it to my nose, inhaling the scent of the ocean. Everything in me wanted to pursue this. Hell, there was no way I could stop pursuing it... But how would she feel if she knew my whole story? How would she feel about Slayer?

At the same time, it was possible I was expecting too much. She could just be in this for fun, a few dinners, a roll in the sack, and back to friends.

No, I knew that wasn't the case. It went against all the signals she'd been sending.

Allowing my mind to travel back, I thought of how she looked when I first saw her tonight. The red dress she wore hung on her slim body in a way that drove me crazy. I wanted to slide those spaghetti straps off her shoulders, lift that filmy skirt and explore everything underneath. Topping it all off, she had on these insanely sexy shoes. I was seriously bummed about taking those off her feet.

She was so tiny without them. Her funny old-fashioned hairstyle was like something a former beauty queen would wear, a little lump with gentle curls spilling down her back to her waist. That's not right. A beauty queen would be all platinum and pink, and Kenny was jet-violet and red. Damn I loved her boldness.

It activated that possessiveness in me that I'd tried to curb. I wanted to pull her hair back and claim that mouth. I wanted to claim every inch of her, but I knew from my experience to take it easy.

Only a few times I wavered, lost control. She seemed turned on by it. When I took her like a fucking animal our first time, she cried and twisted, wrapping her legs around me and pumping her hips against mine. It was so hot. I was fucking the shit out of her, and her body was begging for more.

The memory provoked a semi under the sheets, but *damn*. I could've only been surer if she'd told me, yet she seemed as bewildered as I was by our intense connection. I was a self-centered prick, but I loved the idea that she hadn't been with anyone in a while. It made me imagine her waiting for me — as much as I'd been waiting for her.

"Hmm... Slayde?" She turned her head, and my heart stopped. Was she calling for me in her sleep?

Lifting her head, she blinked a few times, but I couldn't tell if she was awake.

"What's wrong, baby?" My voice was so tender, I almost hoped she was asleep. If not, my feelings would've been far too evident.

She took a deep breath and bent her elbow. Eyes still closed, a slender hand moved to her forehead, and she pushed a dark lock away. "Is it okay if I spend the night?"

Chuckling, I wasn't sure if it was possible for me to feel more for her until this very moment.

289

"Yes. I'm not letting you go anywhere tonight."

She sniffed and cuddled closer against me on the bed. She was off of me now, but her head was tucked into my ribs against the white tank I wore.

Glancing over her shoulder, I could see the length of her long, pale back, so elegant and beautiful. I traced my finger from the base of her skull all the way down the line to the top of her ass. A tiny shiver moved through her, and I remembered the way she'd shook when she came for me tonight.

"Goodnight, beautiful," I whispered before kissing her head and closing my eyes.

* * *

One to Protect *and* **One to Love** *are both available as eBooks on Amazon, iTunes, Nook, Google Play, Kobo, and AllRomanceeBooks.*

Paperbacks are available online at Amazon, CreateSpace, Book Depository, and Barnes & Noble.

ABOUT THE AUTHOR

Tia Louise is the Amazon and International Bestselling author of the One to Hold series.

From "Readers' Choice" nominations, to *USA Today* "Happily Ever After" nods, to winning the 2014 "Lady Boner Award," nothing makes her happier than communicating with fans and weaving new tales into the Alexander-Knight world of stories.

A former journalist, Louise lives in the center of the USA with her lovely family and one grumpy cat.

Also by Tia Louise:
One to Hold (Derek & Melissa), 2013
One to Protect (Derek & Melissa), 2014
One to Keep (Patrick & Elaine), 2014
One to Love (Kenny & Slayde), 2014
One to Leave (Stuart & Mariska), 2014
One to Chase (Amy & Marcus), **coming June 2015!**

Amazon Author Page: **http://amzn.to/1jm2F2b**

Connect with Tia:
Facebook
Twitter (@AuthorTLouise
Email
Pinterest
Instagram (@AuthorTLouise)

Keep up with the guys on their Facebook Page: *The Alexander-Knight Files.*

* * *

Milton Keynes UK
Ingram Content Group UK Ltd.
UKHW030624111124
2736UKWH00020B/88